"A sensual romance steeped in nature with a suspenseful undercurrent that's tensioned with loss, danger, and lust. A must-read for romantic suspense enthusiasts." JP MCLEAN, author of *Blood Mark* and *The Gift Legacy Series*.

"An engaging and mystifying novel which tells a story that brings readers to a place of compassion, understanding, and relation. The ever-changing emotions, and idiomatic expressions that W.L. Hawkin represented left me feeling as though I was one with the character." ALEXA BLYAN, Indigenous mentor, activist, and motivational speaker.

"A redemption story with an engaging suspense plot, plenty of action and a strong, sexy "mountain man" CJ HUNT, author of the *Rivers End Romance Series*

"A book for those wanting to find romance, love and acceptance for themselves, and a sense of home. Blending characters readers will connect with, a strong sense of place and mystery, readers will turn pages until the very end." EILEEN COOK, author of *With Malice*

"A finely drawn romance with unique characters and a vivid sense of place. *Lure* doesn't shy away from the grittier aspects of small-town life, but it will sweep you away nonetheless." AMANDA BIDNALL, editor

"A suspense-filled romantic story about unique and intriguing characters, who are also highly relatable. This story will stay with me." DANIKA BLOOM, USA Today Best-Selling Author

PRAISE FOR THE HOLLYSTONE MYSTERIES

"The whole narrative plays out like an HBO show waiting to be developed, combining elements of LGBTQ+ and adult storytelling into a complex character study of those who seek the answers hidden within the most complex systems of our universe, from historians and archeologists to Wiccans and Pagans." ANTHONY AVINA, *Reader's Entertainment Magazine*

"Hawkin writes with such fluid prose that the stage upon which she places her magical tale becomes visual and near cinematic. Superb characters and a keen sense of history and mythology blend with romance in this involving galaxy of a novel. Highly recommended." GRADY HARP, *Reader's Entertainment Magazine*

"Highly literary, occasionally surreal, and grounded by characters clipped, matter-of-fact voice, *To Sleep with Stones* is a dark murder mystery that readers will have trouble leaving behind. The buzz for this novel is deafening." JOHN KERRY

"Hawkin's tight and well-paced writing and knowledge of Celtic myths, combined with multi-layered characters, lush language and plot twists and turns, draw the reader in. The hallmark of this novel is the author's seamless interweaving of myth and reality. She appeals to our intellect and desire for vicarious adventure. GAIL M. MURRAY, *Blank Spaces, Ottawa Review of Books*

"Sweeping emotions and meticulous but seamlessly integrated socio-cultural backstory of a historical romance, the sharp edges of a psychological thriller, and the exhilaration of an epic adventure." JUNIPER GREER-ASHE

A LURE RIVER ROMANCE

To Auntie Dora,

LURE

JESSE & HAWK

*Enjoy,
WLHawkin*

W. L. HAWKIN

BLUE HAVEN
PRESS

Lure: Jesse & Hawk
A Lure River Romance (Book 1)
Copyright © 2021 W. L. Hawkin
Published by Blue Haven Press

Issued in print and electronic format
ISBN 978-1-7772621-2-9 (paperback)
ISBN 978-1-7772621-3-6 (eBook)

Published by Blue Haven Press
Edited by Eileen Cook & Amanda Bidnall
www.bluehavenpress.com

Dedicated to missing Indigenous women everywhere.
May you find your way home and may this madness end.

DEERSLAYER

Jesse held her breath, her muscles as tense as the trees hiding her. Through the telephoto lens on her old Nikon F2, the buck appeared close enough to touch. Angled perfectly, he browsed a patch of wild strawberries at the edge of the thicket. Sunlight broke through the pines and stretched across the glade, framing the deer in a golden glow. Jesse was downwind. The light was ideal. The moment was perfect.

The buck glanced up, uneasy. Perhaps perceiving her presence with some intuitive force known only to animals surviving in the wild.

Stay with me. I won't hurt you. I only want to show the world how beautiful you are.

The faintest crackling twig, blurred wave, scratch, or yawn would send the buck dashing, white tail erect. She knew he'd bolt at the first click of the shutter and was glad of it. His wariness would keep him alive. But the first shot had to be the best.

He dropped his head to browse, and she sipped in a breath. Then he raised it again, turned his thick neck, and stared in her direction. The white rectangular patch on his neck matched that of his inner ears and the edge of his black button nose. Jesse focused on the eyes. Black and intense, they bored straight through her soul.

Pressing her finger to the shutter, she heard the motor drive fire. *One. Two. Three.*

Then, a soft whoosh. A muted thwack.

Glazing hard, the black eyes slid from view as she stared through the lens, heart racing, mind spinning.

The buck crashed to his knees, shaking the earth as he hit the ground.

Letting go of the shutter release, Jesse sprang from the bushes. But her right foot caught one leg of the tripod and sent her sprawling into a patch of stinging nettles. Cursing, she picked herself up and ran to the deer, wringing her throbbing hands.

Smeared berries marred the buck's moist black nose. The dead eyes stared. She knelt and touched the tip of his thick bulbous antlers; they'd not yet hardened into points. He was young and healthy. Tears burned in her eyes. Working as a nature journalist, she encountered wounded and dead animals at times, but each one broke her heart.

"You poor thing. What happened?"

When she noticed blood beneath the buck's left foreleg, she used both hands to shift the body. A broken arrow jutted from a gash. Head up, she took a quick breath. *Hunters. Where?*

Glancing around the glade, she searched for camouflage or neon flashes. Seeing nothing, she stared back down at the deer. Studded with the feathers of a red-tailed hawk, the arrow was blood-spattered and driven into the soil. Its sapling shaft had splintered under the buck's weight. Had the arrow pierced its heart?

She hadn't expected to encounter hunters here on the reservation. Deer season didn't start until September, and it was only June. Shaking her head, she fumed. *Unbelievable! Hunting out of season and with a homemade arrow.* Then she realized that the whoosh she'd heard had been the arrow whizzing past, and her stomach flipped. He'd been standing behind her the whole time. *What if his aim had been off and he'd hit me instead?*

Jesse's flesh prickled as she sensed his presence. The great hunter had come to claim his kill. Reaching out, she curled her fingers around a jagged rock. She'd chosen to live out here, alone in the bush, and she would take a stand—for herself and the deer. This beautiful head wouldn't adorn some killer's wall if she could help it. And if he tried to take more than a trophy, she'd give him a fight.

Thrusting out her chin, she threw back her head defiantly, turned and yelled, "Murderer!"

But her first glance sent her sliding back onto her hip. Backlit by the sun, the man was shrouded in gold, his face obscured by shadows. Wavy blond hair hung long and loose well past his thick shoulders. He'd braided red-tailed hawk feathers down one side. A small bag hung from a rawhide thong around his neck and lay against the blond hairs on his muscular chest. A skin quiver packed with arrows dangled from his shoulder. He was naked except for a rag of buckskin laced low along his pelvis.

Jesse's breath caught, and she coughed. Then, catching herself staring, she glanced down at the deer to calm her racing heart. Her gut told her the man wouldn't harm her, and she trusted it. She had to, living out here.

He only wants the deer. So give him the deer. The voice in her head was confident and condescending. *Undeniably Alec.* Sweat trickled into Jesse's eyes, and she rubbed it with a fist. *No. It's not right.*

She tried to predict the hunter's next move. He was movie-star hot. Perhaps they were filming on the reservation, or he was engaged in some historical reenactment. When he approached, she saw his boots: deerskin moccasins with puckered seams. She'd bought a pair like that at the local trading post, but hers were tall to her knees and decorated with fancy beadwork. His were plain and laced tightly around his ankles—decidedly homemade. Pale yellow hairs feathered his tanned legs. The man was clearly not Chippewa. But what, then? An actor? An eccentric? A lunatic?

A rush of adrenaline tightened her gut and brought her up to her knees.

The hunter's hot breath brushed her neck as he reached down to claim his kill.

Incensed, Jesse turned, and their eyes locked. A rush set her fingers trembling. Then, regaining her composure, she flung her arm around the buck's neck. "No! Leave it." She pounded the ground with her free fist.

Rocking back on his heels, the hunter laughed and shook his head in derision.

Jesse squeezed the rock, wanting to smack the smug grin from his face, even knowing he was armed and could best her. Tall and wiry, the man seemed as innate to the bush as the buck, the two somehow conjoined. Was this how he lived? She wanted to know.

"Can't you speak?"

Still, he stared at her with that crooked mocking grin and said nothing, though his arrogant eyes spoke reams.

What's your story? Do you live out here on the land? Is this how you survive? Her mind flung questions she couldn't voice.

She ran her fingers between the deer's dead eyes and thought of the soldiers who'd shot thousands of buffalo and left them rotting on the plains. A murderous means to a murderous end—a strategy intended to starve and cripple a people.

But what if this man *needed* to eat? She thought of his moccasins and that deerskin rag around his hips. He wasn't just a trophy hunter. He was something else; something she didn't understand.

Huffing, she released her grip on the buck.

Seizing the deer, he hefted it over his shoulders, turned, and swaggered into the forest.

"Murderer!" she yelled again, claiming the last word to soothe her indignity.

When he disappeared, she stood and brushed herself off. As she stamped back to salvage her camera gear, she chastised herself for giving in to this raw-skinned stranger. It galled her that he'd ridiculed her for something she truly believed in—saving animals by showing the world their beauty.

4

Still, she couldn't get her heartbeat to slow—or his face out of her mind. Nostrils flaring from a long, sharp nose. Slender cheeks pulled taut over high bones. Full lips pulled straight between heavily bearded cheeks. And those eyes. Lucid and entrancing one moment, dancing disdainfully the next, and silver as moondust.

He'd hefted the buck over his shoulders like it was a mere hide, when it must have weighed at least a hundred and fifty pounds. And what was he wearing? He looked like some Viking warrior playing at being seventeenth-century Chippewa. No one dressed like that. It was all denim and cotton tees. This was twenty-first-century America.

Baffling and beguiling, the man had effectively paralyzed her without uttering a word.

Embarrassed that she'd given in so easily, Jesse vowed that, if she ever saw him again, she'd hold her ground. But the thing that gnawed at her the most was how much she wanted to see him.

BROTHERS

Padding along the scrubby game trail that swept the lake, Jesse swatted blackflies from her burning cheeks. The bloodsuckers seemed to sense her heightened emotions. Perhaps the heat from her flushed face attracted them.

As she emerged from the forest, one of the feral cats skittered off the bleached gray steps of her porch in a black-and-white streak. Weathered by countless storms, the log cabin had been built by trappers in the 1850s—at least that's what the ad had said. Jesse had always wanted to live in a cabin in the bush, and now here she was. This was her haven, at least until the fall. Growing up a Seattle woman, she couldn't commit to a Midwest winter alone in the woods in this rustic cabin. There was no electricity or plumbing, and the old plank outhouse was a haven for spiders. Still, the lake was glorious, and she could rough it for a summer.

She'd focused relentlessly on her freelance career and finally secured a contract with an international magazine. The reservation teemed with wildlife, and she'd promised photographic essays for several spreads. But more importantly, with Alec gone, the assignment gave her an opportunity to contemplate her future.

A puff of smoke belched from the old stone chimney. Someone was stoking the fire. *He wouldn't follow me home, would he?* A rush of goosebumps careened up Jesse's bare arms at the thought of *him* being here in her cabin. The daring part of her hoped he was, but the other part wanted to throw up. She peered through the grimy window as her best friend turned from the stone hearth. *Rainy.* Jesse released a breath as a perplexing mix of disappointment and relief swamped her heart.

The metal latch screeched when she hefted it, and she shoved open the heavy wooden door with her shoulder. "Hey, I love your surprise visits." Jesse set down her camera gear on the planked floor, and they hugged as old friends do.

When they parted, Rainy gave her a sideways glance. "What's going on, Jess? You look weird."

"Well, I just had a very weird encounter."

"With what?"

"Not a what. A *who*. A man. A rather stunning man. And that's just how I acted. Stunned. He must think I'm a lunatic, but then again, *he* was acting like a lunatic. Standing over me, all haughty and self-assured, like God's gift to the bush."

Jesse knew she was ranting, but she couldn't stop herself. She had to get it out, and Rainy would be nothing but supportive. They'd been best friends forever, having grown up in Seattle as next-door neighbors. Social Services had farmed Rainy out to a foster home far across the country, and she hated everything and everyone but Jesse. As soon as she could, Rainy had fled back home to the reservation, where they now stood.

"You're still stunned. Like, deer-in-the-headlights stunned. Tell me what happened—slowly, and in great detail."

"Deer. Yes. But first, tea." After checking the cast-iron kettle for water, Jesse set it on the grate over the fire and added another log. Daytime temperatures soared at the end of May, but nights could dip to fifty, and the old cabin had only two tiny windows to let in the sunlight. Smoke deterred the bugs, and the fire gave her comfort. Plus, it smelled better than the small propane stove. She took down two mugs from a shelf above the table and shook a little orange pekoe into each one.

"So . . . stunning man in the woods . . ." Rainy waved her on.

Jesse exhaled. "Right. Well, I was photographing a white-tailed buck, and I had the perfect shot, and then this man . . . he just . . ."

She threw up her hands. "Well, he shot it with a bow and arrow. I got the whole thing on film, and that murder sequence is definitely going into one of my spreads. It's not even deer season." She pointed to her camera bag and shook her head. "And you should have seen what he was wearing . . . or not wearing, I should say. And this arrow. It was straight out of another century and decorated with hawk feathers. When I ran over to the deer, he stalked out of the bush, pretty much naked, with feathers braided in his long blond hair, and this bushy beard—"

"Oh my God. You saw Jed." Eyes sparkling, Rainy clapped her hands excitedly. "It had to be him."

"Jed? You *know* him?" Jesse leaned forward.

"Jedediah VanHouten." Rainy emphasized each syllable dramatically, obviously entertained by Jesse's exuberance. "Jed is Matt's little brother, and you had a rare sighting. I don't think anyone's seen him since he left Lure."

"You never mentioned him before." Jesse crossed her arms over her chest and waited for more. If you measured peoples' relationships by six degrees of separation, her mystery man had just jumped the queue. From "stranger" to "brother of best friend's boyfriend" in seconds.

Rainy shrugged. "Jed's something of a taboo subject. Matt's two years older, and I think he feels guilty he couldn't stop him from leaving."

Jesse bit her lip. In her experience, there was nothing you could do to stop someone bent on leaving. "Why? Why did he leave?" This was the story Jesse wanted. There was pain in those moondust eyes.

Rainy shook her head. "All I know is, his girlfriend died—"

"Died how?"

Rainy released a heavy breath. "He was delivering their baby."

Jesse's hand flew to her mouth. It seemed incredible that a woman could die in childbirth in the twenty-first-century, unless perhaps they were out in the middle of nowhere. Her heart thudded in her ears. She knew grief. She'd escaped to the woods herself and was still grieving Alec's death. But she sensed this man's pain was different. He'd fled to another century.

"When? How long?"

"Three years."

Jesse's breath caught. "Three years! He's been hiding in the woods for three years?"

Alec had only been gone a little over a year. She thought of her fiancé's obsession with Mount Everest. The spring storm. The avalanche. The photos of the snow where his body—

"Jesse?" Voice sliding upward like a key change, Rainy called her back.

"Sorry. I just . . . I get it, you know. I feel bad for him."

"I know." Rainy had been supporting Jesse since Alec's disappearance, and she'd finally convinced her to come to Minnesota so they could be closer together.

Jesse picked up the steaming kettle, filled the cups, and stirred a teaspoon of honey into each one. After handing Rainy a mug, she sat on the floor, clutching her own, and leaned back against the cot. Rainy joined her on the rug beside the stone hearth, and the two women sat silently, watching the steam rise.

When a blue jay squawked, Jesse glanced at the window. She'd been photographing a pair of them, their courtship, nest-building, and egg-laying in the pine tree outside the cabin. Ornithologists said they mated for life. This pair was working to keep their fledglings fed and protected from the feral cats.

"What happened to the baby?"

Rainy blew on her tea. "Her parents took him."

"God." Jed's girlfriend dies while he's delivering their child, and his son gets taken away. He lost them both. What guilt. Jesse wrinkled her nose. It didn't seem fair. "Tell me something good."

Whenever things got too intense, that was their cue to lighten the mood.

"That's easy. I *came* here to tell you something good." When Rainy smiled, her face lit up like the sun. She'd been ironically named after the lake where her grandmother was born, and it didn't match her personality at all.

"Yeah? What?"

Rainy raised her left hand and waved it in Jesse's face. "Matt proposed last night."

"No!" Reaching out, Jesse grasped her friend's hand and scrutinized the engagement ring by the light of the fire. "Is that an emerald? How did I miss this?"

"Too preoccupied with the wild brother in the woods." Rainy laughed.

"Wow. This is a serious stone." The huge emerald sparkled in myriad facets. Tiny diamonds encircled it like a ring of ice.

"You know my ranger boyfriend and his love of all things green."

"It's gorgeous. I'm so happy for you!" Throwing her arms around her friend, Jesse hugged her. "When's the big day?"

Rainy scrunched up her nose and stared at the ring. "Maybe this winter?"

Matt had a dangerous job. He was a forest ranger, and wildfires rampaged through the needleleaf forest over the late summer and fall, when the woods were hot and dry and lightning played roulette with the bush. He was away frequently.

Rainy beamed. "I can't wait."

Seeing her best friend so happy brought tears to Jesse's eyes. Rainy had never had a serious boyfriend until she came home to the reservation and met Matt VanHouten in Lure River.

"It looks like I'll be staying for the winter after all. I hope I can take part?"

"Hello, maid of honor. There'll be plenty for you to do."

Jesse smiled. "Start making a list."

"Oh, I will. And, hey, if you see Jed again, be sure to tell him his big brother's getting married. Matt would be thrilled if he came to our wedding."

"*If* I see him again." Jesse shivered as a ripple ran through her belly—a ripple that shouldn't have been there so soon after Alec's death. "Do you think I might?"

"You're both living out here alone, so odds are . . ."

Jesse threw her arms around Rainy and hugged her again. "You and Matt are the perfect couple."

Rainy smiled. "Thanks, friend. But are you really all right, way out here by yourself?"

"Of course." She didn't want to worry Rainy by mentioning the flash of fear she'd felt when Jed crept up behind her in the bush. It didn't seem to matter now anyway. "I haven't seen anyone lurking around here besides those feral cats." She winked and sipped her tea. "We're still going into town tomorrow, right? I should pick up some kibble for the poor things."

"Every Saturday, girlfriend."

"Good." Slipping the film from her camera, Jesse packed it in a cylinder. "Is there somewhere in town to get this developed?"

"You sure do things the hard way." Rainy shook her head. "Ever hear of digital?"

Jesse smiled. "Yeah, but analog far outweighs digital, and my grandfather left this camera for me to use." Her grandfather had been a famous Seattle photojournalist, and Jesse had always admired him. "Besides, I have no power and no computer. And just wait until you see these prints."

"Did you get one of *Jed?*" Rainy said in a playful tone.

Jesse shook her head. The only picture she had of Jed was the one she couldn't erase from her mind.

PREDATOR & PREY

Hawk treaded down the weedy trail, muscles bulging under the weight of the buck slung across his shoulders. Veering west at a quartz outcropping, he wended his way through the scrub. The tiny clusters of spring-green tamarack needles would glow burnished gold by fall.

The thought reminded him of the woman's hair, and he scoffed. Images of her toppling that expensive camera equipment, falling on her face in the stinging nettles, and embracing the dead deer played in his mind. Still, he couldn't help but admire her passion and grit.

Dropping the carcass, he took a deep breath and rested back against a tall black spruce. He was in no hurry. There were no clocks, crowds, or deadlines here, only the natural ebb and flow of the seasons. Life spun in circles as each species renewed itself in its own time, and all species were interconnected to create a balanced whole. If one became disproportionate, all were affected through the chain. This was ecology, the natural order of things. Predator and prey. Hunter and hunted. He was a hunter. The deer was his prey. And this was *his* kill. Case closed. Ah, but why was he trying to justify his actions with philosophy?

He scratched his back against the bark, crushed a few blackflies buzzing his ears, and wiped the sweat from his brow. The woman's face appeared again in the darkened theater of his mind. Her brown-and-gold-streaked hair shone in the sunlight. He liked her thick bangs. Her eyes were a deep blue with yellow orbs that spiraled from dark centers like tiny suns. The effect turned them green, the aqua green of a stormy lake. He tried to dislodge her image from his mind, but it lingered. Her lips were full and soft, even in her anger, and her silky cheeks scorched red with rage. She was high-spirited. Potent. She screamed "murderer" as if it were an incantation to strike him dead. If only she knew the truth in that accusation.

He glanced down at the bulging deerskin below his belly and scowled. He'd come here to escape the allure of women, and now this doe-eyed beauty had invaded his domain. Did she really care that much about the buck? Nah, she was likely a walking contradiction—one of those fanatic naturalists he'd met at college who wore T-shirts proclaiming death to hunters but drooled over the surf and turf at fancy restaurants. It was best to forget her.

Still, his best friend Joe had taught him to honor and protect women. That was the old way. Women had the power to bring life into the world, and this special gift should not be abused. He'd learned that lesson the hard way when he let Shen die. Now he was destined to walk alone. He should never have agreed to deliver their baby in Joe's cabin. He'd honored Shen's request for a home birth but neglected to protect her. They'd completed their medical training but they weren't licensed, experienced doctors. He should have listened to his gut and insisted on a hospital. His arrogance had cost her life.

Eye's burning, he sniffed and ran his fingers down the white scar that divided his left wrist from his palm. He'd cut so straight and deep he'd nearly taken his hand off that night. It was no mistake. He knew exactly how to severe an artery. After Shen died, all he'd wanted to do was join her.

Ironically, it was his passion to die that saved his life. He took his time. Prayed and grieved. Wanted to sever his hands from his body—those hands that were meant to heal and had only brought harm. But Joe heard his prayers, caught him in the act, and stopped him.

The old man was livid. Grabbing the knife, he flung it to the ground. "Jedediah can die, but Hawk must go on living in *this* world. I dreamed it, just like I dreamed what you're trying to do now."

Jed looked at Joe strangely. He had no words.

"The first morning I met you, I saw a little hawk with eyes that took in all the world." As he talked, Joe bound his wrist with cotton strips from a ripped pillowcase to stop the bleeding. "Those eyes still have much to see."

With pressure, the bleeding slowed. Joe pulled fishing line and a needle from his pouch while Jed sat silently, shocked by divine intervention. "You're going to stitch this skin tightly back together and never try this again. Every time you see this scar, you'll remember that these hands are a gift. You're going to heal many people with these hands."

Joe sat beside him all night, drinking tea, and by morning Jed was dead and Hawk very much alive. "One day you'll fly beyond this grief. But until then, you must walk with it. Be with it. You can't escape by dying. There's no honor in that."

Hefting the carcass to his shoulders, Hawk walked on. He had to honor Joe by being the best man he could. And that meant keeping one eye on the green-eyed woman who'd invaded his woods, no matter how she made him feel.

A hundred yards from the cave, he arrived at the grassy glen where he skinned and butchered his meat. After hanging the deer from a sapling, he secured its head by a rawhide thong and braced the weight with three green poles, tripod fashion. Then he unsheathed a ten-inch hunting knife and slit the buck along the underside of its legs and up the belly to the chin. Guts poured out onto the mossy grass. They would feed the wild ones—the wolves, ravens, and other scavengers. All bellies would be full tonight and the remains gone by morning. There was a food chain in the bush the woman knew nothing about.

He skinned methodically, listening to the eerie cries of a pair of mating loons on the nearby lake. After spreading the hide hair-side down on the ground, he packed the choice saddles and tidbits inside. Then he gathered up the edges of his simple sack and walked the remaining distance to his home.

Joe had brought him to this high dry cave when he was just a boy. Hawk's primal instincts, plus the skills Joe had taught him, enabled him to survive in the bush as a predator, not prey.

The woman was clearly prey. She had no idea what could happen to her out here. What was she doing on the reservation with all that expensive equipment anyway? Likely, she was some kind of journalist, sticking her nose into places it didn't belong. Places where she could lose it. But below her nose were those thick pink lips. Lips he ached to kiss.

"Damn feisty woman." Her passion had ignited a blue flame that seared his heart and sent a forgotten urge riveting up his thighs.

SISTER

Hawk smiled as Sister dashed from the cave, alert to the vibration of his footfalls. Scenting the bloody bundle he carried in his hands, the white timber wolf jumped up on him from behind, nuzzled her muzzle under his arm, and kissed his face with long wet licks. He grinned and, encouraged, she lay on her belly, muzzle to paws, awaiting her share.

"Missed me, huh?"

Her turquoise eyes flashed when she heard his voice. She seemed to love its deep timbre and his tough fingernails scratching her ears and belly. A strong bond had developed between them during the seasons they'd shared the cave.

He'd found her whimpering in a shadowy corner. A runt abandoned by the pack, she was starving and fearful. Her daintiness had reminded him of Shen. He'd been grieving hard for her then— her and the child. So, with unyielding love, he raised the wolf, calling her Sister because he longed for family.

He dropped the hide to the ground and retrieved a hind leg from his pungent parcel. "Here you go, girl. Today we feast."

Next, he scooped up the deer's brain and placed it in a canister. He'd crafted the vessel with Lake Superior red clay and engraved it with the profile of a hawk, hook-beaked and eerie-eyed.

The morning he'd left Lure River, he'd taken nothing but his Swiss Army knife. He needed to begin again and sculpt a new life with this new identity. In the dark forest, days before, he'd stood, sullenly fondling the medicine bundle Joe had made him as a boy and strung around his neck. Joe had taught him everything he needed to know about survival over the many years they'd been friends.

Since they'd never married, Hawk had no legal rights. Shen's parents had claimed her remains and used their power and influence to also claim his son. He saw then why she'd hated them and fled to college. The years hadn't dulled the memory or the feelings.

He'd rambled in the bush for days, then gone to the cave. As soon as he entered, he knew he had to stay—how long, he didn't know. He knew only that this sacred place would heal him. When he returned to share his plan with Joe, the old man was pleased. Joe gave him an iron kettle, an axe, a metal match, a hunting knife, and a packet of steel needles.

"Everything else you can make yourself." And he did. "I'll come see you," Joe promised. But so far, he hadn't made it. His wife's cancer had returned, and he was spending every moment with her. Hawk wanted to stay and look after Effie too, but Joe said, "No. You go and live for us all." So Hawk went. He'd proven it was possible to survive with a vacant heart, though he wondered at times if he was truly alive.

The sound of the churning mountain stream drew his thoughts back to the task at hand. He set the covered cannister in a stream of clear, cold water twenty feet from the mouth of the cave. It flowed from an underground spring into a hollow below. The stream never froze, so provided a year-round supply of drinking water. Plus, it doubled as a cooler.

Later, when he'd scraped the deer's hair from the hide, he'd mash the brain and rub the paste into the skin to tan it. Nearby, he'd constructed a four-foot-high platform stand from green sticks. Now he built a small fire just inside the cave opening and placed the stand over it. He sliced the tender venison into strips and hung them to dry along the green poles. The fire kept the flies at bay. The sweet, smoky jerky kept indefinitely and could easily be packed for storing and traveling, then rehydrated with boiling water to make a fine nutritious soup.

Because he was a lone man, Hawk didn't hunt often. One kill lasted many weeks. He built a second fire in his hearth and hung the iron kettle from its sturdy tripod. A venison stew flavored with wild onions, mushrooms, and herbs would fill this pot. Later, when it had simmered, he'd refrigerate it as he'd done the brain. Thus, the deer was honored by its use.

Hours later, when all the meat was dealt with, he placed the hide in a huge birchbark vessel of water to soak for a few days. Jerky smoking, stew bubbling, Hawk looked at his bloodstained skin. It was dry and itchy. He smelled his armpits. "Sister, I need a bath. Let's go."

He bundled up fresh clothing and they padded downhill to the waterfall below his cave. The sun hung low in the western horizon like a golden sphere and painted the sky in tangerine clouds, while the moon rose to the south. Her full, round face shone like a polished silver locket. At this moment, both were apparent in the dusky sky. It was a sacred time when Grandmother Moon and Grandfather Sun joined together in the heavens. Bats swooped and fluttered from the trees, catching night flies. A great gray owl hooted from the shadows, and the wolf pack howled. Hawk pictured them sitting back-to-back in a circle, tails wagging and touching in the center, their bellies bulging with fresh deer.

The waterfall was frigid in May, but Hawk stood naked beneath it, scrubbing the stench of the kill from his skin.

Sister stopped gnawing on her leg bone and joined the wolf chorus. Her howling seemed more mournful than usual, an anguished longing for her own kind. Hawk knew she'd leave soon. She was past two and would soon come into estrus. Then she'd go looking for her mate—if he didn't find her first. Perhaps she heard his howl even now and was answering him. In the wild, all had mates.

He felt a sudden tightness in his chest and thought of the blonde woman. Did she have a mate? Why was she living alone in the bush?

Bouncing up the stony bank, he shook the water from his mane. As the cool air dried his flesh, he pulled on buckskin pants and tied the drawstring around his waist. Then he slipped a hide jacket over his shoulders, leaving it loose and open. The night breeze caressed his chest. He felt good. Ravenous. He punched Sister playfully, and they bounded up the hill together.

"A woman tried to take our deer today." His lip pulled into a lopsided grin as the wolf cocked her head, trying to understand. Sizzling venison steaks dripped juice on the cooking fire, causing tiny explosions of flames. "If she'd had her way, we'd be eating berries. I know you like berries but think how many it would take to fill our bellies for the next month."

Hawk feasted on the venison and lay back against his thick bed of cedar boughs and rabbit skins, absorbed by the dancing flames. He shook his head to dislodge the vision but couldn't get the woman out of his mind. He could see her amber hair, shining like honey in the sunshine. It framed her ruby face and stormy eyes. Beneath a pale slender neck, her breasts shook from running and strained against her turquoise shirt. It didn't escape him that she'd been braless.

His thighs tingled, and he scoffed. "I don't want another woman." But even as his words died in the shadowy cave, he knew it was a lie. He wanted a woman. He wanted her. There was something irresistible about her, something beyond her obvious beauty. An inner spark that ignited his cold, lonely soul.

Closing his eyes, he imagined the woman. Her passion and daring. Every inch of her cried out to him, and his spirit heaved in answer.

The fire flickered in the darkness, casting shadows on the damp cave walls. Above his head, the story of an ancient deer slaying was painted in stone. And across from it, on the far wall, was a more recent tale, painted by him, of a hunter killing a black bear—an eternal expression of his battle to the death with *Makwa*, whose winter residence had been this particular cave.

The huge black bear had swaggered into the cave that first November just before dawn. Eight hundred pounds of predator. Surprised to scent man and wolf in his usual winter den, he'd stood in the doorway, stretched to his full height, clacked his teeth, and growled.

"Stay back, Sister." She'd waited in the corner, eyes wide and ears flat.

He turned to the bear. "There are plenty of caves, Makwa." Hawk hoped the bear was bluffing. Most black bears he'd encountered hadn't attacked. He talked to them, and they backed away, leaving him unharmed. But here, in the cave, he couldn't back away. There was nowhere to go. "Just go back the way you came. Go on, now. Get."

Raising an arm, the bear growled a second time, louder and more aggressively. Then the arm came down and pounded the ground.

This was more than a bluff. Unprepared to be the bear's last meal before his winter sleep, Hawk stood to his full height, growled from his core, and unsheathed his hunting knife. There was no element of surprise. The only chance he stood to win this fight was to make it past those keen claws.

Shrieking, Hawk had sprung from below, his knife pointed up. He felt the bear's arms close around him in a fierce hug. Smelled the fetid breath. Heard the teeth gnash. Felt his flesh rip as the bear stroked his arms with steel claws. Then he'd plunged the knife into its throat.

Air, saliva, and blood bubbled from the wound as he twisted with deft movements, severing tubes and arteries. The bear's guttural bawls faded as it lost consciousness, and when it fell, the earth throbbed her sorrow.

Hawk slid down himself, drawing deep lungfuls of oxygen. Staring at the bloody black bear, his eyes filled with tears, and he tapped his forehead to touch the bear's.

Makwa would physically sustain him through the winter ahead. His fur, fat, and flesh would provide food, fuel, and warmth. But of greater importance was Hawk's victory. He was protected by the spirits of this cave. Having slain Makwa, a creature who symbolized strength and courage, that powerful medicine became his. The bear had become one with the hawk. Hawk had become one with the wild. He would survive.

This is what the painting said.

LURE

Sam parked his pickup and sat for a moment beside Ira with his elbow still hanging out the open window. A moist river breeze rattled the rain-rusted hinges on his office shingle. The sign read *Samuel F. Flanagan Insurance* in six-inch black, glossy letters. Down in the bottom right-hand corner, scratched in letters half that size, it read *Federal Indian Agent*. Although the original Flanagan had been relieved of this post in the 1860s, Sam kept the sign. He felt it lent his business notoriety and character. Besides, a man needed a sense of his own history, especially in a town like Lure.

Lure River was its official name on account of the massive waterway that ripped through the land, but everyone who lived here just called it Lure. It was like any other sleepy town in the Midwest—except for one thing: it straddled the Chippewa reservation, which bordered the other side of the river, like a crow on a fencepost. Lure was a fertile town of trees, lakes, and contradictions. Many of the residents were descendants of immigrant settlers who'd worked this land the last two centuries. But lately, a host of back-to-the-landers had fled the nearby cities to take advantage of cheap old fixer-uppers in Lure. Jobs were scarce, so most of them hooked up to the Internet and worked from home or built lavish artist-studio additions to their country homes.

Sam didn't care one way or the other if he could sell them insurance, which he believed was an essential part of life. And some of the women were young and pretty, a welcome sight in Lure. Beyond that, there were the trail guides and outfitters who serviced the hordes of hunters and fishermen who arrived seasonally, loggers, and the few white-collars, such as himself and old Doc VanHouten, who tended to personal needs.

Main Street boasted Hanson's General Store, Hank's Roadkill Café—the local butcher's greasy spoon, which served the best rabbit stew west of Superior—Biff's Barbershop for the fellas, and Millie's Beauty Salon for the ladies. Gold Corp Trust, a bank that had been manned for generations but was more a dream than a reality, mirrored the Superette. Sam's father, Sheriff Flanagan, hung his hat beside Gold Corp, though he mostly cruised around town in his pickup.

Gus VanSickler's garage and filling station had been around forever. Their gothic house topped the hill and crowned the town with a sense of old-world mystery. Sam thought it would make a great backdrop for a horror movie. Across from the gas station, Teddy Shanks, a realtor with high hopes and a low bank balance, caught visitors as they came and went from the highway. Sam's closest neighbor was Chin's, a restaurant by the river with a cook who spoke only Cantonese and offered a sweet and sour buffet seven days a week.

For anything else, you had to cruise the numbered side streets. Main Street dead-ended at the river, where you were forced to cross the bridge onto the reservation, drive east along River Road, or head west toward the mill–turned–cannabis farm and distillery.

The town served all their needs. Well, mostly. There were three churches, all of which had declining congregations. The few white-hairs that still believed plunked their butts down on the wooden pews religiously, but most people, Sam included, couldn't give a preacher's ass about the Bible anymore. There was a tongue-wagging Pentecostal church that caught the rollers; a Protestant holdout for the Germans, Dutch, and Swedes who'd settled Minnesota; and a Catholic parish that paid homage to the voyageurs and the Irish. Sam's longtime friend Ira Griswold had a good

Catholic mother who attended mass and confession with the regularity of a saint, and she saw to it that Ira did likewise.

Sam got out of the pickup and shut the door gently. Pearl was vintage—a cherry-red 1988 Chevy Silverado—and Sam loved her to bits. He'd refurbished Pearl himself and tended her for over twenty years. His mother had loved the dark-red velvet bench seats and matching carpeting. She said she felt like a rodeo queen when he drove her around town in Pearl, and that made him laugh since she'd never ridden a horse or even been to a rodeo. Jenny Flanagan had never made it out of Lure, and now she was buried here. Planted for good. He should have taken her on a road trip, and he would have if it weren't for the old man.

Sam scooted up the stairs, but, behind him, the veranda's wooden floorboards creaked and groaned under Ira's weight. Once, long ago, Ira Griswold had held a title—Heavyweight Boxing Champion, 2001. He'd been only nineteen years old at the time, and with his flaming red hair, green silk shorts, rippling muscles, and six-foot three-inch frame, he cut a striking figure. No man could take him down. Folks still called him Griz, though never to his face. No one dared taunt that wild Irish temper. Sam had figured on managing his career until Ira slugged a logger one night at Billy's Bar and killed him. He got sent up for manslaughter, and when he returned to his ma ten years later, he'd lost his innocence and found God.

Now Ira's muscle had turned to flab, and the heavyweight boxing champion was an ordinary red-haired madman. Ira had turned his parents' farm into an auto wrecker's and managed to survive among the rubber tires and rusty frames. It was rumored—a rumor propagated by Sam—that the Griz could still bend a steel frame in his bare hands if he got mad enough. But nobody had the guts to verify it.

Sam hung around with Ira for protection as much as anything

else. At five foot six and one hundred thirty pounds, it didn't hurt to have a big man in your corner when things got out of hand at Billy's Bar. Plus, they were old friends and clung to each other as old friends do.

Sam unlocked the door while Ira crouched to clear the six-foot doorframe. Then Ira's arm brushed the closed venetian blinds, and a dusty clamor shook the stifling room.

"Couldn't you get in here just once without hitting those goddamn blinds?"

"Don't curse. Take 'em down if it bothers you so much." Ira sneezed and wiped his nose on his shirtsleeve. His allergies had been raging all month.

"And have the whole town peering in here, seeing our business?"

Ira shook his head. His swollen eyelids drooped. "I'm beat, Sammy. Let's just get on with it."

Sam took a tired landscape painting off the olive-green wall to reveal a large steel wall safe. "I sure am glad my great-granddaddy didn't trust banks after the crash in '29." He clicked through the combination, carefully obscuring Ira's view, and swung open the heavy metal door. "Look at it, Ira! Another few weeks, and we can retire."

He glanced over at Ira, who'd squeezed into the tweed armchair and was dozing like a baby. His mother kept him dosed up on allergy medication to avoid having to deal with his asthma. Ira could rhyme off exactly which trees and grasses were the cause of his misery at any given time.

Grinning, Sam pulled a bulging purple Crown Royal whiskey bag from inside his canvas jacket. He kissed it affectionately and deposited it beside several others in the safe. Closing the door, he listened for that satisfying click. After he replaced the painting, he nudged Ira with his knee. "Wake up, man. You can go home and sleep. Come on, I'll drop you off."

Ira groaned, yet slowly rose. He stretched up a cowhide hand and hit the ceiling fixture with a crack. It swayed, and light spun round the room.

"Christ, Ira. Get out of here before you break something."

"I'm going. I'm going."

A scruffy black cat sprawled in the sun on Sam's top step. Chin's Chinese kept cats to deal with rodents, and it was rumored they were the secret ingredient in his sweet and sour *chicken* balls. Scowling, Sam nudged it with his cowboy boot. "Damn lazy varmint."

The cat yowled and disappeared into the shrubs, and Ira shook his head. "You shouldn't have made it run in front of you like that, Sammy. My ma always says it's real bad luck to have a black cat cross your path."

"Your ma says a lot of things, Ira." Sam's lip pulled to one side. "Just get in the truck."

Saturday shoppers bustled up and down Main Street. The parking lot at the Superette was full. White-hairs in polyester smocks strolled out of the post office, leafing through envelopes and flyers. People stopped to gossip on the street. Sam nodded and said good-day to everyone. That was just how he was.

A pretty blonde woman walked out of the Superette with a satchel slung over her shoulder, and a bulging bag of groceries in her hand. Though she wore a loose pink T-shirt, her curves flexed beneath it. She hurried down the sidewalk toward Sam and Ira, hips swaying in tight blue jeans.

"Lordy. Where'd *she* come from?" Sam's elbow jutted out the window as usual. He leaned against the door and ogled. There were few dateable women in Lure, so to have any kind of sex life at all, he had to drive twenty miles to the casino or thirty to the Handimart, which ran a rip-roaring business for truckers in the back parking lot. Either way, he had to pay for it, which a good-looking businessman on the south side of forty should never have to do. Most nights he made do with a selection of fifteen-year-old DVDs that had lost their luster, though not their effect.

Ira's red eyes suddenly opened wide. "Looks like an angel." He made the sign of the cross near his heart.

Sam cast him a sideways glance and ignored the gesture. "Looks real enough to me." The girl had big green eyes, a wide square jaw, full lips, and an Angelina-Jolie swagger.

Sam slid out of the truck and hoofed it up to her while Ira lagged behind. "Excuse me, miss. Do you need some help with your groceries?"

She smiled coyly. "No, thank you. I'm almost there." Her gaze traveled beyond them to an old baby-blue Jeep Wrangler with the top down. A good-looking Chippewa girl was sitting in the driver's seat.

"All right, then." Sam tipped his ball cap. "But if you ever need anything . . . anything at all . . ." He handed her his card.

"I'll be sure to call, Mr. . . . ." She peered down at his card, then stared up with those big green eyes. "Flanagan. What does the F stand for?"

"Fearless." Sam didn't miss a beat. "Anything you need, you be sure to call. Day or night."

She stuck the card in the pocket of her jeans, and he swallowed hard as he watched her walk away.

THE KISS

The wind-licked cabin smelled of conifer smoke and kerosene. Moonlight streamed through open fissures in the cracked clay long packed between hand-hewn logs. The night wind mingled with the hoots and screeches of night flyers.

Jesse cuddled in her flannel sleeping sack, transfixed by the crackling embers of the glowing fire, and thought of Jed. *The poor man. Tormented by grief and self-imposed seclusion, he must be so lonely. No wonder he acted so strangely.* She couldn't imagine what it would be like to lose the people you loved and then not talk to another human for three whole years. She'd only been out here a couple of weeks, and before that she'd had Rainy.

Finally, her heavy eyelids closed, leaving her soul vulnerable to the spirits of her dreams.

She was deep in the boreal forest, trudging through a black spruce bog. It sucked at the bottoms of her bare feet as bristly boughs reached out to fondle her flesh. She walked and walked, trying to touch the full moon, which hung like a silvery beacon just out of reach. She was weary and sore when the bog suddenly morphed into a grassy glade bursting with wildflowers. Lying on her back in the thick grass, she inhaled their sweet scent and stared up at the moon. When from out of its depths a shadow plummeted to Earth, her body froze. The sleek silhouette slipped closer and closer until she was staring into Jed's steely eyes. With taloned fingers, he gently plucked her from the field and flew her into the starry heavens. Crushed against the warm flesh of his neck, she inhaled his scent, her breasts heaving against his as their bodies merged.

Jesse moaned and shuddered, awakening feverish from her dream, the details still vivid. Would this man leave her no peace?

Must he invade her mind even as she slept? Truth be told, it was a pleasing escape from her recurring nightmare of the avalanche, where she ran endlessly through piles of snow, searching for Alec. Still.

When she opened her eyes, dawn was breaking, lighting her cabin with glints of gold. She sipped from a cup of cold tea as she pulled on her jeans and turquoise sweater.

As she left the cabin, one of the feral cats, who'd been sleeping on the porch in a sun streak, darted into the bushes. She'd seen several ferals since moving in and wondered how they'd survived with no one to feed them. The cabin hadn't been used in years. This cat was white and burnt orange, wild and beautiful. The tin plate of kibble she'd set out last night was already empty. "Sorry," she said, as she walked down the steps. "No more until suppertime."

Her dream had left her skittish, and when a ruffed grouse flapped suddenly across her path, she bounced backward and nearly fell. Her heavy camera gear often unbalanced her delicate frame. After steadying herself, she took a couple of deep breaths and continued down the trail. As she walked along the lakeshore, the emerging sun shimmered across the water. Buzzing, honking, and chattering—the sounds she loved—brought comfort.

She positioned her camera in a rush blind she'd recently erected adjacent to the river mouth. This gentle pool was sheltered from the lake winds and deeper currents and protected by sweeping softwoods and papery birches. It provided a quiet haven for forest and river creatures. A flock of green-winged teal dived in the shallows, the drake's chestnut and emerald head patches reflecting the sun's early rays. From out on a far tamarack, a belted kingfisher rattled and descended beak first, speared a crayfish, and returned to his perch.

Jesse caught it all on film, shutter clicking, her trained eye pressed to the lens. Now and then she paused to write in her journal, accurately recording each of the many bird species, from robins to ravens. Hordes of whistling spring frogs seduced potential mates in the rushes, and the haunting laughter of loons drifted in from the lake.

She felt her tense muscles soften as she relaxed into doing what she loved. Rainy had been right about Lure River. This was a good place for Jesse to heal from Alec's death and decide where and how she wanted to live. Of course, Rainy wanted her to stay. But only time would tell.

The southeast corner of the pond harbored an old beaver lodge adjacent to a reedy cove. A red-winged blackbird perched on a velvety cattail, singing. Turquoise dragonflies coupled and spun through the rushes and yellow water lilies.

Jesse maintained her vigil, quietly focusing, zooming, and snapping photographs for another hour. When, from the corner of her eye, she saw something dark slip into the pool along the opposite bank, she held her breath and waited. A trail of bubbles arose a few feet distant. She exhaled and, camera looped around her neck, crept cautiously on hands and knees toward the bank. A head popped up. Bristly whiskers twitched on a broad brown muzzle, and dark eyes observed her suspiciously.

A river otter!

"Don't be—" she whispered, but before she could finish, the otter sank silently straight down, leaving scarcely a ripple to mark the spot. A squirming flash of brown near the lodge caught her eye. Was the otter there so soon? Or was there another one? Perhaps they were a pair.

She hunkered down cross-legged and smiled. River otters. What an opportunity. They were secretive, yet she knew of naturalists who'd studied them, even lived with them. Humans swam with dolphins. Could she one day swim with otters? That would make quite a story, especially if she could photograph them up close and underwater. It would take time and trust. She had the time. What she needed to do was gain their trust.

The river otter had been trapped into extinction during the fur trade years and only started to come back during the 1980s. Now that there were more of them in the wild, the government allowed trapping during the fall and winter. It might be different on the reservation, but Jesse doubted it. They were safe for the moment, but for how long? There was likely a pup or two tucked away in the lodge. If she could increase awareness through an emotionally appealing spread, perhaps she could save some of them and give her work real meaning.

She worked quietly for a couple of hours, shooting macro shots of insects on flower heads. The otters might be watching, and she wanted them to get used to her. When the sun rose high in the sky, she decided they'd retreated for their daily siesta. Her stomach rumbled, and she reached into her pocket for a bag of trail mix. After a few handfuls, she washed it down with water from her canteen. It was a long walk back to the cabin.

As she turned to dismantle her camera gear, she spotted a flash of white near a blackberry thicket. A timber wolf crouched, ears pricked, sea-blue eyes staring intensely. The breeze riffled the silvery blaze that painted its muzzle and ran down the neck and chest.

A surge of adrenaline rippled through Jesse's limbs, but she took a breath and calmed herself. It was just watching. That was all. Turning the tables, she snapped a few photographs of it. Then she just stood still, impressed by the wolf's feral beauty. Warily, she scanned the surrounding undergrowth for others. A hungry pack might rip her to shreds, but this wolf appeared to be alone, and intuition told her it wasn't a threat.

Still, she picked up a hard butt of driftwood from the bank and set it near to hand. It was a meager defense, but something just the same. She packed her gear up slowly and kept watch on the white wolf whose eyes followed her every move. Then she headed home. This forest held many surprises.

Her random thoughts were interrupted by the discovery of a large bark dish sitting on the veranda in front of her cabin door. She peered inside. A bloody venison roast slumped in the dish, buzzing with flies. The stink of raw flesh spasmed her stomach, and she gagged.

Impulsively, she picked up the dish and hurled it across the glade, where it crashed against a spruce, split wide, and sent its bloody contents thudding to the earth. "I don't want your stinking meat! How could you butcher that beautiful creature, you murderer? You, Jack the Ripper!" Flinging her arms wildly in the air, she kicked at the loose planks on the veranda floor.

In a flash of white, the timber wolf burst into the glade and sank its canines into the roast.

Jesse leapt back toward the door. Then, catching the wolf's true intent, she stopped and glared into the forest as the wolf hauled the roast into the trees.

"I know you're out there! Lurking in the woods like some perverted Peeping Tom." Sniffing, she threw back her head. "You're no man. A real man wouldn't hide in the woods. A real man would face me."

It was a ridiculous taunt, but he triggered some passion in her she couldn't control. To her surprise, Jed stepped forward into the sun, naked chest gleaming with sweat. He stood poised, muscles taut, waiting. The look of daring etched on his face mirrored her own.

Jesse sat down on the top step of her veranda like a haughty queen. But when she looked at Jed, standing so vulnerably before her, compassion tore a hole in her heart. She remembered what Rainy had said of his grief and suffering. He was Matt's little brother. His girlfriend was dead. His son gone.

She sighed one long, frustrated sigh. "Look, I don't eat meat. I'm a vegetarian, and I think it's wrong to kill animals. All right?"

Jed glared at her from across the glade and said nothing.

The man needed to revive his social skills. He'd been too long alone in the bush. But he'd brought her what he considered to be a gift. "My name is Jesse Jardine." She bit her lip and waited. Nothing. "You're Jed, right? Jedediah VanHouten?"

His gray eyes burned into hers. "Jed is dead."

Jesse choked—she was not expecting that—and stared at her tightly clenched fists. Should she mention Matt? Remind him of his family?

She opened her mouth to speak and then he was there, bright and hot as the sun.

"So you're a killer of plants, and that makes you better than me." His voice was low and raspy, like he'd been partying all night, though she knew that couldn't be the case.

A killer of plants?

"The spirit of this strawberry is no less sentient than the spirit of a deer," he said, opening his hand to reveal a tiny red fruit.

Where did that come from? Is he a magician?

He held the strawberry between his thumb and fingertip and popped it reverently into his mouth. "I'm thankful for *all* life that sustains me. Do my beliefs make me a murderer? Do my beliefs make me less than a man?"

What could she say to that? This man—the way he spoke, the words he used—baffled her. She continued to stare silently at her hands.

Leaning forward, he cupped her face in his palms and raised her eyes to meet his. "I asked you a question, Jesse Jardine."

Her dry throat ached. Trembling from his touch, she saw her tense face reflected in the black mirrors of his eyes. With pouting lips, and panicked eyes fighting to hold back tears, she called to him.

His mouth closed over hers. And then his tongue was running along her moist lips, parting them tenderly only to fill her with his passion. She couldn't resist him. She tasted the sweet berry on his tongue and smelled his smoky, earthy musk. The kiss went on and on, and Jesse fought to control her desire, to stop her hands from touching, to stop her body from bending into his. A moan escaped from someplace deep in her throat, and he ran his fingers down the damp flesh of her neck and touched her there. Every pore in her body screamed for him, though she dared not move.

At last, and too soon, his lips released, and he whispered in a husky voice, "I *am* a man." Turning his sinewy back to her, he sauntered into the bush.

"That does not make you a man," Jesse murmured.

But only the wind heard her words.

APPALOOSA

Jesse's stomach rumbled, but she felt no desire to eat. It was late afternoon, and she hadn't eaten a thing since morning. She'd felt the pounds slipping away over the last few days but couldn't seem to lose the anguish that gripped her guts and squeezed. Was it fear? Anger? Loneliness? Or perhaps it was a mingling of all three, repressed for months and now surfacing since she was finally alone with her thoughts. Three weeks in, and she was a mess. She'd chosen to live alone in this cabin to *find* herself but wasn't sure she liked what she was finding.

And then there was that kiss. She'd been obsessing about it, about *him*, for days. *"I am a man."* Well, there was no doubt about that.

Alec, her fiancé—the man she'd promised to marry and love forever—had been dead just over a year, and it seemed too soon to think about someone else with this kind of intensity.

Alec had flown into Kathmandu last March to get a jump on the hundreds of climbers determined to scale the south side of Mount Everest from Nepal. A West Coast stuntman, Alec was in demand because people in the business knew he'd do anything. When he heard rumors of a new mountaineering film, he thought adding Everest to his résumé would not only land him a role in the film but help him break into Hollywood as an actor. After an unusually warm spell, he persuaded his Sherpa to take him up. That was the last she'd heard from him. News and photos of the avalanche arrived in May. They'd yet to recover his body.

The wound was still raw; yet, here she was, kissing a stranger on her porch steps and enjoying it. *Really* enjoying it. More than she'd ever enjoyed kissing Alec. She gnawed at the skin inside her cheek. This was bad. Really bad.

She rummaged around in a cardboard box packed with books and pictures until she found the old photo album. Leafing backward, memories leapt from the pages. Alec's bearded face and twinkling eyes smiled from beneath his snowy parka. That was when he'd been training that last winter for Nepal.

Alec and Jesse had been friends since childhood—shoveling in the sand, boating and swimming, building snow forts, horseback riding. If there was action, Alec was in the midst of it. Later, they'd spent summers hiking the backwoods trails and peat bogs, searching for orchids to photograph for their collection.

It was Alec who'd inspired Jesse to become a nature journalist and photographer. Although she'd always been at home outside in nature, he'd convinced her that she could make a living doing something she loved. And she had.

How could she betray Alec's memory by kissing Jed?

They'd canoed the still waters and rafted the white waters. Alec had been her energy. Her life force. *He* was the animal rights activist. The vegetarian. He had an inner strength few could match, and though her passion for him had never come close to what she'd felt in her dream or on her front porch last week, Alec was her anchor. *Damn him for leaving me. It's not fair.* Jesse bit her lip and huffed. Closing the album, she lay back on her bed and hugged it to her chest.

When she heard the growl of a truck's engine outside the cabin, she dropped the photo album and hurried to the door.

"Rainy! Matt! I didn't know you were coming."

"Of course you didn't. You don't have cell service out here." Matt smiled to soften the tone.

"Ignore him. We brought you a surprise."

From the trailer behind the white pickup, Jesse could hear

stomping and swishing. She bolted down the veranda steps. "A horse? You brought me a horse?"

Rainy beamed. "You're going to love her. She's the most contented horse I've ever met."

"Content to stand and eat." Matt winked.

Jesse grinned. "What's her name?"

"Reba." Matt smirked as he walked by Jesse and opened the back of the trailer.

"As in McEntire?" The only Reba she'd ever heard of was the famous red-haired country singer.

"You guessed it."

When Matt led the horse down the ramp, Jesse was thrilled. She was white but wore a leopard pattern as if she'd been splattered in copper paint. "An Appaloosa!" Jesse had harbored a mad love for the spotted ponies since she was a little girl.

Rainy poked Jesse with her elbow. "Matt's uncle is crazy for country, and the night before this filly was born he went to a Reba McEntire concert."

Matt walked the horse around so Jesse could admire her. "Yep. When he saw the color of her spots, it was obvious she was a Reba."

Jesse stroked the mare's nose. "Hello, Reba. We're going to have a great time together."

"She responds well, especially to sugar cubes." Matt took a handful from his jacket pocket and passed them to Jesse. "My uncle was going to pasture her for the summer—"

"So we talked him into letting you keep her here."

Jesse smiled. Rainy was finishing Matt's sentences. It was cute.

"She's old, and she's slow."

"And she's beautiful. I love her. Thank you both so much."

"Well, there's a catch . . ." Rainy raised her eyebrows. "Now you've got transportation, you can ride over and visit."

"Deal." Jesse placed a sugar cube on her palm and held it flat under the horse's soft flickering muzzle.

"I brought you a big bag of oats. Don't give her too much. Well, I don't have to tell you about horses."

Jesse stroked the mare's shoulder with one hand and tickled her velvety nose with the other. She and Rainy had spent half their lives riding Jesse's father's horses. They were one of his passions. The other was women, who he treated on par with his horses. A succession of *aunts* had lived with them after Jesse's mother died, but none stuck. Jesse escaped with Alec, Rainy, and the horses.

"You won't need a saddle or bridle with her," Matt said. "We thought you could stake her out in the daytime and put her in the old shed at night. She'll let you know if there are any predators around."

Predators. There were a few big cats wilder than the ferals that lived around the shed—bobcats, lynx, even cougars. Not to mention bears and wolves. An image of the white wolf flashed through her mind.

"I saw him again," Jesse said.

"Already?" Rainy's mouth dropped open.

"My brother?" Matt's eyes lit up.

"I told him," Rainy confessed.

Jesse nodded. "Come inside, and I'll make tea." She wanted to know more about the man who'd chosen to live in the bush.

Matt led the mare to a grassy spot beneath the trees. "I'll be right there. Don't start without me."

"So?" Rainy thrust her hands in the air as soon as he'd turned.

"He kissed me."

"What?" Rainy raised her palm and waited for a slap. "You obviously liked it, judging by your face."

"Yeah, well . . . Yeah."

"He just showed up here and kissed you? What happened?" Rainy always wanted the details.

"He came by last Sunday morning with a venison roast."

"Oh. Big mistake."

"Yeah, and he thinks he won this round."

"Jesse." Rainy clicked her tongue in a scolding way.

Matt bounced into the cabin and made himself comfortable on a rag rug by the stone fireplace. There were no couches or armchairs. Jesse's bed was the only padded surface in the room, and the lumps didn't count for much. "So, what's the news?"

"Jed kissed Jesse."

"What?" Matt chuckled and shook his head. "Go, little brother."

Jesse glared at her friend. "Rainy!"

"Hey, we're engaged. We share information." Rainy shrugged.

Jesse wasn't upset, really. This was just very new and exciting, and she didn't know what to make of it . . . or Jed.

"Tell me something, Matt. Has he always been weird? He talks like he's back in the seventeenth century. I mean, how do you fight with someone who compares the spirit of a deer with the spirit of a strawberry? And he's so intense."

Rainy laughed, but it came out in a bit of a choke.

"What? *I'm* not intense," Jesse said defensively.

"No, not at all." Rainy's eyes were wide, but her quivering lips fought back a smile.

"Yeah, well, my little brother's a very unique individual." Matt drew in a big breath. "I remember the day my mom brought home *Dances with Wolves.* You remember that movie? Jed was seven, and we couldn't get him away from the television the whole weekend. He kept watching it over and over."

"Yeah, well, he's got his own Two Socks now," Jesse said, thinking of the wolf Kevin Costner befriended in the film.

"That doesn't surprise me." Matt shook his head. "Right after that, he started running off to the reservation. We kept finding him in the bush or hunting with this old Anishinaabe man named Joe."

"Anishinaabe?"

"That's what we call ourselves," Rainy said.

Jesse nodded, and Matt continued his story.

"My mother used to say she regretted naming Jed after her great-great-grandfather Jedediah Duchesne. He was a French fur trader who married a Dakota woman back in the 1800s."

Rainy gave him a quick backhand to the shoulder. "You never told me that."

"Yeah, well, wait till my mother gets out her genealogical charts and records. She's got paper on everyone dating back to the Stone Age."

Jesse liked the idea of a family history. Her parents had never said much about their relations beyond the grandparents she met as a kid, and she had no idea where they came from.

"Anyway, my parents finally made a deal with Jed. He could spend weekends and holidays with Joe if he didn't run off and focused on his schoolwork when he was home."

"So, some old Anishinaabe man got joint custody of your brother?" Jesse giggled. The man she'd met in the bush was starting to make sense.

"Joe and Effie pretty much adopted him. He stayed with them every holiday he could manage. All summer vacation. Long weekends. Easter. Christmas."

Jesse got down the cups and lit the small propane stove. "Is that why he talks like it's the seventeenth century? Did he get that from Joe?" She spooned tea into the chipped mugs.

Matt shook his head. "Nope. That's one-hundred-percent Jed. He told me once he was born in the wrong place and time."

Jesse bit her lip. "He said something really strange and creepy. It wasn't just *what* he said, it was *how* he said it." She mimicked him in a low monotone. "'*Jed is dead.*' Any idea what *that* means?"

Matt's lips pressed thin. "My brother was destroyed after Shen died and he lost his son. Maybe he felt dead inside."

For a moment, Jesse regretted asking. It seemed too sad. Too personal. But sometimes a story is so tragic you need to hear it all to understand. She glanced at her friend to gauge her reaction and was surprised when Rainy asked the very question she wanted to ask.

"What went wrong, Matt?"

"I don't know, exactly. They'd both just finished med school and thought they knew what they were doing. Shen wanted a home birth, and Jed agreed to it. They set up a room in Joe's house near the medical center and thought they had it covered." He shrugged. "It happened so fast, there was no time to even call for help."

"Does he blame himself?" Jesse's eyebrows furrowed as she leaned forward.

"There's no one else." Matt's eyes grew cloudy.

Jesse shook her head, filled the mugs with boiling water, and stirred in honey. She'd gone too far and upset Matt. As she served the hot tea, she gauged his reaction. He seemed recovered, so she tried a gentler tack. "What about Joe? Where's he now?"

"Still here." Matt picked up one of the steaming mugs and blew on it. "He's not well, though. His wife, Effie, died a couple of months ago, and Joe took it hard."

"Did they have kids?"

Matt snorted quietly. "Just Jed."

"Do you think Jed knows that Effie passed away?"

Matt shrugged. "We don't hear much from Joe."

Rainy took Matt's hand. "Jed must be so lonely. He might have survival skills but living in the bush *alone* is unnatural. In the old days, you only lived alone if you were banished from the tribe for doing something horrible. Jed must know about the wendigo."

Jesse felt a ripple through her gut. "The what?"

"The wendigo. It's a cannibal monster that possesses humans it finds alone in the bush."

"Jesus, Rainy!" Jesse stood up and knocked over her mug full of hot tea.

Matt grabbed a towel to sop it up.

When Jesse glanced at him, she saw the grin on his face. "It's not funny, Matt. I have enough weird dreams living out here. I don't need to be thinking about cannibals and monsters that possess people."

Rainy touched her arm. "Don't worry, Jess. The wendigo wouldn't come to your front porch and kiss you. That's all Jed!

MAKWA'S TOOTH

Hawk awoke bleary-eyed in the starkness of the cave. The fire was dead. The raw chill of an early-morning rain tugged at his bones while the cold sweat of his dreams clung to his flesh. He'd relived his bloody battle with the bear once again. This time, however, after the kill, the honey-haired woman had been standing in a corner of the cave. Makwa's spiked teeth fell from his gums and rattled onto the stone floor at her feet. Hawk picked them up and handed one to the woman, who took it and vanished.

He fingered his medicine bundle where the bear's incisors lay in a skin grave. The dream was an omen. The woman needed protection from something. He didn't know what, but he was determined to ensure she came to no harm.

He left immediately, thinking of her as he jogged the two-hour trail. He felt a surprising source of power emanating from her. In her own mysterious way, she'd turned his life upside-down, made him do things he didn't understand and feel things that he wished would stay unfelt. Yet he followed his intuition as he followed a new trail, knowing it would either end or fork.

Crouching in the shrubbery, he waited for Jesse to leave. He hadn't seen her in days, though she scarcely left his thoughts. Already summer was painting the earth, and he felt the passing of time more fervently than ever before.

When a pale-blue Jeep Wrangler pulled up, Jesse emerged from the cabin, her tawny mane shining in the first rays of dawn. She still had the thick bangs but had braided her hair down the back. Her skin shone with a reddish-brown hue that enhanced those big green eyes. And her curves flexed beneath a tight, scooped-neck, lime-green T-shirt and pale denim jeans. He couldn't look away. *God, she's beautiful. And she's right. Here I am, spying on her from the bushes like some Peeping Tom.*

He wanted to approach her and talk as if they'd never met before—or fought. He wanted a do-over, a second chance. But no. He was too frightened. Terrified he'd ruin her life like he'd ruined Shen's. He had to stay far enough away that he could never hurt her.

Jesse waved to the woman in the Jeep, then went to an old shed and opened the doors. She had a horse! Not just any horse, but Reba, an Appaloosa that belonged to his uncle. What was that horse doing here?

He watched her pat the mare on the neck and walk her down by the leafy banks of the creek where she'd have water and shade. After staking the mare out on a long line, she threw her arms around the horse's neck and gave her a hug. Finally, she climbed into the Jeep and disappeared.

When Hawk emerged from the bushes, he felt a storm brewing. The eastern sky backlit the cabin in a bright-pink glow, but he could sense electricity in the air. A metallic taste made his teeth jump. Hopefully, she'd be back before the storm hit.

He hustled up the creaking wooden steps and lifted the metal latch. As he shoved open the plank door, he smelled an intriguing mix of scents. The heartening aroma of oatmeal and cinnamon made his mouth water. He hadn't had a decent cup of tea in three years, let alone porridge. He could also smell woodsmoke, kerosene, and propane. She'd been burning cedar, likely deadfalls. Plentiful but inefficient. An oily kerosene lamp sat centered on a graying, knife-scarred pine table. Two hand-hewn chairs perched around it. The hearth mantel was loaded with scented candles, at least eight or ten, though they didn't mask the other scents.

He lifted a pink candle to his nose and drank in its rosy scent. It was nothing like the wild roses that rambled through the valley, but somehow it reminded him of Jesse. Her beige flannel sleeping bag stretched over the single pine bed frame. Beside it, on a tiny tabletop, were her hairbrush, a silver hand mirror, and an intricate quill box. He resisted the urge to look inside. It felt too private, too personal, like his own totem sack.

Four boxes crammed with books stood against the north wall, and several framed photographs hung from rusty nails. One was in black and white, a mustached man hugging a pretty little girl. Jesse with short hair squared around her chin. He recognized those bangs, and those pouty lips. Was the man her father? There was a resemblance. Something in the eyes.

Another photo showed Jesse with a bearded man, standing in front of a mountain lake and looking romantically windblown. So, somewhere, she had a man. He had intense eyes but didn't look like anything special. Hawk turned away from the photograph, feeling an unfamiliar pang of jealousy. It was unfounded. Jesse was nothing to him but a woman living alone in the woods who needed protection. Still, he wondered why she was here alone and where this man was now.

Her clothes hung from stumpy branches on a handmade clothes tree. Chopped from a birch, it stood braced in a pail of soil. He recognized the turquoise sweater. She'd been wearing it last week when he'd kissed her.

He needed to apologize for that. When she'd responded to his demanding lips, he'd almost lost control. It was all he could do to turn his back and walk away before she became aware of the passion she aroused in him. He held the sweater to his lips and breathed in her scent. And suddenly he was aroused again. How could her scent affect him so much? But it wasn't just her scent. Everything about her called to him. *Damn her.* Even if she wanted him, as her kiss suggested, he couldn't have her. He would not ruin another woman's life. He hung the sweater back on the branch and turned away.

The southeast corner of the cabin served as a kitchen and held odd utensils, a kettle, pots, plates, racks of tools, two blue tin waterpots, soap, and towels. Several jars of beans, grains, herbs, and jam stood on a pine shelf. Though the cabin was sparsely furnished, it was clean and orderly. He liked that. She took good care of her things. The energy was clear and strong, yet as turbulent as the rapids.

Taking Makwa's tooth from his totem sack, he held it between his damp palms. Then, closing his eyes, he prayed. *Protect this home and let no evil enter this woman's heart.* He stuck the tooth into a chink in the log wall just above the cabin door. Here the bear would guard the cabin. Even if evil entered the room, it would not enter her heart. It would strengthen her spirit so she could walk her path with honor and courage. No one could harm her in this place.

Hawk took one last look around the room, breathed one last breath of her intoxicating scent, and left.

STORM

Rainy cocked her head curiously as Jesse packed a spade, rake, and watering can into the back of the Jeep. "What's with all the tools?"

Jesse held up a three-pronged cultivating fork and shovel. "I saw these in the window at Hanson's General Store and couldn't resist the lime-green handles. They match my shirt." There was a sunny flat glade close to the lake that would be perfect for a garden. Beneath the pine needle carpet was rich black soil. "I'm going to plant vegetables. I bought seeds."

"What'd you get?"

As Rainy pulled the Jeep out onto Main Street, Jesse glanced out the window and saw the same two men staring at her again. When the short man tipped his baseball cap, her flesh broke out in goosebumps. "Ugh. Do you know who *they* are?" She gestured to the two men slumped against Biff's Barber Shop. The giant red-haired man with the twisted nose looked as vacant as a yam.

Rainy squinted and shook her head. "No idea. But I miss most of the local creeps by living out of town."

Hanson's also had a gun rack. If those two were here gawking at her again next Saturday, she'd see the sheriff and get a permit for a handgun. They might be harmless, but then again, they might not be. She'd checked out a couple of Rugers but hadn't said anything to Rainy. Her friend was already worried about her living alone in the cabin. Male intruders weren't her only concern. Reba was bait to any wild animals, and if Jesse had to defend herself or her horse, she would.

"So, what seeds did you buy?" Rainy asked again.

"Oh, right." Opening the paper bag, Jesse pulled out each packet as she rhymed it off. "Gourmet butter lettuce. You know it costs four dollars a head?"

Rainy gave her a thumbs-up.

"Carrots. Zucchini. Green beans. Mini cucumbers. Kale." Jesse sniffed. "Oh, and basil, parsley, dill, and cilantro."

"Yum. I can't wait for those gourmet dinners."

"I'll make you one right now. Lunch, at least."

In front of the cabin, the old Jeep sputtered still. Jesse made a huge salad from fresh vegetables she'd purchased in town (including one of those four-dollar butter lettuces), and the two women sat out on the large flat rocks by the lake to eat. Jesse had picked up a couple of baguettes from Giselle's, the new gourmet shop run by a baker from the city. Brushed with olive oil, salt, and rosemary and stuffed with jalapeño goat cheese, they were delicious. With the influx of city entrepreneurs, Lure River was beginning to have a little more allure.

A flock of over fifty geese honked through the cerulean sky and splashed down feet first in the lake to settle among the blue-winged teal that frequented it during nesting season.

"I can understand why you like living here." Lunch over, Rainy was stretched out on the flat rock in the sun while Jesse perched beside her, arms clasped around her knees. "It's a little like paradise."

"Except for the wild man in the woods."

Rainy squinted through one eye. "Have you seen him since—?"

"The kiss? Nope." Jesse shook her head. "God, that kiss was good." Her belly hummed just thinking about Jed, with his voyageur charm. He was a bad boy, an outlaw, and so unlike anyone she'd ever met.

Rainy's lips curled up in a sideways grin. "If Jed kisses anything like Matt, I know *exactly* what you mean."

"I feel pretty guilty about enjoying it as much as I did, given that Alec has only been gone just over a year." She couldn't say *dead*—not yet.

"Alec left you sixteen months ago to pursue his dream. He'd want you to be happy and live your life to the fullest."

Rainy always seemed to know exactly what Jesse needed to hear.

"What did Alec always say? 'Do it or die trying?'"

Jesse bit the inside of her lip. "Well, he did that."

Rainy rambled on. "What *you* need is closure, Jess. No body. No funeral. It's hard enough to let someone go, but when you have no proof they're really gone . . ."

The photograph of the mountain of snow passed through Jesse's mind. That seemed like proof enough.

Rainy brightened. "Hey, we should throw a wake for him. That might give you closure."

"Seriously?" Rainy had a point. It almost felt like Alec had gone traveling and been detained in a foreign country.

"Why not? Alec lived his life exactly as he wanted, and you're not to blame for anything. You need to say goodbye, Jess, and stop living like a nun." Sitting up, she stretched and stared into the woods. "Do you think Jed might be out there watching us right now?"

"God! Will you *stop* trying to creep me out?"

Rainy punched her and laughed. "I'd like to meet him, that's all. He sounds badass."

Jesse felt her heartbeat quicken. *Badass. Rebel. Outlaw.*

After Rainy left, Jesse spent the rest of the afternoon digging and raking the dark soil in the sunny glade. By dusk, she'd prepared an eight-by-eight-foot square. Tomorrow, she'd plant. She appraised her dirt-encrusted fingernails and grimy clothes. Her neck and ears were black where soil clung to the oily patches smeared with repellent. Her face was gritty. *I'm a mess. But the lake's likely warmer than the air*, she thought, feeling the descending chill.

She walked back to the cabin, brought in a good supply of dry wood, and started a fire in the stone hearth. Then, carrying towels, biodegradable soap, and a fresh flannel nightshirt, she skipped to the lake's edge. It was darker than usual, the sky moonless, starless, and cold. Mosquitoes plagued her. To dodge the bugs, she stripped fast and then plunged. Finding the rock ledge with her toes, she balanced so that her torso was out of the water, then scrubbed her hair and bumpy flesh. She dived and splashed in the cold water to rinse and then clambered out through the rocks. After drying off, she wrapped her hair in a towel and pulled her nightshirt over her damp skin. Everything else she threw in the towel and raced back to the cabin.

When the chill left, she heated tomato soup. By the time she'd sipped it and eaten the remains of a cheesy baguette, her eyelids were drooping. Fiery shadows danced across the cabin walls. Ice-blue flames sputtered and flared. Huddled in her sleeping bag before the hot bright flames, she watched the crackling coals. *How early man must have revered fire*, she thought. *How Jed must love it now.* And then she was dreaming again.

She floated naked on tepid waves of herbal mist, watching a troop of dancing bears. The soapy smell turned musky as she listened to the murmuring bears. She felt no fear, only comfort, even as they exposed their ivory canines in a toothy smile. Then Jed appeared, plummeting from a silvery moon. Her heartbeat quickened as he plucked her from the pond, water droplets spraying in the moon glow. Holding her wet flesh against his hot body, they soared. She tasted the salty flesh of his neck and inhaled his potent, musky scent. Tilting back her face, she opened her lips to take his kiss. They swooped and hovered like hawks, catching the thermals, entangled in ecstatic flight. Her body ached for him. She wanted to cling to him and never let go.

Jesse fell off the narrow cot with a thud and woke up trembling.

Cold rain pelted the tin roof and splattered down the open chimney, causing the fire to spit and hiss. Brittle cedar branches screeched against the windows. Forked lightning flashed through the wooden shutters, followed seconds later by a blast of thunder that brought her to her feet. She hadn't seen this coming. After lighting the kerosene lamp, she fed the dying fire a few dry logs. And then—

Reba! The poor mare was tied in that dilapidated old shed. *She must be terrified!*

Throwing a plastic poncho over her head, Jesse raced down the steps. The black rain blinded her as she felt her way through the slick trees and threw open the doors.

Reba hovered in a corner, looking spooked and bedraggled. Jesse edged her way in, speaking gently to the spotted mare. She took the soaking canvas halter in her hand and coaxed the mare out of the stall and toward the cabin. When they reached the steps, Jesse started up but Reba hesitated and backed away.

"It's all right, girl. It's warm and dry inside. Trust me. Please."

As if she understood, the mare clomped onto the veranda and into the cabin. Jesse patted them both dry with towels and left the horse standing by the stove. She cuddled back in her sleeping bag and stared at the horse as the storm raged around them. At last, she closed her eyes, and, in that moment of peace, Jed enveloped her again. She tingled deep inside, wanting more, wanting to make love to him.

Why, oh why, in this terrifying storm, am I yearning for Jed and not Alec?

BONES

Jesse slept late the next morning. Dawn didn't awaken her in its usual kindly way, with golden streaks of sunlight breaking through slits in the slanted shutters. Dawn didn't seem to come at all. There were no bright rays to burn the dense fog off the lake. The mist clung to the glassy surface, slippery banks, and vernal hollows.

As she led Reba down the front steps toward the shed, Jesse noticed that she'd left the double doors wide open to the storm. Water had pooled on the dirt floor.

"Well girl, you have two choices," she crooned to the mare. "Hang out here under the soggy trees or come with me to Otter Pond. This was supposed to be planting day, but we'll have to give the ground time to dry."

The mare snorted.

"I agree and would appreciate the company."

She left the horse standing at the base of the steps while she went back inside to collect her camera gear. Using the step, she slipped onto the back of the mare, and they started off.

Mist clung to Jesse's skin along with the swarms of mosquitoes that had sniffed out her scent. "Bloodhounds. That's what they are." Uncorking her repellant, she slathered it on thickly as the horse plodded along the spongy ground. Now and then, she had to duck beneath rain-barrel leaves that soaked her jean jacket. She could see only a few feet ahead, but the morning birds created a cacophony of warbles and trills that brightened their way.

The walk to Otter Pond had become a morning ritual. Perhaps the chickadees, warblers, and jays recognized her now. She sometimes dropped sunflower seeds and peanuts along the trail as tokens.

By the time they reached the pond, she was damp through, but a southeasterly breeze was beginning to blow across the water and buffet the fog. Jesse dismounted and left Reba tied under a tree, then stripped off her wet clothes and hung them over a birch branch to dry. If she was ever going to swim with the otters, they'd need to get used to her being in their pond.

She waded in. The velvety water felt wonderful, warmed by many days of June sun despite last night's storm. After a shallow dive, she swam a few yards, surprised to see how well she could see below the surface. The pond was crystal clear and alive with darting minnows and scurrying crayfish. No wonder there were otters living here.

Flipping onto her back, she floated on the tepid surface, arms and legs outstretched, and gazed up into the misty heavens. When she first heard the chitter, it reminded her of childhood stories of faeries and elves. Then she realized it was coming from the muskrat lodge. Otters didn't build their own dens but simply moved into the lodges of other creatures. A stocky little otter pup stood atop the lodge, whiskers twitching, merry brown eyes beaming fearlessly at a potential playmate.

Jesse found her footing on a submerged rock and balanced carefully, observing him. He tissed once, and then again. His brown coat looked as soft as cattail velvet, and his tiny leathery hands were almost human.

"You don't look so shy, little otter."

But the unfamiliar voice sent him scampering off the lodge roof and behind a gnarly pine tree. She waited to see if his curiosity and natural desire to play would bring him back. Suddenly, the mother otter's muzzle appeared like a periscope beside the lodge, not six feet from Jesse's perch. She barked a sharp warning that sent Jesse splashing across the small expanse of pond. Sitting on the bank, she tried to catch her breath. "Too soon. I'm sorry, Mama. I won't come that close again."

Although the pup had little fear, the mother must have encountered humans before on her travels. Otters were gypsies with an insatiable urge to seek out new territory.

Everything seemed to have a home but her. As she dried herself and pulled on her damp clothes, thoughts rambled in Jesse's head. She'd given up her flat in Seattle and put her stuff in storage. There were too many memories there she couldn't get past; it had left her feeling as dense as the morning fog. Her father had just fallen in love again and didn't want his grown daughter hanging around— not that she'd ever live in her father's house. Lure River wasn't home, although she liked the small-town atmosphere. So, it seemed, this cabin in the bush was home, at least for now. There was nowhere left to run and no one to run to. Here, she had to face herself. That was why she'd come to the reservation in the first place. No longer defined by Alec but feeling moored by his memory, this haven was exactly what she needed to discover who Jesse Jardine really was and what she wanted from life. Cliché or not.

She was roused from her daydream by an odd sound. Reba was stamping her hooves. Horseflies were attacking the poor mare in droves, and she had nothing but a tail to defend herself.

"Let's get out of here." Jesse mounted the mare and, camera gear untouched, they loped along the trail back to the cabin.

"Ah, damn. The raccoons stole your oats." Jesse surveyed the makeshift barn. "At least the puddles are drying. If you can manage—Hey. What's this?"

It looked like some animal had been digging in the dirt floor. There were paw prints. *Dog? Wolf?* And something white protruded from the hole in the ground. Squatting, she brushed the earth carefully away from the object. *That's a hand. A human hand.* A chill swept through her body, and sitting back on the damp ground, she stared at the pale fragile bones. *There's a body buried in my shed.* Though a wolf had been at it, she could clearly see the bones of a thumb and four fingers. The urge to start digging herself was strong, but she knew better than to disturb the site.

This was when she should have whipped out her cellphone and called 911, except she didn't have a phone. The only thing she could do was ride until she found someone who did.

But I need to cover and secure this. And I need photos. Christ! Who could be buried here in the shed? And who buried them? It was unlikely that the shed had coincidentally been built over some burial ground. It was more likely the killer had buried the body in the shed to keep it from being dug up by animals in the woods and discovered. *Is this a murder victim?* Goosebumps shivered up her arms.

Jesse unpacked her camera and took several photographs of the hand protruding from the muddy floor. She looked at the fingers and, placing her own hand beside it, snapped a few more pictures. Their hands were similar in size. Too similar. This was not the hand of a man. "I'm sorry," Jesse whispered. Her chest tightened, and for a moment she couldn't breathe. Considering the location, chances were this was a woman from the reservation. Too many young women went missing and were never seen again. Somewhere she'd heard that the number of Native American women found murdered was ten times higher than other races. Their cases were rarely investigated for all kinds of reasons—none of them adequate.

Jesse placed her hand gently on top of the bones. "You poor thing. I'll get the tribal police. I'm sure they'll find out what happened and take you home to your family."

The sheriff was in charge in Lure River, but the reservation was managed by the tribe. Jesse mounted the mare and followed the dirt road to the paved highway that connected the reservation east and west. After about an hour, she came to a cluster of homes and a handful of kids playing ball in a driveway.

"Does anyone have a phone I could borrow?"

One of the kids pulled a cell phone out of his pocket. "I like your horse." When he smiled, she saw his two front teeth were missing.

Jesse nodded and jumped down. "Her name's Reba. Can you look after her for a few minutes?" She handed the reins to the grinning boy and turned away, not wanting to alarm the kids with talk of bodies, murder, and police.

Staring at the phone, she punched in 911.

PROM NIGHT 1

June 2000

> The three little kittens, they lost their mittens,
> And they began to cry,
> "Oh, mother dear, we sadly fear,
> Our mittens we have lost."
> "What? Lost your mittens? You naughty kittens!
> Then you shall have no pie."
> "Meow, meow, me oh my."

His mother used to cuddle in bed with him and sing that song when he was a kid and couldn't sleep. And now, here they were. Three little kittens cuddled up to their mama like he used to cuddle up to his. A gray one. An orange one. And a fluffy black one with white tips on its nose, ears, and tail.

He touched the black one's soft forehead with his finger. "Tippy's my favorite." The kitten had sea-green eyes like his mom's.

But now his mother's eyes were filled with tears. "He said he's going to drown them tonight when he comes home." She didn't believe in sugarcoating.

Tonight? Christ! Not tonight. It was prom night. He didn't have a date, but he still wanted to go. It was the last dance of his last year of high school—the night the few virgins left in school gave it up to celebrate their freedom. And he was hoping to be one of them.

But he couldn't stand to see his mother cry. "Can't we give them away? Find them homes?"

"Before supper?" His mother sniffed and twisted her long

blonde hair between thin fingers with nails bitten to the quick.

"I'll put them in a box and take them into town. Put up a sign. *Free Kittens.*" The prom didn't start until eight o'clock, and the best parties happened later.

She shook her head. "Not in Lure. Someone will tell him."

That was the problem when your father intimidated everyone. He remembered there was a rat in that song about the three little kittens. He knew all about rats. Touching the green bruise along his mother's cheekbone, he wished he could make it disappear. Or make *him* disappear. Despite her scars, his mother was still the prettiest woman in Lure.

He sat for a moment, thinking. She was wearing that cologne he liked. Vanilla Dreams. His father wouldn't allow her to buy it, but her best friend Millie ran the beauty salon where his mother shampooed hair, and sometimes she gave her open bottles. The old man seemed oblivious of the scent.

"What if I drive them out to the reservation, Mom? Someone out there might want a kitten for mousing."

"You're so clever, baby!" She brightened, and his chest puffed with pride.

"Oh, but my truck . . . I'm still waiting for that muffler." He was a decent mechanic, but sometimes it took weeks to get parts from the city.

"Take *my* car, and mind he doesn't see you." When she patted his cheek, he leaned into the warmth of her touch. "You're such a good boy. I don't know what I'd do without you."

SWEAT LODGE

Hawk spread the final deerskins over the wood frame and adjusted the weighted hide that hung across the entrance. As he gazed at his finished Sweat Lodge, boyhood memories surfaced. His first kill. A young whitetail, maybe a hundred pounds. Joe's pride. His first Vision Quest. The fear and joy of a twelve-year-old boy alone in the wild.

He'd always felt more connected to Anishinaabe culture than that of his parents, like he was born into the wrong time and place to the wrong people. Joe never questioned it, just accepted him as he was. He belonged here with Joe and Effie, and they all knew it. When other boys on the reservation were going on Vision Quests, Jed asked if he could too.

Joe left him in a valley by a stream with only drinking water and a blanket. He fasted four days and nights, cleansing his body and opening his spirit to other dimensions. He didn't see an animal like some of the boys. He just kept seeing his hands. Sometimes they were pale and normal; other times they were covered in blood. Once they sprouted claws like a cougar and then talons like a hawk. Joe told him to always protect his hands. That's why he'd been so angry the day he found Hawk trying to sever them from his body.

Hawk felt in need of a vision again. He'd thought his path was to become a doctor, marry Shen, and raise a family. Then everything changed in one horrible moment. After, he'd found a balanced life in the bush with Sister, and he felt satisfied until the wolf started to wander. Then the woman appeared. A storm brewed around him, and he knew his ordered life was about to turn upside-down again. He'd considered going to see Joe but knew that Joe would only tell him to sit with it in the lodge. That was Joe's answer to everything. *"Sit with it. Listen."*

So Hawk would sit.

He'd wandered for days in search of the right place. Only yesterday, he'd climbed a steep rocky grade and discovered this perch. It had existed for eons and had no doubt been used by others before him. It encompassed a spectacular view of the country, a granite wall carved by a marauding glacier, a regal rock cliff energized by the elements, and a lofty peak of pines.

Sister lay perky-eared in the cooling shade of a chunky cedar, panting lightly in the late June heat. She'd dogged his trail for days. He knew she felt his turmoil just as she'd felt his grief as a pup.

Night was falling. Stern sentinel pines encircled the glade in black silhouette. The ceiling shone indigo with silvery moon and stars, and, as peace enveloped him, Hawk sighed.

At last, he stood and massaged the cramped muscles in his legs.

He fed the fire he'd built outside the lodge, and it crackled and popped in its rocky pit. As the wood burned into a bed of glowing coals, he used sturdy branches to carry the hot stones from the fire into the lodge and place them in the central pit. He closed the door and sat, then sprinkled the stones with water.

Sweat streamed down his face, tickling his closed eyelids and the nerves in his neck and chest. He prayed and sang, gave thanks to the Creator, and asked for direction, for he felt lost.

At last, he crawled on hands and knees out through the flapping door and emerged. He poured fresh water over his head and bathed his hot flesh. Gazing at the sky with outstretched arms, he stood and gulped great breaths of fresh air. Then he lay naked on Makwa's skin in the center of the glade.

Sister sauntered over, muzzle blood-rosy, gut full, and laid at his feet. Her soft, silvery fur tickled his toes. He smiled and breathed a low pleasurable growl, and together they passed the night.

LURE

When they awoke at dawn, they were wet with dew. Mosquitoes had ravaged his sweat-cleansed body. His throat was parched, and everywhere he itched. From his lofty perch, he could see a silvery stream meandering through the canyon below.

He bounced down the steep canyon wall like a mountain goat and plunged into the water. The frothy current whisked him along. Bracing himself on a huge flat rock, he opened his mouth and drank in this cool sweet gift. Then he picked up handfuls of gritty sand and scrubbed his scalp and body until the blood pinkened his skin. Diving and snorting, he rinsed himself clean.

When he stepped from the river and shook, a balmy southern breeze caught the shimmering droplets and dried his glowing skin. Plucking plantain leaves from the sand by his feet, he masticated them between his teeth and applied the juice to the worst of the bug bites. Then, humming, he scaled the canyon wall.

Sister frolicked by his feet, talking in excited yips. His answering yipes caused a wrestling match as she jumped up and planted her leathery pads on his chest. He caught her shoulders and they fell, growling playfully in the grass. "This is a good place. Let's stay for a while."

WILD MINNESOTA

The tribal police cruiser passed Jesse as she was riding back up the lane to the cabin. Rainy pulled in behind it in her old blue Jeep. What was she doing here? Did news travel that fast on the reservation?

By the time Jesse dismounted and staked Reba out under the trees, the police chief and two of his officers were taping off the shed.

"What the hell happened?" Rainy bounced out of the Jeep and ran over.

"I found bones in the shed."

"Bones?"

"Yeah. Human bones. I called the police. Any idea who could be buried here?" Jesse sat down on the front step of the cabin.

Rainy stood in front of her and made a puffing noise.

"Matt might know." Jesse stared at her fingers. "It was a hand. A small hand. I think it might be a—"

"Don't even say it." Rainy crossed her arms over her chest.

"I know sometimes women disappear." Jesse chewed her bottom lip.

"Too many times. *Jesus!* All this time you've been sleeping in this cabin with a body buried out in that shed." Shivering, Rainy rubbed her arms.

"I know." Jesse's stomach lurched, and she swallowed. "Come on. I'll make tea."

The police chief knocked on the door a few minutes later, shoved it open, and nodded. "I'm Chief Chase." When he extended his hand, Jesse shook it. "I need to ask you a few questions." He seemed young for a police chief. Good-looking, focused, and pleasant.

"Of course." Jesse motioned for him to take a seat. Rainy was pacing the room.

"I don't recognize either of you ladies. Are you renting this place?"

"I am," Jesse said.

His bottom lip pushed down when he nodded. "How did you find the rental?"

"I found it," Rainy said. "And, for the record, I live here with my family. The Harpers."

"Oh, right. You came home a couple of years ago. Work at the school. I know your brothers."

He seemed to relax, and Jesse was glad her friend had arrived when she did. Finding a body was awkward, but finding a body in a place you'd lived only a few weeks was unnerving. What else was hidden beneath the surface?

Rainy brightened. "Oh, is basketball your game too?"

"Whenever I can find the time." Rainy was proud of her younger brothers, who she called the Harper Hoopsters. "So how did you find the rental? Don't tell me it was listed on Airbnb."

Rainy giggled, and Jesse was glad to see her smile despite how she must have been feeling. Too many Indigenous women went missing and were never seen again. It was a lot to take in.

"Close. It was on the Wild Midwest rental site. I knew where it was from the description, so I came up and checked it out."

"And I sent an electronic funds transfer," Jesse added.

Chase turned to Jesse. "That easy."

"Yep. That easy."

"Do you remember the email address you sent the money to?"

Jesse shrugged. "It was cabinfever something at Hotmail."

Chief Chase snorted in a way that said, *I know exactly who placed that ad.* "Can I ask how much rent you're paying?"

"Three hundred a month, and I'm paid up till September with an option to renew. I hope I'm not going to have to leave now."

Sniffing, he surveyed the room. "What is it you're doing here exactly, Miss"—he glanced at his notebook—"Jardine?"

"Jesse. I'm a wildlife photographer."

His lips flattened. "We'll station a team up here for security and bring in forensics. The college may send an archaeological team too. It would be best if you made other arrangements, at least for a few days."

Jesse clenched her jaw and glanced at Rainy. Where could she go? There was no room at Rainy's house. "I'd rather stay here. I'll stay away from the shed. Would that be a problem?"

Chase shrugged. "Suit yourself. You said you found the bones this afternoon?"

"Yeah. I brought the horse into the house last night during the storm."

His eyebrows rose, and Rainy snickered.

"Hey, it was really bad out there. I forgot to close the doors to the shed, and when I checked this morning it was flooded, so I left it open to dry out. When we came back from our ride this afternoon, I checked again and that's when I saw the . . . fingers." She swallowed and glanced at her hand. "Something had been into the oat bag, likely raccoons, and there were dog or wolf tracks in the dirt around the—" She thought suddenly of the white timber wolf that hung around with Jed. *Had it been here? Did this have anything to do with Jed?*

Chief Chase saw the change in her expression. "What?"

"Nothing. It's just . . . the hand. It looked small. Like a woman's or even a child's."

"I can't comment on that."

"Has anyone gone missing from here? That must be public

knowledge." Rainy's hands went to her hips, and she sent Chase a look that said, *Come on. Give us something.*

"People usually turn up eventually or call home. There was one girl, though. Must be twenty years ago. I was just a kid." Chase glanced away. "They sent out search parties for months."

"What was her name?" If there was any chance that fragile hand belonged to her, Jesse had to know.

"Ruby Little Bear."

Jesse turned the name over in her mind, trying to imagine the girl who might be buried in her shed.

"She was fifteen," Chase added. "But don't jump to conclusions."

Jesse'd already made the jump. It had to be her. Ruby Little Bear. All this time, the poor girl had been buried right here in the shed.

"He gave us a lot of information for a cop that can't comment," Jesse said, after Chase had folded up his notebook and left. "Thanks for giving him that little nudge." She put another mug of tea down on the table in front of Rainy.

"Nothing current, though. Ruby Little Bear's disappearance would just be part of the story of this place. Everybody knows everybody here. Just like Chase knows exactly who 'cabinfever' is. That made his day."

Jesse sighed. "Ruby Little Bear. Part of me hopes it's not her, but the other part knows her family must still be wondering what happened to her." She sipped her tea.

"Yeah. If it is her, they can at least bury her properly. Hold a ceremony. Make things right."

"Maybe they can even find out who killed her." Another shiver ran through Jesse's body. A murderer had been in this place, maybe even in this cabin. What if he still lived in Lure River? She thought of those two creeps by the barber shop. The next time she went into town, she was buying that Ruger.

Rainy's hands flew up. "I completely forgot why I came here."

"I just thought you'd heard about the body in my shed."

"Right. Moccasin telegraph is faster than Wi-Fi." Rainy winked. "So?"

"Joe."

"Jed's Joe?"

"Yeah. Joe's sick. We don't think he's gonna make it. Matt's trying to find Jed. He might want to see his friend before . . ."

"Jeez. I don't know where he is." Jesse stood up. "Maybe somewhere east of here?" She gestured toward the hills.

"Are you up for searching? We could go together. Take Reba."

Jesse nodded enthusiastically. "Sure. She can carry us both."

The two women set off in an easterly direction and followed the river trail. They called Jed's name until they were hoarse but saw no sign of him or the white wolf. By dusk, they'd backtracked to Jesse's cabin. The weather had cleared, so they left the horse pastured out by the trees. As promised, two tents were set up, and the officers were sitting around a campfire holding tin mugs. The women were too hungry and tired to care.

"I'm exhausted, Jess. Can I bunk here tonight?"

"If you don't mind spooning on my cot, please do." As much as she hated to admit it, Jesse was unnerved by the body in the shed. She kept glancing at her hand and wondering what had happened to Ruby Little Bear. "And don't worry about finding Jed. I'll head out again when you leave for work. Chase as much as told me to vacate anyway. I'll just keep following the river east up into the hills. He's gotta be up there somewhere."

"That's dangerous country, friend. Nothing up there but trees and caves and critters. What if you get lost? Or hurt?"

"I'll be careful and keep the river in sight. That way I can always backtrack like we did tonight. I'll take a week's provisions. Give the sheriff time to sort out what happened here."

Rainy scrunched up her face. It was her *I don't like it* look.

"You said it yourself: Jed needs to know about Joe." She knew what it was like to lose someone and never say goodbye. "If I'm not back in a week, send a search party."

"A lot can happen in a week. There are bears, wildcats, and wolves in this bush."

"There are wolves right outside my door. A wolf dug up those bones this morning while I was out photographing otters."

Rainy opened her canvas backpack and took out a ten-inch hunting knife in a leather case. When she pulled it from the sheath, Jesse's jaw dropped. "When did you start carrying that?"

"I bought it for myself when I moved back here."

"Have you ever used it?"

"Not to kill," Rainy said gravely, "but I would if I had to."

Jesse nodded and thought about the Ruger. "I saw some handguns at Hanson's. I should have filled out the permit. Next time I'm in town . . ."

"Take this for now." Rainy sheathed the knife and handed it to Jesse.

At dawn, Rainy helped Jesse pack provisions. They devised a way to lash the pack onto the mare's back but leave enough room for Jesse to ride comfortably in front, sitting on her sleeping bag for some padding. Then they hugged and, after many promises, parted ways.

Jesse followed the river toward the distant hills. With Rainy's knife tied to her belt, she felt brave and bold. A woman on a mission. Indestructible.

QUEST

The feeling didn't last. Although Jesse was a fit, experienced hiker, she'd never traveled so far into unknown territory alone. A sense of foreboding clung to her like the mist. The Appaloosa plodded along the sandy ridge, leaving tracks Jesse hoped someone would be able to follow. When the sandy stretch ended abruptly, Reba was forced up into the bush. A trail veered north, but Jesse decided to keep along the river as planned. If Rainy and Matt came looking, she wanted them to be able to find her.

Horse and rider wound their way slowly through masses of ferns, the tips of which tickled Jesse's toes. She appreciated her new knee-high moccasins now more than ever. Deerflies were drawn to Reba's strong sweaty scent, and they ripped chunks of flesh with razor jaws whenever they weren't scattered by her sweeping tail. But the tall moose-hide boots were laced tightly to Jesse's legs and padded her calves.

Her repellant did nothing to discourage deerflies, although it helped deter the mosquitoes that swarmed around her face. She wished she had one of those net hats to tuck inside her jacket. Each step roused the devils from their resting places, and they joined the hungry throng.

Jesse was beginning to have doubts. She'd left quickly that morning on a quest to reunite a dying man with his adopted son. At least that's how it had seemed. Joe was Jed's mentor, if not his real father, and if the old man died before they could see each other one last time, how would that affect Jed's already fragile psyche?

She knew what it was like to miss that last goodbye, and she would save him that pain if she could. She barely remembered kissing Alec goodbye. It had been a rushed departure, a peck on the lips when she dropped him off at the airport with all his gear. Alec often put himself in dangerous situations, so both refused to acknowledge anything bad could happen. It was the only way to live with an adrenaline junkie who took risks daily.

But here in the bush, with a day's ride behind her and far from comfort, Jesse began to question her impulsive decision. If she found Jed, which seemed more doubtful by the hour, he might just tell her to mind her own business. And he'd be right. She wondered how much she was doing this for him and how much for herself. If she were honest, she wanted Jed to leave the bush. Even though he loved his solitary lifestyle, a part of her wanted him to be somewhere close. Somewhere *normal* like Lure River. She caught herself imagining a double-date with Rainy and Matt, even going to their wedding as a couple. She gave her head a shake. She was exhausted. Starving. And possibly overdosing on insect repellent.

She decided to quit for the day and made camp in a stand of elegant silver birches, using bits of their fine, papery bark to kindle a fire. Then she boiled river water and stirred in instant miso. After she'd filled her empty stomach with biscuits and cheese, her eyes grew heavy. She considered bathing, feeling swollen and crusty with sweat and repellant, but decided to wait until morning. Her stench might keep the night crawlers at bay. After staking out Reba on a patch of grass under the trees, she crawled into her sleeping bag and sank down in the eider-like forest lichen.

Darkness fell like the heavy red velvet curtain in Lure River's historic theater. Rainy had taken her there when she first arrived. Intimate and ornate, it held only fifty people yet played first-run movies. She wouldn't mind being there right now, watching some adventure film in which she wasn't the star.

The fire crackled and lulled her into a trancelike sleep. No breeze stirred the pine boughs or slapped the stream. It felt as if the earth were suspended. She opened her eyes a few times to glance at the fire and the stars, but they were gone, concealed by stratus clouds. When the drizzle started, she tucked inside her sleeping bag like a turtle and drifted.

Jesse awoke suddenly, heart racing. Reba was nickering anxiously and pulling at her halter, desperate to free herself from her tether.

Something's out there.

Then she heard it. A tremulous wail like the low-toned bleat of an infant. Shivers ran up her arms, and she reached for the knife beside her.

Cougar. The sound was unmistakable. She'd heard it once in the Cascades and would never forget it. *Make yourself big. They don't usually attack humans.*

She stood and stretched her arms above her head, clutching the knife with her right hand. A cougar's normal prey was the white-tailed deer. But a hungry young male, or a female with a den of kits to feed, might go for a horse.

"Easy girl. I won't let it near you." Jesse walked over to where the horse was tied and stroked her neck with one hand. "Just breathe. We'll be okay." She glanced around the glade, taking stock of the situation. The fire was almost out. It would help to build it up into a decent blaze. "I think you're in the best place you can be," she assured the horse. "I can't untie you. I don't want you to bolt. You might panic and get lost." She talked loudly to let the big cat know who was alpha here.

What else could she remember? They were solitary and nocturnal. And secretive. Most human deaths were caused by hikers venturing into their territory. Well, that could be the case here. This certainly wasn't Jesse's territory. They ambush by striking the neck or the throat.

"I'm just going to throw a few more sticks on the fire and get a blaze going. I'm sure—"

When the cougar cried again, she swiveled. The cry wasn't quite as loud, and it emanated from the west, in the direction of the Dakotas. She knew cougars were established and breeding there. Perhaps this was a lone male exploring new territory.

"I think he's heading west, girl. I'm gonna build up the fire, though, just in case."

After, Jesse dozed fitfully. When she awoke the drizzle had stopped, but everything was wet. In the east, a low glow rose over the hills. She built up the fire as best she could using dry branches from under the trees, then spread her sleeping bag and clothing over branches to dry. At last, she dug out crackers and cheese and stood, craving a cup of tea. Black and really sweet.

The horse was quiet, the danger passed. After breakfast, she packed her gear and rode upstream using a well-used game trail. Near a quiet pond she spied a beaver colony. The wind was blowing from the northeast and swept her scent away. Shielded by boulders, she sat quietly on Reba's back and watched. The creatures gave her comfort.

The beavers had cut many of the trees from the pond site, leaving brittle pencil-point stubs. Their dam was at that moment being repaired by one of the smaller rodents. The largest, no doubt the patriarch, stood upright on the shore, using his thick leathery tail for balance. He munched a handful of duckweed in his front paws.

As the sun rose higher, the beaver's orange incisors glinted. She dug out her Nikon and snapped a few shots, wishing she'd been able to pack more gear. There simply wasn't space for heavy lenses and tripods. The tiny kits emerged, breaking the surface with webbed feet and rudder tails. Birds sang in the pines and thickets, and she felt her body relax.

When a hawk glided through the gray dawn, she thought of Jed, high in the hills that stretched out before her to the east. It was a sense clearer than anything she'd felt yet. He was there, and she had to go to him. She could do this. She could find him.

INJURED

By the evening of the third day, both horse and rider were fatigued. The exuberance Reba had displayed in the early morning dissipated by late afternoon. Now the mare plodded heavily, hooves and tail swishing as she tried to dissuade the deerflies that plagued their every step.

Jesse had seen no sign of Jed. That sense she'd felt so clearly still seemed too real to ignore. But where was he?

Her muscles ached. The trail had suddenly vanished the previous morning, and since then she'd led the mare on foot through thick sedges and shrubs. They were far from the river she'd promised to follow and were climbing steadily upward. The land grew rockier as she closed in on the hills that loomed before her like great stone mountains. Would she ever find him? Would he somehow find her? Listening to the thrum of a thousand lonely acres, she prayed they'd find each other.

Each time she thought of turning back, she remembered the photograph of Alec buried in the snow—Alec, who died alone with no way to say goodbye—and she refused to give up. After losing his partner and their child, Jed deserved the chance to say goodbye to the man who'd been his friend and mentor. She wanted that for him.

After stopping for supper and a rest in a shady copse, Jesse led the mare and walked slowly beside her. Reba had stumbled on a rock shelf and was favoring her right forehoof. It was likely just bruised, like a stubbed toe. Still. What if she went lame? Could Jesse kill the horse if she had to? Slice her throat with a knife? She couldn't leave the mare alone in the bush for wolves to ravage.

They'd been dogging her trail the past two days, slipping through the spruces like shadows, spectral canines yipping in the night, stealing her precious sleep. They, too, had sensed the mare's weakness.

Yesterday, they'd killed in a violent strike that echoed through the woods, filling Jesse and the mare with dread. Perhaps their appetites were satiated for the moment. She made herself believe they were only hunting white-tailed deer, which were plentiful here, and that she was imagining their pursuit due to fear. A fear compounded since the dawn of time by myth and legend.

As night drew near, she fought her way through the dense bush, skirting rotten logs, smacking flies, enticed by the sound of a river. Somehow, she'd circled back. *Thank God.* Its rhythmic song soothed her soul and drew her thoughts away from the predators who crackled twigs in the black woods.

As she entered an open grassy space, she noticed a game trail along the bank that she'd somehow missed. Slipping off Reba, she let her free-range. With food and water close, the mare wouldn't wander far. Jesse dropped her pack and sleeping bag on the ground and stretched. It was a pretty little glade, but a sense of uneasiness still niggled at her gut.

Standing very still, she closed her eyes and listened. Nothing but the river's whisper and the usual chatter of birds at dusk. It seemed safe enough. What she needed was a campfire, supper, and a good night's sleep. She set about collecting dry deadfalls.

A rock-walled fire pit had been built by campers who'd shattered whiskey bottles and left the sharp smeared glass as testament to their drunken trip. In three days of steady travel, she'd not detected the presence of man, yet here he was—a menace in these beautiful, sacred hills.

She pulled off her dirty T-shirt and slipped on a clean one. Then she picked up the scattered glass with careful fingers and wrapped it in the dirty shirt. Assured there were no sharp edges, she stashed it in a side pouch of her backpack. The last thing she needed was an injury way out here.

With her campfire clean, it was easy enough to build a fire with bark kindling and deadfalls. She lit it with a waterproof match, then sat back and sighed. She stank. She needed a bath. But she was also starving. Perhaps a bowl of ramen and a cup of tea, then a dip before sleep. It would be pitch dark in another hour.

She slipped Rainy's knife off her belt and tucked it into her pack to keep it safe. Then, kneeling by the riverbank, she dipped her canteen into the stream. Its clear warmth beckoned. The water rustled around and over smooth gray rocks, creating whimsical waterfalls and deep dark pools where fish lurked. She could see why people came here. A ripple careened up her spine, and she thought again of that creepy pair from town. But she was still on the reservation, hell and gone from Lure River. She assured herself it was too far for that pair to be partying in the bush.

Then she spotted a lodge on the far bank about ten yards distant. Muskrats? Otters? Glancing around, she looked for signs. And then—

Oh my God! Gasping, she leapt back and dropped her canteen. It caught in the current and disappeared downstream.

A large otter had been all but decapitated in a rusty steel-jaw trap hidden beneath the surface of the water close to a willow scrub. Jesse shuddered. It could easily have been her hand in that trap, perhaps only partially severed at the wrist. Just enough to hold her in agony while she bled to death in the water. *Bloody drunken trappers!*

In her madness, she ripped off her moccasins and stalked into the stream. She wrestled the metal in a futile attempt to dislodge the poor otter, jerking the trap wildly until the frayed head fell free. Lunging sideways to avoid it, she winced as something sharp pierced her thigh. She glanced down. It had ripped right through the thin cotton fabric of her pant leg—and her flesh. Blood poured from the wound, mixing with the otter's blood.

Holding the torn flesh of her thigh, she staggered from the river. *Damn! No first aid kit. No antiseptic. Not even a bandage.* That was a stupid mistake, one she knew better than to make. She'd left in such a rush, distracted by that skeletal hand and her fervor to tell Jed about his friend, that she hadn't packed properly.

She made padding with a pair of underwear and a cotton shirt, using the long sleeves as ties. But the blood seeped through in a crimson streak. The gash was wide and deep. Dazed, she climbed into her sleeping bag by the fire, teeth chattering, body shaking. Curling up in the fetal position, her mind told her to move, but her body refused. Soon, she passed out.

Twice in the night she stirred to hear wild chanting in the hills and loud, sorrowful cries. The deeply resonant tones pierced her soul, and she sobbed. Then she passed out again.

When she awoke hours later, her thigh throbbed. Blood soaked her sleeping bag. The horse glanced up from grazing, backlit by the orange light of dawn, then went back to browsing. Jesse crawled to the river, splashed water on her face, and sipped from her open palms. Her belly growled with hunger. She found her damp, discarded moccasins and pulled them on over her cold bare feet. When she crawled back to her pack, dragging her injured leg, she found it empty. Clothing scattered. Food gone.

Collapsing in a heap, she cried. She couldn't walk. She had no food, no canteen to port water. She was badly injured, sick, and alone. Miles from home. It would be at least three more days before Rainy sent a search party, and days before they found her. *If* they found her. She could be dead by then, ravaged by wolves or cougar or whatever predators grew frenzied at the smell of her blood. Or the bloody trappers might return to check their bloody trap. *Damn.*

Damn. Damn. She'd tried, really tried, to tell Jed about Joe. She spit the bitter funk of failure from her mouth and stared at the horse.

If she could get on Reba's back, maybe the mare could find her way home. Horses could sense what humans could not. She crawled to a fallen tree and whistled for the mare. When Reba ambled slowly toward her and stopped, Jesse threw her good leg over the mare's back and used all her strength to pull herself up, gritting her teeth as the pain shot through her injured left leg and up into her chest.

She had to concentrate to keep her balance on the horse's back. Leaning forward, she gripped Reba's mane in her fingers and drifted into a semi-conscious stupor as the mare plodded up one hill and down the other side, stumbling over the odd rock that cracked against her stiff hooves like a pistol shot.

Jesse heard herself moan. She felt like a hot sack of grain. Saw images of flowing water and moaned more. The last thing she heard was the horse's loud nicker.

BUSH DOCTOR

The mare shied when the skins of the sweat lodge flew up and Hawk peered out. Her sudden movement jarred Jesse, who slid off the horse.

"Jesse!" When Hawk saw her lying so still and lifeless, face down in the dirt, he ran to her. Placing his thumb against the blue veins in her wrist, he panicked. "Come on, woman. Don't die on me." The faint pulse sent a chill through his body that raised his flesh. The man in him felt triggered, but the doctor prevailed.

He examined her prone body. The laceration on her thigh was by far the worst. He loosened the long-sleeved shirt she'd bound around it. (*Are those lace panties?*) The wound gaped. It was still oozing blood. Thank God the cut was so close to her glutes. If it had nicked her femoral artery, she'd be dead. He re-bound it and checked her spine. Finding no significant damage, he eased her onto her back.

Jesse's eyelids riffled. Her skin was pale gray and peppered with bites, her lips blistered and peeling with fever.

He unsheathed his knife and slashed down the side of her pant leg.

"No," she cried, awakened by the action. Then, "No," she cried again, when her eyes focused on him, kneeling over her, clutching a knife.

"You're safe, Jesse. I'm going to help you."

She whined. "Sleep. Die." She was delirious with fever.

"Die? There's no way I'm letting you die."

"Alec . . ." she breathed.

"Alec will have to wait." Hawk's voice rose with a pang of

jealousy, and he berated himself for feeling such a thing. Jesse was nothing to him but an injured woman in need of help.

When she tried to pull away, he tightened his grip, and she beat him with her free fist. Tears streamed down her dirty cheeks.

"You're one lousy patient." He shook his head.

And then she passed out.

"Good. Sleep." He rechecked her pulse. This time it was stronger, racing from the surge of emotion. He carried her into the lodge and laid her down on the bear hide. It would provide some protection from the elements. Her skin was cold and clammy despite the fever. The wound was deep and, in this summer heat, a mecca for flies. He draped a doeskin across her body, then sat close and placed his palm on her forehead. "Please help me heal this woman," he whispered.

He went outside and stoked the fire. The horse stood nearby, swishing her tail, one hoof tucked up. Her eyes were heavy. She was exhausted.

"How long have you been on the trail, Reba?" This was one of his uncle's horses. He remembered when she was born. His uncle had joked about the splattered copper that covered her white coat "like a shit storm." But Hawk had seen something in the foal. Intelligence. And it appeared he was right.

When he touched the mare's neck, she nuzzled her soft mouth against him, searching for a treat. "You remember me, don't you, Reba?" Every visit he'd fed her apples and sugar cubes. "Is that why you brought her here to me?" He touched his forehead to the mare's. "You *are* a clever girl." The mare nickered. Taking her halter in one hand and his pack in the other, he walked her down the hill. "There's water and grass here, and you'll be safe in the cottonwoods."

He left the mare grazing and set about collecting herbs. At the river's edge, he picked plantain and yarrow, wrapped them in skin, and stowed them in his pack. Then he filled his canteen with fresh water. The moon was waning, but it afforded enough light to guide him back up the hill in the gathering dusk. Deciding he'd rather not move Jesse again, he made pine-resin torches to light the lodge. After cutting two straight, solid green sticks, he split the ends of each one several times. He always carried pine resin in a bark container for emergencies, along with waterproof matches and a metal match that had been a gift from Joe. "Use technology selectively," Joe said. "Metal's our friend." At the cave, Hawk kept a few sewing needles for crafting, but he had none with him now. He'd need to improvise.

He put on water to boil in a small iron kettle. Then he readied his pine torches by stuffing resin into the split ends. He'd jam them into the earth inside the lodge and create enough light to work on Jesse's wound. He couldn't afford to wait for daylight.

He crushed plantain and yarrow leaves in his hands and dropped them into the boiling water, then set the kettle on the earth to cool. The only way to stop that bleeding was with sutures. She'd lost too much blood already. He remembered seeing a mess of gnawed rabbit bones in the bush, probably left by Sister. Pulling a burning stick from the fire, he went to find them.

There were several splinters. Two were quite good, slender and already sharp to the touch. He brought them back to the firelight and tried to puncture a tiny hole in the end of one. But he used too much pressure and the splinter broke in his hand. "Damn!" He'd nicked his finger and drawn blood. Puncturing a hole in the bone wouldn't work.

He laid another splintered bone on his leg against a piece of wood. Then, scraping gently with his knifepoint, he wore a tiny hole through the bone. He sharpened the end of the bone needle and tested it by easing it through the scar tissue on his inner arm. It slid in easily, so he left it wedged there where he could find it when he was ready. The pain would keep him alert and focused.

He set another kettle of water on the fire, gathered his supplies, and crawled back inside the lodge.

Jesse lay motionless. He planted the torches in the earth on either side of her and lit them. The resin sputtered, and light flooded the lodge.

He masticated several plantain leaves to make them pliant and release the juices, then set them on a clean piece of doeskin. If she awoke during the procedure he'd need to finish quickly, perhaps even hold her down. There was no knowing how she'd react. The largest plantain leaves he left until last. Since he had nothing with which to close her wounds, he'd need to make his own sutures. Carefully, he extracted the large main veins from the centers of several leaves and laid them on the doeskin.

When he crawled back out to retrieve the kettle of boiling water, he paused a moment to think about what he was about to do. Did he have everything he needed? Once he started there was no stopping, and there was no one here to help.

Back inside the lodge, he took a deep breath, untied her makeshift bandage, and examined the wound. It was four inches long and maybe half an inch deep. Something sharp and straight had penetrated the skin. *Axe head?* Had someone attacked her? It had missed the femoral artery but nicked a vein. That was what had caused the bleed.

He tested the boiled water and dribbled some over the wound, following with the herbal tincture.

Then he pulled the bone needle from his arm and held it to the fire. He threaded the plantain vein through the hole and ran the whole thing through the boiling water, ignoring his burning fingers. It would help to sterilize his hands.

Pinching together Jesse's gaping flesh with his left hand, he eased the needle through her skin with his right. She jerked and moaned but didn't regain consciousness. He made his first tie with the plantain vein and continued. The skin held together. He sutured the first inch, tied it off, then repeated the process with a second vein. He worked deftly, sealing the wound and tying sutures all along its length. An hour or more later, he appraised his work. It didn't look bad, and it would hold. She'd likely have a scar but, hell, that would give her a story to tell. He couldn't imagine how she'd got such a gash.

Finally, he placed a thick poultice of masticated plantain and yarrow leaves over the wound, to help heal any infection, and bandaged it with doeskin. Placing his palm across Jesse's forehead, he looked at her dirty, tear-streaked face. The woman had been through hell. Her shirt was filthy. Her pants were in bloody shreds, mostly thanks to him.

He cut a small piece of doeskin, dipped it in the cool tea, and wiped her face and neck. The firelight cast dancing shadows over her cheeks. After removing the rest of her clothing, he sponged down her body. Her flesh prickled in the chill.

How beautiful she is and how very vulnerable. He kept looking at her, looking away, and looking back. *I'm here to protect her and help her heal, and that's all.*

After spreading the doeskin over her, Hawk lay down beside her and tried to sleep. It was an emotional time, and he typically didn't allow for emotion. Once he'd released his passion and desire, and he'd got hurt. Now he protected his heart by staying away from anything and anyone who could make him feel.

Yet *they* were coming to him. First this woman, and then, last night in this sacred lodge, Joe had appeared. Joe, who Hawk hadn't seen since he walked into the bush three years ago. Joe, who was his father, teacher, confessor, friend.

"I'm leaving now but will one day see you again, Little Hawk." Hawk's lips had trembled, and he'd wailed. "Don't despair. I'm going to join Effie. Your grief will pass, and soon you will return. People need you."

Hawk's gut ached when he thought of the responsibility that involved. He didn't want to be needed. Joe was dead. Effie was dead. Shen was dead. His son was gone—taken by the people Shen had tried to escape. And now this woman lay beside him, hurt and needing his help. A living responsibility.

It wasn't just her physical beauty that attracted him. It was something more. And he fought it because it scared the hell out of him. The smell of her. The sound of her voice. Even the thought of her. *How can I help people when I can't even help myself?*

Lying beside her, he pillowed his right arm under her neck and placed his left palm across her heart. He needed to feel it beat.

BUNNY BROTH

Jesse awoke lying on her back. She heard even breaths. Smelled wood fire and a virile scent. Felt the heat of a body against her right side. The last thing she could remember was climbing on Reba's back. And pain . . . excruciating pain. Then terror, because she was injured and alone in the bush. She still felt that pain emanating from her left thigh, but she wasn't as scared. Perhaps because of the stranger breathing into her right shoulder.

Opening her right lid just wide enough to focus, she peered from the corner of her eye. *Jed. Yes.* She recognized the blond beard and high cheekbone just above it. *I found him. Or he found me?* She let out a breath she didn't know she was holding. *But why is he touching me like this?*

She moved her hand slowly beneath the cover to touch her growling belly. *I'm naked? What happened? Oh, God. Did we . . . ? Why can't I remember?* Easing away, she tried to roll to her knees, but a head rush sent her sprawling.

Jed caught her and held her while she struggled. "Why must you always fight me, Jesse?"

"You took my clothes off," she said indignantly, and clutched the soft cover to her breasts.

"Yes. You were a mess. Bloody and soaking wet." His voice was gentle. Caring, even. She'd never seen him like this. He sat up and stared into her eyes. "How do you feel?"

Was it not obvious? She'd no strength to fight or walk or even talk, but . . . "I-I have to pee." She sighed, humiliated.

"Me too." Releasing her, he stripped off his deerskin shirt. "Your clothes are ruined. Here. Sit up."

She did, and let him slip the soft shirt over her head. It was big and bunched up at her hips but rich with the warm scent of him. The sleeves hung past her fingers, and the slit in the neck was laced together with a buckskin thong.

Jed took a deep breath as if collecting his thoughts. "When you come back, I'll check your wound."

She turned onto her right knee and tried to stand. A sharp pain skidded through her left thigh. Staring down at her legs, she saw the bulging deerskin bandage. *Oh, God. The otter.* The memory of fur and blood and bone was too much. She swayed, caught in a wave of nausea, and gagged.

He leapt up to steady her and waited. "Stomach settled?" he asked at last.

She nodded. It wasn't really, but she refused to vomit in front of him, even if he was a doctor.

"You lost a lot of blood. I'll carry you."

She shook her head to protest. "I can walk." She hated feeling this weak and helpless. Gritting her teeth, she stared up at his face. He was tall and strong and unbearably handsome.

"I'll carry you," he repeated calmly.

"No, I can—" But the moment she moved her leg, pain shot through her body, and she wailed and fell into his arms. She felt his potent strength under her back and knees as he scooped her up.

He had to duck and crawl out of the lodge on his knees, the opening was so small. But still he held her firmly in his arms and, for a moment, she wished he'd never put her down. Then, with long strides, he moved through the morning air. Opening her mouth, she gulped oxygen and felt fortified.

After setting her down behind some bushes, he held her shoulders for a moment, making sure she was steady on her feet. "I can wait here or . . ."

"I'm fine," she assured him. There was no way she was going to pee in front of him. "The fresh air helps."

"Call me when you're done." His steely eyes flashed in the sunlight that pierced the dawn. And then he turned and walked away.

She limped back to the tent on her own, using a dead branch as a crutch. Spiderwebs sparkling with sundrops hung in the bushes. The ground was wet with dew, and it soaked her bare feet. Gazing around, she took in the dawn sky, fractured gold emerging through a rippling tree line. It seemed they were camped on top of the world.

Jed wasn't there, and she felt a staggering sense of relief and disappointment. Too much had happened. Too much she didn't understand. She needed sunshine and fresh air and to lie down before she fell down.

Reaching into the tent, she grabbed the bearskin and dragged it along the ground to the small campfire. The night chill still clung to her skin, and she was glad he'd built up the fire. Easing down onto her right hip, she stretched out and closed her eyes. *If I'm careful, I can manage.* The bear hide was thick and inviting . . . and then it hit her. *These are dead animals!* She pushed up onto her elbow. *I'm wearing buckskin, just like that deer he killed the first time I saw him. And look at this poor bear. Did he kill it too? Alec would be horrified if he saw this. And where's my sleeping bag? I can't remember. Why can't I remember?* Her throat tightened, and she swallowed to ease the dryness and stop the tears. The last memory she had was of climbing onto the back of the horse. *Reba! Where's Reba? Did she bring me here?*

Jed appeared, clutching a limp rabbit by its hind legs. He nodded. Then he leaned over, took out his knife, and began disemboweling the rabbit.

"*Oh, please!* Don't do that. It's making me sick."

"You need food. You're weak."

"Well, I'm not eating *that*." Jesse rolled her eyes. "Poor thing. I haven't eaten meat in years."

"Fine. You can sit here and chew on pine boughs till someone comes along and carries you home." His voice was cool.

"Why can't *you* take me home?"

"I'm not traveling with an injured woman too stubborn to heal herself."

Stubborn? How is standing firm in your values stubborn?

Bunny disemboweled, he further mutilated it by slipping the skin off in one piece like a glove.

Jesse's stomach flipped when she saw the pink, naked creature. She turned her head and took a deep breath. "That's just wrong." When she turned back again, he'd laid the corpse on a flat rock and was focused on building up the fire. Leaning her cheek on her fist, she watched him to keep her eyes averted from the poor rabbit. She sighed. It could be worse. She could be laid up somewhere, alone and bleeding. At least with Jed she felt safe.

Once the fire was crackling, he poured some brown liquid from an iron kettle into a tin cup and offered it to her. "Here. Drink this."

"What is it?"

"Tea."

She held it to her nose and sniffed. It smelled bitter, but her dry throat ached. "What are these twigs?"

"Just drink it." Huffing like an old bear, he shook his head. "It's *vegan*."

There was no bargaining with him. He lived simply. Spoke little. Meant what he said. And she had no doubt he'd leave her behind if she didn't do what she was told. She sipped the tea.

"You score zero for bedside manner."

"You didn't mind my bedside manner last night."

"What?" The word escaped before she could catch it. Had something happened between them? Is that why everything felt so awkward? She wanted him. Bad. Perhaps in her delirium she'd seduced him and forgotten. No, she'd remember *that* no matter how sick she was, and Jed wasn't the kind of man who'd take advantage of an injured woman out of her mind with pain.

He ignored her question, and she felt relieved.

She sat watching as he sliced the rabbit into chunks and put it in a kettle to boil with water and herbs. He was deft with that knife. Would have made a fine surgeon. Then her eyelids grew so heavy that she lay back on the bearskin and closed her eyes.

When the stew bubbled and she caught the scent, her mouth watered and she hated herself for it. *Bunny broth.*

"I need to check your wound." Leaning over, Jed blocked the sunlight.

She was too tired to argue.

He untied the deerskin bandage and gently eased back the poultice.

"Are those leaves?"

"Yes."

She wrinkled her nose and turned her face away as shivers riveted up her thighs.

"The stitches are holding well."

"Stitches? How did you stitch it?" He pointed at the bone needle stuck through the doeskin shirt she was wearing. "What's it made from?"

"Rabbit bone."

"You made a needle from a rabbit bone to stitch up my leg?" She saw a sudden image of the bone needle piercing her flesh as he sutured her wound, and a tingling sensation passed through her groin.

Nodding, he narrowed his eyes. "You ask too many questions, woman." He adjusted the bandage and started feeding sticks to the fire.

"Well, this *woman* owns this body. Just because you're a doctor doesn't mean you can do anything you want to me." Her jaw tightened. "Don't you have to ask permission before performing medical treatment on someone?"

"I did. You were unconscious."

Passive-aggressive. And ornery too. But he *had* fixed her injury, and God knows what would have happened if he hadn't. "Where's my horse?" she said, remembering the Appaloosa.

He gestured down to the valley where a river glinted through the trees. "Why do you have Reba?"

So he knew the horse. "My friend Rainy is your brother's fiancée. They loaned me your uncle's horse, and . . . Oh. Joe." The thought hit with a force that made her head pound for a brief second.

He stopped prodding the fire and stared at her. "Joe?"

"Yes. I came to tell you about your friend Joe. He's really sick. He might—"

"Joe's gone." Jed was quiet for some time, and she left him to his thoughts. Perhaps these two had a stronger connection than she imagined—a psychic connection.

Then, suddenly, he cocked his head. "You came all the way out here alone to tell me about Joe?"

"Well, yes. I thought you'd want to see him. Say goodbye." Jesse sighed, and, for the first time, Jed pulled back one corner of his mouth in a smile.

TRAVOIS

Hawk poured some of the pale brown liquid into a clay cup, raised Jesse's head, and held it to her lips. "You need broth. Sip it." He spoke softly—he didn't want to upset her. Her condition was deteriorating, and he didn't like what he was seeing.

"Bunny broth." She flicked her stormy eyes at him, opened her lips, and sipped.

He touched her forehead. She was still feverish. They couldn't stay here. She needed medical treatment, not makeshift bush remedies.

He'd left her sleeping on the bearskin while he built a travois out of straight, strong pine poles. The hides from his sweat lodge padded the base. Then he'd bound it to the mare using hide thongs. Down near the river, where he'd found the mare grazing, he'd noticed pussy willow shrubs. Joe had told him they once used the bark in a tea for headaches. It contained salicylic acid, the base for aspirin, and was a remedy for pain and inflammation. With his knife Hawk had cut several branches, peeled and sliced them, and boiled them in a small kettle of water. He wasn't sure of the dose, but he hoped the decoction would help bring down her fever.

"We're leaving, Jesse. I'm going to pick you up now."

She looked at him oddly but didn't protest when he scooped her up in his arms and carried her to the travois. After laying her gently in the skins and covering her to protect her from the sun, he lashed her down using thongs. She was too sick and weak to protest, and that scared him more than anything else.

Grasping Reba's lead, he started walking. The travois was new to the mare, but she didn't seem to mind. He glanced around for signs of Sister. The wolf would find him. She always did.

Stepping quietly, he gave the mare rein but directed her around rocks and holes that might cause her to stumble or turn a hoof. If she went lame now, they'd have more trouble than they could handle. He followed the trail left by the mare the previous day. Jesse might have left her gear where she'd been injured. If she had, he'd pick it up. Mostly, he was curious how she'd hurt herself so badly.

They were in hill country, traveling steadily down a rock ridge toward the river valley. It was slow going, skirting boulders and lichen-covered rock floors that rose and fell in unending crevasses. Time passed with scarcely a sound save the mare's footfalls and the cawing of crows who seemed to be everywhere like a trembling black cloud. He felt his heartbeat quicken. Crows were messengers, and so many cawing loudly together meant only one thing to Hawk: it was an omen. And omens meant change.

Joe had passed, and Jesse had come into his life. It didn't escape his analytical mind that he'd gone twice to her cabin—once with venison and again to offer her the protection of Makwa's tooth.

Hawk glanced at Jesse bouncing along on the travois. *Who was this woman? A lesson? A test? A mate?* He was certainly attracted to her physically. But he hadn't seen a woman in three years, so it could just be lust. A man could only go so long. But even as the thought rolled through his mind, he knew he was wrong. It was more than lust. All of these things played on his mind as he paced through scrublands and thickets, coming at last to the still, silent woodland.

The horse was tiring. She was old, this mare. He'd been just a kid when she was born. Still, what she lacked in stamina she made up for in heart. They followed Jesse's trail to the river. Its gurgling sweetness beckoned, and the mare nickered to let him know it was time to drink and rest. He released her from the travois so she could browse, and made camp beneath a stand of swamp oak.

Jesse stirred and rubbed her eyes. Her color was high—perhaps with sun, perhaps fever. She tried to move and winced. Her muscles were likely sore from lying bound to the jouncing travois.

"You okay? How're you feeling?"

"Like a prisoner."

He undid the skin straps that bound her to the travois. Then he found the canteen of willow bark tea and held it to her lips. "This is organic aspirin. It will help with the pain."

"I'm so stiff. Everything hurts."

Hawk laid his palm on her forehead and looked into her eyes. "Your skin's hot from the sun." Rather than take his hand away, he ran it down her hair and kneaded her shoulder and behind her neck.

"That feels good. I feel like I got hit by a train."

He laughed. "I've never traveled tied to a travois myself, but I can imagine the bouncing might mess with your muscles. Roll that way onto your stomach," he said, pointing away from him. He didn't want to aggravate the wound on her left thigh.

"I don't know if I can."

"Here, I'll help." Lifting her gently, he eased her over, then rolled some hide into a pillow. "Lift up," he said, catching her hips with his hand and thrusting the roll beneath her pelvis. The pillow would take the pressure off her lower back by rounding her spine.

Kneeling, he kneaded her neck and shoulders.

Jesse sighed. "Your bedside manner is improving, doctor."

He grunted, but massaged her tight muscles and walked his fingers up and down her spine, releasing the tension and adjusting each vertebra.

Her long low sigh made him feel good. He remembered why he'd become a doctor and how much he liked making people feel better. He continued working her neck, squeezing and rubbing, and finally ran his fingers across her skull and hair in featherlight strokes. When her breathing deepened, he realized she'd fallen asleep. *Good. That will give me time to catch supper.*

He caught a glimpse of Sister's white fur just before she disappeared over the riverbank. Perhaps she was traveling with her new pack, but she was keeping him in sight. His eyes teared up, and he rubbed them with his fist. *Weepy? Why am I weepy?*

He took out his knife and walked toward a stand of tall maple trees near the river. After choosing a straight sapling about six feet tall, he hacked it through a few inches from the ground. Then, using downward strokes, he commenced sharpening one end into a fishing spear.

A man did not get weepy over a wolf, even one as loyal as Sister. The next thing he knew he'd be tearing up over the woman. *No more tears.* He'd stopped crying when Shen died, and he'd never cry again.

Taking his spear down to the river, he found a flat rock in a still place near willow roots where the walleye would go to rest. He'd caught seven and eight-pound walleye in this river before. It was clear as glass, and he could see their shadows. All it took was patience and skill.

He lay flat on his belly along the rock and dipped the sharpened head of his spear into the water. Keeping his eyes on the shadows, he pushed himself forward until he was close enough to put his face in the water along with the spear. A man trying to spear from standing would be tricked by the refracted light.

He took a deep breath and held it, then put his face in the water and opened his eyes. He could see the fat fish sitting there about two feet below. His muscles tensed as he readied the spear. *Hold. Hold. Strike!* The impact of spear into flesh rippled up his arm, and he held on tightly with both hands as the walleye struggled to break free. Head, torso, and both arms in the river, he balanced his hips on the rock and held the fish to the bottom. Then, reaching down, he scooped it up, still impaled on the spear.

It was a beauty. A fat walleye. Over two feet long, weighing eight or nine pounds. He'd speared it right below the gills, so its mouth was wide open, showing a mouthful of tiny razor-sharp teeth.

He cracked it over the head with a rock to stop its floundering and set it back from the water in a crevice between two rocks. Then he stripped off his wet clothes and jumped into the river. Squatting on the stony bottom, he massaged his body. His muscles were in tight knots. He scrubbed his face and scalp firmly, bringing the blood to the surface. He rinsed his wet clothes too. Then he climbed out and hung them on maple saplings to dry in the breeze.

He stared at the fish and beamed. He couldn't wait to show Jesse what he'd caught them for supper.

PROM NIGHT 2

June 2000

He drove over the bridge and parked his mother's '85 Chevy Celebrity in the gas station lot. It was a beater, already fifteen years old, rusted and falling apart 'cause the old man wouldn't buy her a new one. Didn't want her "going too far." Feared that one day she'd pack up and leave.

He hoped she would. He hoped she'd take him with her.

He looked over at the cardboard box beside him on the front seat. When he opened it, the mama cat blinked but didn't move. Her kittens were all attached and sucking. They were only six weeks old. He and his mom had kept them hidden in the attic so the old man wouldn't find them, but this morning he went up there to get his musky gear. Saturday was opening day, and he planned to pull out a fish as long as his arm.

He put his hand in the box and gently pulled Tippy off the tit. His little eyes opened, and he mewed, just a faint sleepy squeak. Holding the soft warm ball to his chest, he whispered, "Don't worry. I won't let him drown you." The kitten blinked, and he rubbed it against his chin.

When the girl walked by, she took a quick look in the car. He held Tippy out the window for her to see, and she stopped and smiled. "Aw, so cute!"

She was short. Big brown eyes almost even with the car roof. Slender and pretty. Light brown hair. Beaded earrings—black, white, red, and a yellow as bright as mustard.

"I'm looking for homes for this one and two more. Wanna see them?"

She shrugged. "Okay."

"They're in the box," he said, gesturing to the passenger side.

She walked around and opened the door. "Oh my God. They're adorable. Can I hold one?"

"Sure." He pried the orange one free and gave it to her. The body warmed his hand like one of Hank's coffees.

Holding it in both hands, she giggled. "You're just the cutest thing."

"You can keep it," he said, and smiled hopefully.

"Aw, I'd love to, but we've got two pit bulls that would . . ." She scrunched up her face rather than finish that thought.

"Too bad. My father's going to drown them tonight if I can't find homes for them."

She bit her lip with perfect white teeth. "Why don't you drop them out near a farm? People always need cats to eat mice and rats."

He pulled down his lips in thought. "You know anywhere good?"

"Maybe."

"Can you show me?"

TRAPS

Ira was standing knee-deep in the pond, straining, and panting. Sweat curled his hairline and stung his eyes.

"Jeez, Ira. You're as strong as you ever were. I bet you could take any man in the state—probably in the whole *goddamn* country." Sam exaggerated almost as much as he cursed.

With his cowhide hands, Ira was trying his best to pry apart the rusty steel-jawed trap, but he wasn't gullible enough to believe his friend's praise was anything but fuel to get him to try harder.

They rarely caught enough animals to warrant selling pelts, but Sam relished trapping. He said it made him feel connected to his ancestors, but Ira thought it had more to do with hating his father than celebrating his granddaddy. The traps were rusty antiques Sam had discovered a few years ago in his attic, along with the gold-mining tools.

Ira didn't care one way or the other, but he knew Sam couldn't set these metallic monsters himself. And, friends being scarce, he pitched in where he could. Besides, he loved the forest. It made him feel closer to God.

They'd been exploring this part of the state the last while. After finding one of their traps sprung but empty, they'd hiked downstream and discovered the pond. No one who walked with his head down could have missed the otter tracks that dotted the bank around the old muskrat lodge.

"What do you think happened to that other trap, Sammy? I can't imagine anything crawling away from one of these." His voice husky, he coughed and spat.

"God knows. Metal tools are fickle. Sometimes they just

spring."

Ira stared down at his hands. He'd submerged the trap just below the waterline and was about to set it.

"Finish her up, man. I'm curious what else is out here. It's been some time since I've explored this far west."

"We're getting pretty close to the reservation, aren't we?" Ira's mother warned him to stay away from Chippewa girls. Oh, he saw them when they came into Lure, but he hadn't been out on the reservation since high school.

"Hell, Ira. We're *on* the reservation. But don't worry. The girls don't come out in the bush these days. They've all got computers and cell phones."

Ira finished setting the trap and waded out of the pond, feeling like a water buffalo. His ma had him on a "no macaroni" diet, but it didn't seem to be helping. He put on his socks and work boots without properly drying his feet cause Sam was standing with his hands on his hips, tapping his foot and looking annoyed. Now, as Ira followed him through the bush, he could feel his damp socks rubbing against the backs of his ankles. He hoped he didn't blister.

Sam was following a fresh trail. The tracks were small and patterned like a hiking boot. After a bit, they came to a square patch that had been dug up.

"Holy shit, Ira." Sam's eyes lit up. "Do you know who these green-handled tools belong to?"

One tool looked the same as another to Ira, who was colorblind because his head had been punched too many times. At least that's what his ma said. She'd never liked him boxing unless he won money. Ira shook his head.

Sam picked up the cultivators. "You remember that pretty girl in the pink T-shirt we saw in town? I saw her with these very same tools last Saturday."

Ira didn't know pink from green, but he remembered the girl.

She had the face of an angel, and he'd been dreaming about her all week. "You think she lives way out here?" He liked seeing her, but he didn't like coming here to do it.

"That is a distinct possibility. I do recall her friend was a Chippewa girl."

"My ma doesn't want me seeing Chippewa girls."

"Well, that blonde was no Chippewa."

But Ira knew how Sam worked. If they found two girls, he chose the one he wanted, and Ira got left with the other one. It had been that way since high school. Sam in the front seat and Ira in the back. He knew Sam was sweet on the angel girl. Sam's mom died a few years back, but he still had photographs of her at all ages in his flat above the office. And the angel girl looked enough like Sam's mother to be her younger sister.

It felt like they'd been walking for hours, and Sam was practically running down the trail by the time he came out into a glade by the lake. When Sam turned abruptly, Ira bumped into him, and the force of it bounced Sam a few feet backward.

He turned with a look of panic on his face. "Holy shit, Ira. Turn around. Turn around now."

"What? Why? What's going on?" Ira pushed past Sam far enough to see an old cabin in the clearing. Tents had been erected, and police tape rippled in the breeze. "You think she lives here?"

"I don't know, and I don't care. Those are tribal cops, and we don't want them finding us here. They'll ask questions we can't answer."

Sam turned and started walking.

"But what if she's hurt?" Now that he remembered the girl's angel face, he was concerned for her welfare.

"If she's hurt, they've likely packed her off to the medical center. There's nothing we can do to help her."

Sam was practically running through the bush. Branches flew

back and hit Ira.

"Slow down, Sammy. We ain't done nothin'." Ira was wet and winded, and his blisters were biting at his heels.

"You're forgetting about our enterprise, Ira. We're too close now to risk anyone finding out about it. If they see us out here, they'll remember our faces. And if they get suspicious, they'll start asking questions."

"But we were just setting traps."

"Out of season on the reservation. Jeez, Ira, sometimes you're denser than fog on a cold May morning."

"I didn't know that. What about the mine? Is it illegal too?"

"Christ, Ira! Use your brain for something other than keeping your ears apart."

Ira glanced around as they walked, trying to remember landmarks. He wished Sam would just say yes or no. He didn't want to go back to jail. Then he'd never stand a chance with the angel girl.

YOU GOTTA BE KIDDING

It must have been the smell of the fish roasting over the fire that roused Jesse. She was still drowsy, but her empty stomach ached. Glancing around, she felt a weird sense of déjà vu. Then Jed walked out of the woods, wearing nothing but a piece of deerskin tied around his hips, and she forgot everything else. His pecs were more defined than anything she'd seen at the gym or on the beach. Fine pale hair grew down his tanned chest, scarred arms, and muscular legs. When he saw her staring, he grinned. Feeling her face flush, she turned away.

"I hope you like walleye." His tone was teasing and vaguely threatening.

"I don't eat—"

"Yeah, yeah, I know. But tonight you will. Walleye is the lobster of the north."

She'd loved lobster when she was a kid, at least the kind they served at Lobster King, poached in butter. Her dad used to take her there. It was always a special date—one of the only times they were alone and she had his full and complete attention.

"How did you catch it?" He wasn't carrying any fishing rods or nets.

Jed showed her his palms. "With these, and this," he said, pointing to his brain.

She raised her eyebrows and one corner of her lip in a *you gotta be kidding me* kind of look. "Scooped it right out of the river, did you?"

"I speared it first." Taking the roasted fish from the fire, he set it down on a split piece of wood and slit it open with his knife.

Steam wafted out. Using his fingertips, he gently pulled the skeleton out, and the white fish fell in fat flakes.

"You're kind of unbelievable." She swallowed lest he notice her salivating and assume it had something to do with his lack of clothing. Which it did.

He pushed the platter in front of her and took a piece between his fingers and thumb. Closing his eyes as if in prayer, he paused, then popped it in his mouth. A pleasureful growl emerged from his throat.

"Go on. Eat." He nodded toward the fish.

Jesse pulled back, more out of principle than anything else.

He picked up another fat flake and held it to her lips. "You'll feel better. Trust me."

She wanted to trust him. She glanced at her bandaged leg and at the spotted mare happily grazing under the trees. Reba seemed to trust him.

Looking into his gray eyes, Jesse sighed. "Fine." She opened her mouth.

When his lips pulled to the side in a half smile, she noticed the trimmed mustache. Had it been trimmed that day he kissed her at the cabin? In the firelight, his high cheekbones created shadowy hollows above his blond beard. His lips were thick and peaked, almost womanish.

"I could teach you," he said.

"Teach me what?"

She wanted to kiss him. Plant her lips on his and see where it led. Her belly was buzzing.

"To spear a fish." Narrowing his eyes, he stroked his blond beard. "Joe taught me when I was eight. I'm sure you'd catch on. It's really just about angles of light."

Was that arrogance or an attempt at sarcasm? Or both? But the mention of Joe brought Jesse a pang of sadness. It didn't matter that she hadn't known the old man. He'd been a huge part of Jed's life.

"Sorry about Joe."

"I'll miss him." He picked up another piece of fish and held it to her lips. "But Joe lived a good long life, and he's happy to be reunited with Effie."

"So you spoke with Joe recently?"

"Two nights ago." When he looked deep into her eyes, a shiver ran up her spine. He was serious.

"But . . ." She shrugged.

"So, you see, you didn't need to come all the way out here to find me. I already knew. When people are close, they find a way." He nodded slightly, and Jesse touched his hand.

"When my mother died of cancer, all I could smell were butter tarts for days. Everywhere I went. It was like she was there beside me."

She hadn't moved her hand but wanted to run it up his arm, across his shoulder and chest . . . wanted to press her skin against his and share more intimate secrets.

He picked up another piece of walleye and together they put the fish in her mouth. It tasted sweet and salty, smoky and fresh. Much better than the lobster at Lobster King. "You should eat too," she said, picking up another piece herself. "All you've done is look after me. And I should thank you for saving my life."

"Thank Reba. If she hadn't brought you to my lodge . . ." He let his thought drift with the breeze, and they ate awhile in silence.

Finally, Jesse's belly was stuffed with fish. She licked her fingers and wiped them on the hides. "Oh my God. What day is it?"

He shrugged. "I don't keep a calendar."

"Well, how long have we been traveling?"

"Two days."

"I told Rainy to send a search party if I wasn't back by the end of the week." She tried to remember. "I was on the trail three or four days before I got hurt, and then I don't know what happened after that, and we've been traveling two days? We've got to get back and tell them I'm all right. Rainy will be—"

"Relax. I know this river. We'll be back in a day or two, and if my brother comes, we'll get back sooner." With a piece of hide, he wrapped up what was left of the fish and put it in his pack, then took the platter of skin and bones to the river.

When he returned, he was carrying green leaves. "I need to examine your wound and change the poultice."

"Plantain." Jesse recognized many of the local plants and trees she photographed.

Jed nodded and unwrapped the deerskin bandage. "Helps with healing. On a scale of one to ten, how much does it hurt?"

"Seven when I'm resting, but it shoots up to nine when I walk or touch it."

When he pulled back the leaves to expose the wound, a shiver ran right up her inner thighs into her groin. It was a good four inches, the skin red and weeping yellow pus around the puckered edges. "Oh my God! How many?"

"Stitches? I didn't count. Maybe twenty or so?"

"Twenty?" She shivered again when she saw the bone needle sticking through the deer hide. "And you used *this*?"

"Yes . . . and this." He tore apart one of the large plantain leaves and showed her how to extract the main vein. "It's a strong suture."

"Incredible." Without him, how would she have survived with a gaping four-inch slice in her thigh?

"Do you remember anything more about what happened to you?" He popped several leaves in his mouth and began to slowly chew.

"There was an otter in a steel trap. Its head was caught in the teeth, and I . . ." Closing her eyes, Jesse saw the horrific image in her mind.

Taking the soft, wet leaves from his mouth, Jed placed them on the wound. She grimaced but wasn't about to start lecturing him on cleanliness and bacteria.

"You fell?"

"I jumped in the river to try and . . . I don't know . . . release it? I think I must have hit a jagged rock."

Biting his lip, he made a clicking sound. "A river rock didn't do this. It's straight and deep like a blade. Maybe part of another steel trap. These assholes usually use the same places, and they never clean up their mess. When did you have your last tetanus shot?"

She closed one eye and tried to remember. "Oh, I was maybe twelve? A nail went through my running shoe. I still have the scar."

"Get a booster when you get back to town." He cleared his throat and spit. "Steel-jaw traps should be banned."

Jesse nodded. That was one thing they could agree on. "I feel like it happened near here." She couldn't shake that sense of uneasiness she'd first felt at the campsite.

Jed tied her bandage. "I'll take a walk along the river before dark and see if I can find anything." When he shook his head, she saw something different in his demeanor.

Is he more tender? More caring? Less defensive? Jesse suspected his silence and abrupt manner were a means to distance himself. Perhaps he feared losing control. Whatever was happening, she liked it. The touch of his hands on her body. His gentle voice. He was a nurturing man, even in his gruffness. And he'd saved her life.

"You could have died."

His eyes glassed over, and she wondered if he was thinking of her or Shen. A sliver of absurd jealousy arose, and Jesse bit her lip. "But I didn't."

"Not yet." His face was serious.

She glanced away and hugged her arms. She was competing with a ghost. Rolling onto one knee, she tried to get up. She wanted to do something. Anything but lie here and think about dying from an injury in the bush. "I need to stretch. I'll come with you to the river."

"No." His voice was sharp. Definitive.

"No?" Jesse never did like being told *no.*

"These sutures are delicate, and if your pain is shooting up to a nine when you walk, you don't go farther than the bushes." He pushed a small kettle of willow bark tea toward her. "Drink this."

Narrowing her eyes, Jesse crossed her arms over her chest and fumed. She couldn't walk without him. And now, apparently, she couldn't walk *with* him. Her butt was numb and damp from sitting on the ground, her back ached, her neck ached, and the pain in her thigh had suddenly spiked.

"Do you need to go to the bushes now?"

"I don't need you for that, *doctor.* I can get by just fine on my own."

WOMEN

Hawk pulled on pants and a shirt and padded along the riverbank, swatting flies and muttering to himself about *women* and *who could understand them* and *why try*. One minute Jesse was all doe eyes, and the next she was stormy, and he couldn't figure out why. What had he done to set her off?

It hurts when I walk, doctor.

Well then, don't walk.

Case closed. Except it wasn't.

Hopefully, the willow bark tea would lessen her pain and she'd be asleep by the time he returned. He was missing the solace of the woods. And Sister. He hadn't seen her in hours. Sticking two fingers in his mouth, he whistled. He could handle a wolf. Even a bear. But a woman?

Shen was never like that. They never fought. Not even when she was pregnant, and the baby kept trying to kick his foot through her uterus. Hawk used to put his hand on her belly and laugh when the tiny foot pushed up the skin. He could hold it with his fingers. They had dreams and plans. They'd work together in a clinic somewhere. Maybe here on the reservation near Joe, or perhaps with his dad in Lure, if his dad would have him. Shen wanted to specialize in pediatrics because she loved kids and couldn't bear to see them suffer. He'd been willing to do whatever was needed. Fill the holes. Dole out antibiotics and mend broken bones. Look down throats and listen to hearts.

And then *his* heart broke.

Sister came out of the bush, dragging a canvas backpack. "Hey, what have you got there?"

It was Jesse's. Had to be. The only things left in the pack were a balled-up T-shirt in the outside pocket and a scattering of granola inside, which led him to believe there'd once been a stash. Likely it had been appropriated by raccoons or squirrels. One scolded him now from the low branches of an ash.

"Where'd you find this?"

The wolf walked on, and Hawk followed, keeping a careful eye on the water flow in the river. If he could find that trap, he'd dismantle it so nothing else would suffer like the animals that had been unlucky enough to get caught in it. For years he'd been after his brother, the forest ranger, to campaign for the criminalization of inhumane traps. If anyone saw the results of bad trapping, it was Matty. Sister was following a narrow game trail now, and he always worried she'd get her foot stuck in one of those bloody things. A clean, respectful kill was one thing. Torture was something else, and the animals could linger for days. His gut flipped with the thought of it.

Hawk and the wolf pushed through some willow scrub and emerged in a small glade. Jesse's camp, or what was left of it, stood in the center. Her beige sleeping bag was still there beside the remnants of a campfire. Crumpled, blood-soaked, it looked like she'd only got up for a moment and was planning to crawl back inside. Her clothing was scattered. Wool socks. Underwear. T-shirts. Another pair of cargos. A worn Seattle Mariners ball cap. The turquoise sweater. He scooped it up and inhaled. It still held her scent. He grabbed whatever he could find, including her camera, a ten-inch hunting knife, and a couple of cans of beans, and stuffed it all in the pack.

He saw the mare's tracks nearby and tracked the bloodstains to a fallen fir tree. That was likely where she'd mounted the horse. Thank God she'd been lucid enough to do that. If Jesse had stayed in that sleeping bag any longer, she'd have bled out. There was more blood than he'd expected—too much blood—and it sent a shiver down his spine.

He backtracked to the river and searched for the trap. But it was too dark to see anything in the swift-flowing stream, so he decided to leave it for morning. Now he knew where Jesse's camp was, he could come back and find the bloody thing in the sunlight. What he really wanted to know was how she'd cut her leg. Old rusty metal was more likely to cause infection. She hadn't cleaned the wound, and he hadn't been able to clean it properly. He didn't like the look of it or her rate of recovery. He really needed to get her back to his cave where he could heal her properly, but the way she was now, it was too far to risk it.

By the time he got back to camp, Jesse was asleep. At least she was lying on her right side, facing the fire, *pretending* to be asleep. She'd thrown a few sticks on to build up the blaze and wrapped herself in the doeskin. Hadn't touched the willow bark tea. *Goddamn stubborn woman.*

He sat quietly, watching and considering whether he should force her to drink the tea. She was still awake and likely in pain. He'd listened to her the last two nights—when he couldn't sleep himself for worrying about her—and knew how the depth and rhythm of her breathing changed when she slept. Finally, however, he lay down with his chest against her back to keep her warm, wrapped his arm around her, and closed his eyes.

Jesse was actually sleeping when he awoke at dawn—he heard the deep sough of her unconscious breath. Slipping away, he took up her trail once he'd made it back to her camp. Joe had taught him enough about tracking to follow the broken twigs and grasses that indicated which way she'd walked. She'd turned left and meandered toward a willow scrub. He spotted a muskrat lodge on the opposite bank. No doubt she'd seen that too. With her wildlife photographer instincts, she'd have been searching for shots.

There were two clear prints in the muddy bank where she'd knelt, likely reaching over to fill her canteen or wash. His eyes scanned the ripples, currents, and rocks. Nothing. He stripped off his shirt and pants and left them on a boulder. Then, picking up a strong straight deadfall, he eased into the river. He kept his eyes open and walked lightly, using the stick to test what he didn't trust. He didn't want to get caught up himself or cut his foot. If something happened to him, neither of them would make it home.

His gut told him to wade out near the biggest boulder then turn by the deep pond and walk toward the willow scrub. He was almost on the thing by the time he saw it. Hidden a good foot below the surface, it was barely visible against the brown-gray surge of water. What remained of the otter was trapped below against the rocks, contaminating the river. Jesse had likely moved it from its original position. Standing very still, he surveyed the water behind him and to each side. She would have had to jump backwards, perhaps sideways, to cut her left thigh at that angle. The water would have come about a foot above her knees.

What finally gave it away was a glint of sunlight that broke through the dawn and caught on a piece of metal jutting just above the water line about four feet from where he stood. Using the prod, he waded over. One half of a bloodstained, double-bit axe. The water was clear enough now to see shapes below the surface. A leg-iron trap. The rest of the axe. Reaching in, he grasped the wooden handle and pulled. It was stuck on something. Barbed wire. And another old steel-jaw trap. What the hell? Had these old boys been using this river as a dump? Or had this stuff washed downstream and got stuck here during a spring flood?

He wrenched loose the whole business, which was tethered together, and dragged it across the gravel to the embankment. Then he went back in. He managed to get both the steel trap and what was left of the otter out of the river and onto the bank. Using a fragment of metal, he dug a shallow hole and buried the headless carcass. He took a pinch of tobacco from the medicine pouch around his neck and spread it on the grave as he whispered one of Joe's old prayers.

Then he sat down on the bank and examined the axe. This was the source of the laceration. Both ends had four-inch bits that fit the gash perfectly. They were nicked with wear but sharp enough to puncture her skin if she lurched back and hit hard. Seeing the otter would likely have caused that reaction.

Carefully running his thumb along the edge, he frowned. Bits of rusted metal came off on his skin. Which meant Jesse had rusted metal inside the wound he'd stitched shut. He'd need to cut the wound open again in a sterile environment and debride it properly. He considered leaving her and going for help, but if something happened to her before he could get back, he'd never forgive himself. Besides, what he really needed was the proper equipment and medication, not another bush doctor like himself.

COWBOY SHERIFF

Hawk couldn't run Reba all day, and he knew that if something happened to the old mare, Jesse would never forgive him. His mind mulled over options.

One. Keep Jesse on the travois and slow-walk the horse to one of the more populated areas on the reservation. There, he might borrow a vehicle and get her into town. If he called 911, he'd have to deal with that narcissistic sheriff from Lure who responded to every call whether it was in his jurisdiction or not. Flint Flanagan had been sheriff for over twenty-five years and, frankly, Hawk was surprised no one had offed him yet. He had his fingers in every pie ever baked in Lure, and they were none too clean.

Hawk really wanted to get Jesse out to his cave, where he had a cure that could heal her faster than any known drug. But it was too far, and he was too afraid to risk it. Not with dirty rusted metal in the wound.

Option two was the medical center on the reservation. But Sunday night they'd be closed, and he didn't fancy breaking in, just in case he got caught. The tribal police knew he was living out here on the land and had never hassled him about it. They had a tacit understanding, no doubt due to Joe, who'd referred to Hawk as his adopted son, and he wanted it kept that way.

The last option was to get Jesse as far as possible on the travois, then put her on the horse with him and ride double into Lure to his dad's medical office. He'd find sterilizing equipment there, antibiotics, and tetanus vaccine. He'd lost one woman already, and he wouldn't lose another. This seemed like the best solution for the moment. But first he had to get Jesse fit for travel.

"Please drink this tea. It'll help with the pain."

Jesse kept her eyes shut but screwed up her nose and chugged it down. He helped her into a clean pair of bright-pink panties. He knew she was hurting bad when she raised her hips and didn't try to fight. That, and the eyes that wouldn't open, scared him more than anything else. On some level, she'd checked out.

Still, he kept talking to her. The most terrifying thing for a sick or injured person was to think they were alone. "I found your sweater and your ball cap."

The air was cold and wet with drizzle, yet she was intermittently sweating and shivering.

She let him raise her arms so he could pull off the buckskin shirt. *God. What was this attraction?* She was an injured woman, but seeing her there, topless and vulnerable in her panties, caused a stirring he was glad she couldn't see. He put her hands through the sleeves, pulled the turquoise sweater over her head, and fixed her soft blonde hair. When his fingertips touched her neck, he paused impulsively and counted her pulse through her carotid artery. It was rapid and erratic.

When her fevered eyes flashed open, as bright as the sweater, he took a quick breath. She stared at him for a solid six seconds, then batted her eyelids and slipped into another level of unconsciousness.

Her body will heal itself given time and sleep. Her brain will make white blood cells to attack the bacteria and trigger the release of hormones to heal her tissues. Both will reduce the inflammation surrounding the infected wound. As long as it doesn't spike into sepsis, she'll be all right.

The problem was, he was already seeing symptoms of septicemia.

He dug a pair of clean socks out of her canvas pack and put them on her feet. Then he slid on her moccasins. The pants would never go over the wound, and he didn't want to aggravate it, so he wrapped her legs in deerskin. The last time he'd checked the wound, he'd had to conceal a moment of panic. During his internship, he'd learned to wear a poker face and never get emotional with his patients. A doctor never let a patient see his fear.

Finally, he strapped her onto the travois. He knew she hated to be restrained, but if the horse spooked for whatever reason, it could save her life. The last thing she needed was to bounce off the travois and smash her head on a rock.

"You just sleep now, Jesse, and we'll fix everything at my father's clinic in Lure." He said it more for his own benefit than hers.

But her eyelids riffled, and she exhaled. "Lure?"

"Yeah, we'll be there soon. You just sleep."

The wet drizzle had excited the bugs. The blackflies didn't bother him much, but they'd taken a liking to Jesse. Blood dripped from bites behind both her ears, and one of her eyes was swollen. Taking another piece of doeskin, he fashioned a kind of hood that wrapped tightly around her hairline and neck so only her face was exposed. Then he spread clay on both their faces and fanned smoke over them before setting out.

He stopped mid-afternoon to rest the mare and dose Jesse again with willow bark tea. She seemed slightly better. She even asked for food and didn't fight him when he popped a few pieces of walleye in her mouth. He relaxed enough to eat himself.

They'd be there by dusk, and, if no one was around, he could get her into the office unseen. Sunday night in Lure, the only thing of interest was television. At the edge of the wood, he unhitched the travois from the mare. There wasn't much traffic on the paved road.

He wasn't sure why he cared so much about not being seen in Lure. Maybe it was because he and Shen had ridden the gossip train for years as the main feature. Or maybe it was because he and his father rarely talked. His father had always been jealous of his relationship with Joe. It wasn't something Hawk could help. He'd loved the old man and his culture from the moment they met. Once he found that other world across the bridge, he couldn't stop himself from going there. Joe understood. His father did not.

They'd never fought about it, but his mother told him once how hurt his father really was. That was one of the reasons Hawk chose med school. He wanted to make his father proud. But the bigger reason was his mom. She was a nurse when she met his dad, and she lived to care for others. Hawk wanted to find a way to care for her. She'd loved and supported him every step of the way, even though some days she couldn't get out of bed. She'd suffered with rheumatoid arthritis for as long as he could remember. It came and went. And once, when she was at her worst, he'd promised to find a way to cure it or at least stop the pain. He was still working on that promise.

Jesse's moan brought him back from his reverie.

"Hey. How are you feeling?" He stroked her warm forehead.

Her eyelashes fluttered as she tried to focus. "Sleepy."

"Yeah, you've been sleeping all day. But that's a good thing." He was untying the straps of the travois and rubbing her stiff muscles where he could.

"Hurts."

He nodded. "Yeah, your wound's infected and you've got a fever. Your body's fighting, but you need to chug some more of this tea." He helped her up on her elbow, and she took a few sips. "You think you can stand if I help you?"

Clutching his arm, she struggled up on her feet.

"You need to use the bushes?"

She shook her head.

"Okay. I'm glad you're awake, because we're going to ride the mare into my father's surgery in Lure. You think you can ride?"

She nodded.

He'd yet to see her so accepting, and it concerned him. "Old Reba here's been missing you today." As if she understood his words, the mare turned her head and nuzzled Jesse's arm.

"Aw, hey girl." Jesse stroked the mare's nose.

Hawk made a stirrup by interlacing his fingers, and she slipped her foot inside so he could boost her up over the mare's back. Then he leapt up behind her. He liked the feel of Jesse's back against his chest. He especially liked it when she relaxed into his arms and let her head fall back against his shoulder. What he didn't like was what he was sensing. She was in real danger.

The mare plodded along the gravel road as they headed into town. His father's practice was in the old historic part of Lure River just off Main Street. The one-hundred-and-fifty-year-old house had been divided up into offices sometime in the mid-1900s, when the practitioners started living away from their place of business to get a moment's peace—though that didn't always stop midnight knocks.

His father, Dr. Leo VanHouten, used the entire main floor, which consisted of a large reception area, three examination rooms, an office, two full bathrooms, a kitchen, and a lounge. He'd often talked about taking on a partner, but he never had. Hawk knew why. He'd been waiting all this time for his son to join him. When Hawk decided to go into the medical program, his father had been ecstatic. Then Shen happened, and everything fell apart. Hawk left, and they hadn't spoken since.

He rode the horse up the side drive and into the small, empty parking lot out back. Slipping off, he tethered the mare to a fencepost and helped Jesse down. She gasped when her feet hit the ground, and he knew the willow bark tea was wearing thin. He needed to get some real painkillers into her.

The doors were locked. There was a small drugstore in town, but his father also kept drugs on the premises. Fortunately, Hawk knew which windows could be jimmied, and that's how he broke in. Then he opened the back door and carried Jesse up the steps and inside. Careful to leave the lights off, he fished the emergency flashlight out of the kitchen drawer, where it had been as long as he could remember, and led her into one of the exam rooms.

"Let's get you up on the table." He slipped off her moccasins but kept her sitting up.

"You sound almost like a real doctor," Jesse said, grinning for the first time.

He hated to ruin it. "Let's get you hydrated and feeling better. Are you allergic to anything?"

She shook her head.

He found the key for the medicine cabinet under his father's desk and rummaged around until he found T3s, amoxicillin, and a tetanus booster, along with sterile solution, lidocaine, a few syringes, and a catheter. He wasn't taking any chances. He portioned out the pills and piled everything on a tray with a package of sterile instruments. Then he filled a big glass with water from the kitchen sink and set everything beside Jesse on the table.

"What's all that?"

"Tylenol for pain. Broad-spectrum antibiotics to fight the infection, and your tetanus booster."

She swallowed and sighed. "That's three things and a half-assed answer. I know I'm not okay. You don't have to sugarcoat it."

He nodded. "Fair enough. I'm concerned about septicemia. Your wound's infected, so I'm going to have to clean and sterilize it."

She sniffed. "All right."

"When I went back to your camp, I found what caused it."

Her eyes widened.

"You connected with a double-bit axe head and—"

"An axe head? In the water?"

"Yes. There was a bunch of junk in that river—barbed wire, a pickaxe, traps, and your axe. I cleared it all out and buried the otter. But that axe head was just above the surface and rusty. It's caused an infection."

Her chin dropped. "So?"

"So, I'm going to open up these spectacular plantain vein sutures and clean your wound properly."

"Open up as in . . . cut it open again?"

"Yes. I'm going to flush it out." Her face paled, and he handed her a metal container. "Vomit in here, please." She narrowed her eyes as if he'd offended her by the suggestion, although he knew it was a possibility.

"It's gonna hurt. But the T3s will help, and I'll use a local anesthetic, so you won't feel the debridement."

"Debride . . ." Her face revealed something between horror and confusion.

"Let's get the tetanus booster in you first." He picked up the syringe. "You bothered by needles?"

"You think I'm some kind of wimp? Just cut the damn thing open. I'll bite down on a wooden spoon."

He laughed. "You watch too many cowboy shows."

As if on cue, the light went on in the kitchen and backlit a tall man wearing a dark Stetson pulled low over his eyes. Hawk pulled his lips tight to suppress a laugh. *Sheriff Flint Flanagan.*

The sheriff's right hand hovered over his holster. "Don't move now, kids. You're under arrest."

FATHERS & SONS

Jesse picked up the pills Jed had put out for her and swallowed them fast. After bouncing around all day on the travois, she'd finally made it to an actual doctor's office with drugs and sterile equipment—and now this cowboy sheriff was threatening them?

"Under arrest for what?" Jed, who was still holding the loaded tetanus booster in his right hand, stood statue stiff.

"Hey, give me the shot." After hearing about the rusty axe, the muscles in Jesse's neck and jaw were aching, and she was starting to think lockjaw.

Ignoring her, Jed stared down the sheriff.

"Well, let's see. Breaking and entering. Theft of narcotics." The sheriff made a rude sucking sound out of the corner of his mouth. "That should get you a deuce plus."

"You don't understand. This is my father's clinic, and—"

"Oh, I understand. I know exactly who *you* are, despite all the hair. I know you haven't got a license to practice medicine in this state. And I also know what you did to your girlfriend out on the reservation."

Jed's face flushed, and Jesse cleared her throat angrily. She wasn't about to stand by and let this arrogant jerk shame the man who'd just saved her life. "Listen, Sheriff, I have a badly infected wound, and if I get tetanus because you prevented me from receiving medical care, I will sue your ass."

The sheriff looked at Jesse as if seeing her for the first time. Then, smirking, he glanced back at Jed and rolled his eyes. "You sure know how to pick 'em, kid."

Jed squeezed his fingers so tightly the fluid flew straight out of the syringe and splashed across the floor within inches of the sheriff's boots. "Don't talk about her." The words barely made it past his clenched teeth.

Calmly, the sheriff pulled his gun from his holster and pointed it at Jed. "Like I said, kid, you're under arrest."

A ripple shot through Jesse's belly. "Why don't we call Jed's father?"

"Already did. Leo's on his way."

"Good. Then we can all just relax, and when he gets here, *he* can decide whether anyone should get arrested." Taking a deep breath, Jesse rubbed the tense muscles in her jaw. "In the meantime, I really *do* need that tetanus shot."

The sound of the front door opening seemed to jar them all back from a dangerous edge.

"I'll get another shot." Turning his back on the sheriff, Jed strode boldly into the room where the medicines were kept.

When the sheriff stared at Jesse, she suddenly realized she was sitting on the examination table in just her panties and sweater. Glancing around, she spied a sheet just out of reach. He squinted. He probably needed glasses and was too vain to wear them.

"How'd you hurt yourself, little lady?"

"Little lady? Seriously?" Jesse shook her head. She'd never heard anyone actually say that, least of all a sheriff who looked like he'd just walked off a movie set.

The awkwardness was interrupted by the arrival of a man who had to be Jed's father. Same high cheekbones, sharp nose, and deep-set smoky eyes, and though he hadn't uttered a word, Jesse felt an immediate sense of relief. The man had a calming presence much like his son's.

"Leo." The sheriff nodded and holstered his gun.

Dr. VanHouten took one look at Jesse, sitting up on his examination table in her panties, with a deerskin bandage on her thigh, and grasped his pointed chin with his fist. "What happened here? Are you in need of medical attention?"

Jesse nodded. "Well, yes, and I was receiving it until the sheriff—"

Just then, Jed walked back into the room carrying the loaded syringe. He stopped when he saw his father standing beside Jesse.

"Jed!"

"Dad."

The sheriff cleared his throat, but before he could launch into his story, Jesse said loudly, "Could I *please* have the tetanus shot? My jaw's aching. I think I might have it already."

Both Jed and his dad cocked their heads in a similar way.

"How long since your injury?" Dr. VanHouten asked.

"Not long enough." One side of Jed's mouth pulled up in a grin. "You don't have tetanus, Jesse. Tension, maybe." He picked up the sheet and draped it over her legs. "But if you roll up your sleeve, I'll give you the shot."

She turned her head, tensed up, and felt the pinch. The truth was she hated needles. But the ache in her jaw lessened right away. She took a deep breath and sighed.

"Jesse's had a hard couple of days. She came looking for me to tell me about Joe and ended up with a four-inch laceration. Rusty axe bit. Half-inch deep. She's lucky it was so close to her glutes. I sewed it up as best I could to stop the bleeding, but it needs debridement. Likely rust debris in the wound." He pointed to the instruments on the tray. "I gave her amoxicillin and two T3s. And I'm sorry we broke in, but it was an emergency, and I didn't know what else to do."

The sheriff smirked. "Maybe called ahead?"

Dr. VanHouten only smiled. "So you're Jesse. I've heard a lot about you." He turned to Jed. "You did the right thing, son. Can I assist?"

Jesse wondered how long it had been since Jed and his father had talked. He seemed like a wonderful man, and naturally he'd heard about her. The doctor was about to become Rainy's father-in-law, which would make Jed Rainy's brother-in-law. Jesse hadn't thought of that and when she did, it made her smile.

Jed glared at the sheriff, who was still standing in the doorway. Though he'd holstered his gun, his hand hovered nearby.

The doctor nodded to the sheriff. "Everything's fine here, Flint. Thanks for letting me know. I won't be pressing charges."

"Your boy hasn't got a license to practice medicine in this state."

"Well, he won't need one since *I'm* here, and I do."

Jed touched Jesse's shoulder, and she reached up and covered his hand with hers. "Let's get you lying down on your side."

"Sure." Jed was right. She'd had a hard couple of days. When he tucked a pillow under her head and covered her with the sheet, she closed her eyes and let herself relax into the crinkly paper on the cool metal table.

The sheriff must have left, because she could hear Jed and his father talking quietly between themselves as they unwrapped the deerskin bandage and examined the wound. Then Jed touched her cheek, and she opened her eyes.

"I know you don't like needles, Jesse, so I'm going to clean around your wound with antiseptic and then spray it with a local anesthetic before I inject it."

She wrinkled her nose. "How do you know I don't like needles?"

He raised his eyebrows. "The lidocaine spray should help with the pain, but you're still going to feel a poke and a burn."

She gritted her teeth. It seemed to take forever. She imagined the needle pushing through her skin. And then the pain was gone. It was the first time in two days she'd felt no pain from the wound, and she felt reborn.

"Looks like you caught this just in time. What kind of suture is that?" Dr. VanHouten sounded impressed.

"The vein of a plantain leaf. It's surprisingly strong and flexible, and plantain helps heal wounds."

"Well, that's surprisingly perfect."

Jesse closed her eyes and pretended not to feel the poking and prodding along the lower edge of her glutes.

"Hand me the saline, please, Dad."

They were quiet for several moments as Jed cleaned the wound. Jesse could feel liquid dribbling down her leg.

"Yeah, I was right. Rust particles."

"Well, it'll heal up now. You're doing a fine job. I just got some new absorbable suture that'll work almost as well as your plantain vein."

"The purple one?"

"Yes."

"Sure. Why not? Jesse looks good in purple."

"I'm still here, you know." She felt like she was eavesdropping.

"Almost done. Just got to finish these fancy stitches."

"Your mother will be so pleased to see you," Dr. VanHouten said.

The silence in the room was suddenly thick. She waited for Jed's response, but none came. Did he have a problem with his mother? He seemed to be fine with his father. They'd been chatting like two ER doctors since the sheriff's departure.

"All done," Jed said at last.

Jesse stared down, expecting to see the deerskin bandage, but there was just a light gauze dressing over the wound.

"It needs to breathe now, and you need to sleep."

"Why don't you two come back to the house? We've got lots of room." Dr. VanHouten raised his eyebrows hopefully, and Jesse thought about a warm shower, a hot cup of tea, and a real bed.

"Oh, that would be—"

"I'd just as soon crash here tonight on the couch, if it's all right with you," Jed said. His face had turned cloudy, and she couldn't read him, nor was she sure she wanted to. "But if you could take Jesse—"

"What?" Why was he suddenly handing her over to his father, a man she'd just met?

"Thanks for your help tonight, Dad. Flanagan likely would have shot me."

"Wait a second." She swung her legs down and sat up. "You can't just—"

Jed turned to her, and his eyes held a low smolder. "You'll heal now. I appreciate you coming to find me, but rest in a real bed with a real doctor in a real house is the best thing for you right now."

"No, damn it! *No!*"

TEA & BISCUITS

Jesse was spitting mad. Hawk had never seen her like this. He hoped the T3s would kick in soon and calm her down.

"You can't just give me away! I'm not your property!" She leapt off the table, landed on her good leg, and stood with her arms crossed dramatically over her chest.

He turned to his dad. "Could you give us a minute?"

Dr. VanHouten took the key from his pocket and offered it. "Come by the house or stay here tonight, whichever works best. Lock up when you leave, and drop it in the usual place. I'll be in early tomorrow. Monday always draws a crowd."

"Thanks." Hawk took the key and shook his father's hand.

"I can't believe you're trying to pawn me off on your father," Jesse said, as the front door closed. "Do you really want to get rid of me that bad?"

"Is that what you think?"

"I said it, didn't I?" She glared at him.

"Look. You could have died out there in the bush. I don't think you know how close you were. I want you to be somewhere safe and comfortable."

"How can I be comfortable alone in a house full of strangers? Even nice strangers. I want to be with you."

"Jesse . . ." He didn't know what to say to that. He still had flashbacks of that night when Shen died. Could still see her dark eyes closing for the last time. That moment haunted his dreams and kept him awake at night. The last two days he'd focused on Jesse because he'd never make that mistake again. Never let another woman talk him into something he felt in his gut was wrong. And then the sheriff had thrown it in his face, and now all he wanted to do was run.

She limped into the lounge, settled on the couch, and covered her face with her hands.

Hawk went into the kitchen, turned on the kettle, and found some tea and biscuits. *Bloody hell.* If she was crying when he went in there with the tea tray, he didn't know what he'd do.

It wasn't that he didn't have feelings for her. He just didn't want them.

Jesse was staring at the autumn landscape over the fireplace when he came in with the tray. He set it down on the coffee table and sat at the opposite end of the couch by her feet.

"I really could have died?"

"If we hadn't come here, yes. Possibly. Sepsis. The bacteria gets into your bloodstream and causes your immune system to go into overdrive. You had several symptoms. Fever. Weakness. Rapid heartbeat."

"And now?"

"Now you'll heal, *if you listen to your doctor.*" He tapped his chest. "And stop arguing with him."

She pulled her lips into a grin, picked up the mug, and sipped her tea. "You do make a good cup of tea, doc."

"On a scale of one to ten, what's your pain level?"

She closed her eyes and sighed. "I can't feel a thing."

"Good. After your tea and biscuits, you need to get some rest." They were chocolate digestives. His mother's favorite. He took one, dipped it in his tea, and chewed. There were some things you never forgot. Having tea and biscuits by the fire with his mother was one of them.

"Can we please just stay here tonight? Your dad said we could."

"And then what?"

Jesse sighed. "I'd like to call Rainy and let her know we're all right and then go home. Did he say it was Sunday?"

Hawk chewed his bottom lip. He didn't want her staying out there in the cabin alone, and he didn't want to stay in the cabin with her. Truth be told, he could take better care of her in his cave. He had medicines there that surpassed what he'd used tonight. But just the thought of being alone with her in the cabin or the cave set his body humming.

"Jed?"

"Yeah. It's Sunday night."

"Well, I've been gone seven days and . . . Oh wow." Jesse's eyes widened. "I forgot about the body."

"Body? What body?" He sat back against the arm of the couch and stared at her incredulously. Jesse Jardine was full of surprises.

"Yeah, well, I found it just before I left to search for you."

"You found a body. That's a hard thing to forget."

"Not when you get injured and almost die." When her voice rose, he picked up one of her feet and started to knead it with his fingers. He'd had enough drama for one night and wanted her to remain calm. "Oh God. Are you trying to put me to sleep?"

He raised his eyebrows. "First, tell me about this body. Calmly."

"It's in my shed. At least it *was* in my shed. I left the doors open after it rained, and something dug it up. I only saw the hand. Bones sticking up out of the ground." She glanced at her hand and shivered.

"Did you call the police?"

"Of course. I talked to Chief Chase. When I left, there were police camping there to guard it. He was calling in a forensic team and archaeologists."

"That can't be an old burial ground. Not in the shed like that."

"He mentioned a girl who disappeared twenty years ago from the reservation."

"Ruby Little Bear." Hawk swallowed back a hard lump in his

throat. He was only seven when Ruby disappeared, but he remembered the story. People said she ran off to the city, but that was just denial. A fifteen-year-old girl didn't run off to the city without taking any of her things. She'd been babysitting her cousins that day and simply vanished.

"You knew her?"

He bit his lip and sucked in a breath. "No. But Joe used to talk about her. Ruby was a good girl who looked after her brothers and sisters and cousins. She taught beading classes at the Friendship Center, wanted to be a teacher." Hawk shook his head. "'That girl, she never left.' That's what Joe used to say."

Jesse cocked her head. "What do you think happened to her? You don't think anyone on the reservation would hurt her, do you?"

Hawk sat back. "I doubt it. People here look after each other. But all he'd have to do is drive over the bridge." His face fell as he thought about the annual march in Minneapolis for missing and murdered Indigenous women. He used to go with Shen. Thousands of women and girls, like Ruby Little Bear, simply disappeared. It wasn't right, and not enough was done to try and stop it. "Too many girls go missing. Which is why *you* shouldn't be living out there alone in that cabin."

He squeezed her toes so tightly she jerked and pulled her feet back. "Ow."

"Sorry." He tucked her feet back into his lap and started rubbing them again. "But you don't want to go back out there now, do you, knowing what happened to Ruby?"

"Girls go missing from all kinds of places. And they don't *know* it was Ruby; at least they didn't when I left last Monday."

But Hawk knew it was Ruby. He could feel it. And he could hear Joe's voice. "That girl, she never left," he muttered again.

"Okay. Now you're spooking me."

"You're right." He didn't want to think about what might have happened to Ruby Little Bear or the other thousands of missing Indigenous women. Not now. Not tonight. "How about we pull out the couch and make a proper bed? Let's both try and get a good night's sleep. Then, tomorrow morning, we head out to my place for a few days." If she was determined to go back out to the bush, he wanted her somewhere he could protect her. A place she could heal properly.

Jesse's face lit up. "Oh. So we're going to go live in a cave somewhere?" she asked facetiously.

"Yeah." He gave her feet one last squeeze and stood up.

"Seriously? You actually live in a cave?"

"Hey, it's a high-rent district. Natural heating and cooling. Open fireplace. Water features. Amazing view. Very trendy."

Jesse laughed and raised her arms. "Help me up."

When he pulled her up, he crushed her against his chest. He needed to feel her living, breathing body in his arms. When her chin rested in the hollow of his collarbone and her lips brushed his neck, his heart jumped . . . and that wasn't all.

"Do you need to go to the bushes?" he whispered.

"Actually, yes."

"In there." He gestured to the door. "You can shower but try not to get your dressing wet."

"A shower. God, yes!"

"Oh, and there are clean gowns on the shelf right there." He pointed to a pile of folded cotton near the bathroom. "Do you know how to—?"

"I *have* been to the doctor once or twice. And I'll use two so there are no gaps. Not that you haven't seen me naked already."

She winked, and he swallowed hard to suppress his growing desire. "Right. I'll get the sheets and blankets."

He watched her grab the gowns and limp into the bathroom before he pulled out the couch and made up the bed with fresh linens and pillows. He could hear the water running and running.

Then the door opened and she limped back out, her blonde hair hanging long and wet around her face. Crawling in between the sheets, she put her arms around the pillow and hugged it. "Oh, man. This feels incredible."

Hawk could smell toothpaste. Jesse had obviously found his father's stash of toothbrushes and mini toothpaste tubes under the sink. The dentist upstairs kept him supplied so he could give them out, instead of suckers, to the kids. "What's your pain level now?"

Jesse made a throaty sound but didn't answer, and when he glanced at her again, her eyes were closed.

He went into the bathroom and took a long hot shower with soap. His first in three years. Scrubbing down in a cold pond just wasn't the same. He always told himself he didn't miss anything from his old life, but when he stood under that hot steamy stream, it felt like the most incredible luxury in the world. After that he brushed his teeth twice and combed out his hair and beard. He stared in the mirror.

The whites of his eyes were streaked red. Insomnia was taking its toll. And he had several creases around his eyes. His mustache was out of control. He sometimes used the scissors on his Swiss Army knife to trim it, but apart from that, he hadn't bothered with it. And his bedraggled beard was a good three inches below his chin, dark brown at the bottom and platinum streaked just below his lip, the same shades as his hair.

He tied his hair back in a ponytail and rooted around under the sink looking for a razor. Couldn't find one. If he had, he'd have taken the whole thing off. Instead, he retrieved a pair of surgical scissors from the exam room and thinned and trimmed his beard so it sat flatly just around the sweep of his chin. It felt softer that way too. Then he thinned his mustache and trimmed it so his lips were visible. He checked his teeth. They shone from the brushing. He'd run out of toothpaste long ago, and his old brush was shy several bristles. He took several tubes of toothpaste and a few soft brushes and tucked them into a paper bag to take home.

When he came back out into the lounge, Jesse was chatting excitedly on the phone. Pointing at the receiver, she mouthed the word "Rainy."

For a second, her smile lightened his heart, and then a troubling thought arose. Perhaps Jesse was making plans to stay at her friend's house. He didn't want that. He didn't want to let her go. Of course he would if that's what she wanted, but he wouldn't like it.

He went into the kitchen and dug a few sugar cubes out of the bowl. Then he went outside to check the mare. It was warm and muggy. The temperature was rising. Reba was standing calmly under the trees, her tail swishing occasionally to disturb the night bugs. Opening his hand, he rubbed the mare's face as her soft lips caught up the sugar.

"You want to come out to my place, right, Reba? We're gonna keep Jesse close for the next while. Can you help me with that?"

By the time he turned out the lights and crawled into bed beside Jesse, she was snoring rhythmically in that way she did, and it made him smile. For most of the last three years, he hadn't slept alone. He'd always had Sister beside him, dreaming and yipping in her sleep. Then she'd started disappearing, and he realized he didn't like sleeping alone. Now, Jesse's soft breathing lulled him into a state of calm. He ran his fingers through her hair. Then, pulling up close beside her, he touched his forehead to hers.

I'll never let anything happen to you, Jesse Jardine. I swear.

STALKER

Sam Flanagan was hunched behind the wheel of his red Chevy pickup, puffing on his Winston and watching the comings and goings at Doc VanHouten's office on Second Avenue. He'd been coming here to see the doc for various ailments since he was a kid.

When he was six, he could remember not being able to breathe right for weeks. The doc finally gave him a shot in the ass that hurt like hell, but it worked, and not long after he was back at school. He spent months trying to figure out how his ass was connected to his chest and his ability to breathe. He remembered thinking that farts and burps were both made of air, so maybe it came in and out however it could. He chuckled to himself. For a while, he'd tried holding his mouth and nose shut to see if he could breathe through his butt. That experiment lasted about sixty seconds.

When he was sixteen, he'd snuck back to the doc on his own and begged him not to tell his mom that it burned to pee and that his willy was leaking green ooze. He was petrified it was going to rot off. The doc took a quick look and told him not to worry. Gonorrhea was rampant, and if he'd just turn around, he'd give him a shot that would fix him right up. The doc had a way with a shot in the ass. He asked for a list of people Sam had had sex with, which turned out to be short. One. Penny Lester, who'd graduated Lure River High the year before and now worked day shifts at the Superette and the occasional night shift at the Handimart. She was saving for college, so Sam always smiled and gave her a tip when he bought his Winstons and saw her in the trailer behind the Handimart. When Sam was a kid, his father had smoked so many

Winstons that Sam was probably addicted before he put the first one in his mouth at fifteen. The doc told him to leave Penny to packing groceries and nothing else.

Then, a few years ago when his mother was sick, he'd talked to the doc again on account of sharp chest pains. "Cut back on the Winstons and get a chest X-ray," the doc had said. Sam cut back until the pain lessened, but then his mother died. The Winstons helped to ease his broken heart; leastways the smoke filled a hole.

Sam pulled the silver flask from his inside jacket pocket, unscrewed it, and poured an ounce of CC into his coffee. After swishing it around he took a gulp and sniffed. *Not bad for rye whiskey made by Canadians.* He sat back in the seat and puffed out his chest. His father, the sheriff, had responded to his anonymous call in record time, as Sam knew he would. When he'd spotted the VanHouten kid and that gorgeous girl turning up the doc's driveway on a tired-looking Appaloosa, he knew instinctively something was amiss.

Sam knew he'd never be sheriff. His old man knew enough secrets to re-elect himself in perpetuity. But that didn't mean Sam couldn't keep an eye on his town. After all, he was Sam F. Flanagan, Insurance Agent, and he didn't want to be paying out on any claims resulting from a criminal undertaking—the F standing for *frugal*. And then there was the girl with her honey hair, big green eyes, and thick pink lips. The doc was all right, but who knew what the VanHouten kid was capable of?

Jed was a decade younger than Sam. He'd pretty much lived out on the reservation before he went to the Twin Cities to become a doctor. All Sam remembered about the VanHouten kid was that he wasn't right in the head. When he came back to Lure, talk was he'd botched up his girlfriend's delivery and killed her. Then gave up his kid. Sam wondered if the pretty blonde knew what Jed had done to the last woman he'd been with. The least he could do was warn her.

Clearly, Jed and the girl were a couple. They were glued together on that horse, her up front looking doped, and him spooning her upright. Likely he'd got her stoned on pot. With all that hair, he certainly looked like a pothead, and ever since that Pendergrass woman had opened up her cannabis distillery at the old mill west of town, more and more of those pot-smoking granola-munchers had drifted in. "Holy Herb," she named it, claiming it healed all manner of disease and was sent by God. It still wasn't legal to dispense the stuff to anyone without proper medical certification, but judging from the stench around town these days, the skunk-weed was finding its way into the general population. Doc VanHouten kept narcotics in his office, and that's likely what Jed was after.

Sam's old man leapt out of his black Ford F-150, clutching a key to the front door in his hand. One of his mandates was to fight theft by personally keeping a key to any businesses that might be targeted by thieves in the night. He claimed it allowed him to get in without having to make a fuss or bust anything up, and Sam was grateful for it since he didn't have to pay out on as many claims. But the truth was, it just gave his old man access to all the downtown businesses. No one dared cross Sheriff Flint Flanagan, so they usually surrendered their keys without a fight.

Sam could see the flashlight beams through the chinks in the blinds as the VanHouten kid and the girl moved around the office. Then the lights went on to signal his father's entry. Not long after that, the doc appeared. Things must have got smoothed over, because his father left alone fifteen minutes later. The doc stayed a good hour. Must have had quite the reunion with his prodigal son before slipping out the front door.

Sam had a pretty good idea what the kid and the girl were doing in there now, with all the lights out. He opened the door of the cab and took a slow stroll around the house to see if he could see anything through the blinds. He'd wondered what a pretty girl like her was doing living out in the trapper's cabin by the lake. Now he figured it had something to do with Jed VanHouten. He pulled the silver flask out of his jacket pocket and took another long haul. Seeing nothing in the darkened rooms, he crawled back in his truck and shut the door. He was about to head out when his cell phone rang and made him jump.

Ira. It was nearly 10 p.m. It wasn't enough that Ira had been to mass that morning, Mrs. Griswold had dragged him off to some potluck supper that night as well.

"You stuffed with cabbage rolls?"

"Yeah, Sammy, and I found out something too."

"Oh, yeah? What's that?" Sam hoped one day Ira would find out that the church was an institution bent on taking your money and controlling your mind through fear of death and what came after.

"Remember when we were out on the reservation last week?"

"Yep." Sam tapped out another Winston and lit it.

"Well, those fellas in the tents . . . They dug a *body* out of there."

Sam imagined Ira's eyes widening with the thought. "Oh, yeah? Any idea who?"

"That Chippewa girl who disappeared twenty years ago."

"Is that a fact?"

"Yep. They identified her. Her name's Ruby Little Bear."

In a town the size of Lure, the disappearance of a child became indelibly imprinted in everyone's brain. It was like September 11. You could pretty much remember where you were and what you were doing when you first heard the news. When Ruby Little Bear's disappearance hit the local gossip train, Sam was sleeping off the effects of prom night. He'd taken Christie Carr up into the hills, where they'd split a twenty-sixer of Wild Turkey and celebrated their freedom. He'd come home the next morning wearing her panties and crawled straight into bed. When his mother shook him awake at suppertime, she'd given him the news.

"Do they know what happened to her?" Sam asked.

"Just a minute, Ma." Ira covered the phone and Sam heard him talking in muffled tones to his mother. "I have to go. But ain't that something though, eh?"

Sam shook his head and made a tsking sound out the side of his mouth. His father would be all over it. He'd been Sheriff at the time of Ruby Little Bear's disappearance and had spent considerable time harassing the local boys, including him and Ira, for information. No one seemed to know a thing.

Staring over at the darkened house, Sam chewed his lip and asked, "Who found her? Was it that girl we saw in town?"

"Don't know." Ira paused, and Sam knew he was formulating some point. He could imagine that burly bottom lip curling up as his brain struggled to arrange a thought. Sometimes his thoughts looped back and forth, and you found your own lips moving, trying to help it along as you waited for it to emerge.

"Oh, I know what it was." Ira sniffed loudly into the phone. "Ezra said when they dug her up, she was lying flat on her back and the skeleton of a small animal was in her hand right where her heart would have been. Isn't that something?"

Sam huffed. "Well, I guess if she had to die, holding an animal like that might have given her some comfort."

"Okay, Ma. Listen, Sammy, I gotta go. We working up in the cave tomorrow night?"

"Keep it down, Ira. We don't want your mother knowing our business."

"Yeah, yeah. But are we?"

"I'll meet you after I close the office at five. We can grab a bite at Hank's and head out."

"Be seeing you, Sammy."

"Later."

Sam slumped down further in the seat and lit another Winston. He probably should go home. The two lovebirds were likely steaming up the inside windows by now, which meant the show was over for tonight. He could go back to his flat above the insurance agency, steam up his own windows, and come back with a coffee in the morning. If the horse was still tied up out back, he'd know they hadn't left.

He turned the key and the engine started up, loud and jarring. Then he shut it off again and opened the door of the truck. He'd pretty much drained his whiskey flask, and now he had to drain the pipes. Here was as good a place as any. As he stumbled into the trees, he wondered what the blonde girl's name was.

He liked the name Jenny. It was his mother's name—his mother, who'd died of a broken heart because the man she married turned out to be an epic bastard. He didn't want anything bad like that to happen to this girl. And that meant keeping an eye on her until he could get her alone and warn her about VanHouten.

When the back door of the office opened, he slipped into the shadows and held his breath. *Was it her? No. Damn. It was him.* VanHouten had washed his hair and tied it back. Shirtless and wearing a dirty pair of leather pants, he looked like something out of a B movie. He went over to the horse, talked to it and stroked its nose, then reached into his pocket and gave it something to eat from his hand.

Sam wondered where the girl was. Maybe these two weren't a couple at all. Maybe they were just friends, and Sam still had a chance with her. He'd met lots of girls who just wanted to be friends. Most, in fact. He hoped this one was different. If she wasn't, he'd try to find a way to convince her.

PROM NIGHT 3

June 2000

The girl kissed the orange kitten and put it back in the box, then touched the gray one and patted the mother on the head. "They're awful nice cats. Don't scratch or nothing. I think I know a place."

He pulled the cardboard box across the bench seat to make room. "Get in, then."

By the time they hit the side road, they were talking and laughing. She'd pulled the orange kitten out of the box and named it Marmalade. "Look. It's sucking on my finger."

He laughed. "They *are* awful nice cats."

She tossed her hair back off her neck and the swing of her bright beaded earring nearly made him swing off the road. "I've seen you around. You're a senior at my school."

"Yeah?" He didn't want to admit he'd never noticed her. "I've seen you too," he lied.

"There's a driveway up ahead on the right. Pull in there."

He put the Chevy in park but left the motor running. "Who lives here? Looks abandoned." Nothing but an old log cabin in a tangle of trees.

"That's the beauty of it. We come up here to swim in the summer, so I'll be able to visit Marmalade." She lit up at the thought of it.

He looked around for the pond, then turned the key and the engine stilled. The quiet was suffocating. Made his ears ring. Neither of them moved.

"Who's gonna feed them?" he said at last.

"She'll teach them to hunt. That's what all strays do."

He tugged at his jaw. "Better than drowning, I guess."

"Ah, come on, they'll love it." When she cracked open the door of the old Chevy and got out, he followed her lead. "There's a shed up around the side with a few holes between the boards. Good as a barn."

Picking up the cardboard box, he felt the weight of the warm bodies in his hands. He felt bad about leaving them in a place out in the middle of nowhere. He'd have to come up with a better story than this for his mom. But he didn't want to offend the girl, and she seemed to know everything there was to know about stray cats. Plus, she'd promised to visit. He relaxed a bit. He could visit too.

She opened the doors to the shed, and he put the box down inside. Sure enough, there were a few holes where the late afternoon sun was shining through. They'd be able to get in and out.

She was clutching the orange kitten pretty tight. "I sure would like to keep Marmalade. She's the cutest of them all."

He nodded but didn't want to argue that really Tippy was the cutest. "Well, you know where she is, so if you change your mind you can always come and get her."

"Yeah. I'll talk to my mom and see what she says. It would be like sleeping with a real live stuffy."

They stood awkwardly in the shed for a couple of minutes while she talked to the kitten. Every time she wiggled her finger, it would bat both paws and she'd laugh. The sound made him feel warm inside. Finally, she kissed Marmalade and put her in the box beside the mama cat. "I'll come see you, I promise."

He stopped to shut and bar the shed doors behind her, and when he turned around again, the girl was gone. "Hey!" he yelled, seeing nothing but trees and late-afternoon shadows concealing the old cabin.

"Over here." Her soft voice blew in on the wind.

RIVENDELL

When Jesse awoke, a steaming cup of tea sat on the table along with her pills, a plate of buttered toast, a pot of blackberry jam, and two chunks of old cheese. For a survivalist, Jed set a fine table, and thank God. Jesse was starving—starving and tingling with nervous excitement. Jed was taking her to his cave this morning. That had to mean something. As far as she knew, no one had been inside his cave in the three years he'd been hiding from the world.

When he'd hugged her last night, she'd felt how much he wanted her. And she wanted him. Sure, she felt guilty for wanting him so soon after Alec's death, but *damn*, Alec had never made her feel like Jed did. Then that sheriff had triggered something in him.

She'd seen the guilt and horror and anger on Jed's face when that jackass sheriff shamed him, and she knew it was going to take more than desire to exorcise those demons. He was wavering between running *to* her and running *from* her, which was understandable. There was a big difference between losing someone you loved and feeling like you lost them because of something you did.

Jesse sipped her tea and listened. The house was silent. Too silent. *He wouldn't leave me here, would he?* "Jed?" she called once, and then again. Nothing. Her backpack was sitting beside the couch. She pulled out clean clothes and dressed quickly, relieved to see that her khakis fit over the dressing.

"Jed," she called again as she wandered through the office, searching all the rooms. She relaxed when she saw him outside, wiping down Reba with a dry cloth. His shirt was off, his hair caught up in a ponytail, and his muscles moved as he worked. She stood in the doorway, watching. She wanted to touch him, to run her hands over his bare back and shoulders, to pull him against her. Already the ache to hold him skin to skin was overwhelming. At last, she broke free of her thoughts, opened the back door, and limped down the steps into the yard. Her hip ached, but it was nothing compared to what she'd endured the last couple of days.

"There you are."

He looked up and smiled.

"Wow, it's sweltering."

"Yeah, the heat wave's hit." He stopped rubbing down the mare and nodded to the thermometer attached to a post by the back door. "The mercury's pushing eighty-eight degrees."

She ran her fingers through her long hair, raked it back, and let it fall. "God, it's not even eight o'clock yet."

"How are you feeling this morning?"

"Is that the doctor asking or the friend?" She enjoyed flirting with him.

He huffed. "Both, I guess."

"Well, I'm much better. I woke up starving."

Nodding, he pulled up one corner of his lip. "You do eat cheese, right? You're not a strict vegan?"

"I love cheese. I'm a cheese pig." *And a bad vegetarian. Rabbit and fish. Oh, jeez.* "But I didn't get a chance to eat it yet."

He cocked his head, and she noticed how neat and trimmed his mustache and beard were. It upped his heat quotient considerably. She took a breath. He smelled of soap and toothpaste, but she could also pick up that musky scent that was pure Jed. It made her head spin.

"Well, get it into you. I was letting you sleep, but we should leave before the temperature spikes. It's a long ride, and it won't be easy on Reba." He was all business. "I put the pills in your pack. Did you take the ones I left by your tea?"

"Yes, doctor, and I'll go eat my breakfast right now."

When she came back out, clutching her backpack, he was humming. Was that happiness? She expected he was as happy to be going back to his cave as she was to be invited.

"Thanks for finding my stuff." She'd brushed her blonde hair up into a ponytail like his and was wearing her favorite Mariners ball cap, the one with the turquoise bill.

He looked up. "You from Seattle?"

"Sure am."

"How'd you wind up here?"

"Long story that involves my best friend."

"Rainy."

Jesse nodded. "She was adopted out and ended up living next door to me. I was the only thing she liked about Seattle. But, after college, she came back here to teach and met your brother. So the story has a happy ending."

"You two talked last night. I thought maybe you were planning to go and stay with her."

"No. Rainy's house is full. She has three younger brothers. I'd never impose on them."

Jesse thought she saw one layer of panic vanish from his face. Had he been worried she might leave?

"So you're all ready?" She nodded, and he glanced down at her bare feet. "No boots?"

She padded her pack, grateful that he'd packed her beaded moccasins inside. "Too hot. Besides, we're riding, not walking."

"Can you lock the door and leave the key in the flowerpot by the step? My dad will kill me if I forget to lock up."

She limped there and back again, buzzing from the inside out. He made a stirrup with his fingers so she could swing up on Reba's back.

He swung up on the horse behind her, slipped his hands under her arms, and picked up the reins.

She half turned, needing to see his face up close.

"What's wrong?"

His warm breath and the vibration of his voice tickled her ear and sent shivers down her spine. "Nothing," she said. "Not a damn thing." His strong forearms rested on her hips, and his hands were tanned and flecked with pale-blond hairs, the thumbnails clean and trimmed. With those hands he'd performed a miracle on her thigh and brought her back from death.

"Reba's hoof seems healed," she observed as they headed down the gravel driveway.

"Yep. Sometimes a night's rest is all it takes."

Thoughts haunted her as they rode through town and crossed over the bridge into the reservation.

He saved my life. Is that why I'm falling in love with him? No, it happened before that. Love doesn't happen in a blinding flash like in the movies. It's more gradual. Maybe it started that first day we met, when he shot the buck, laughed at me, and carried it off. Definitely the day he brought me venison and kissed me. And when he fed me fish and made me drink that horrible willow bark tea, it was there too. And when he carried me to the bushes. And built the travois to haul me home. And then he brought me all the way back to Lure River, even though he hadn't come here in three years.

Surely, Jesse thought, *he was feeling it too. You didn't do things like that if you didn't care about someone.*

He wove the horse through forest so dense with undergrowth that a normal man would lose his way. They meandered up rock-strewn hills via switchbacks, past bogs buzzing with frogs and bugs and birdsong. Jesse tried to remember the route but knew she'd never find her way back here again. Or her way back to town. There was nothing but wilderness and him. Closing her eyes, she captured the moment so she'd never forget it.

Hours and miles passed. Once he urged Reba into a shallow rushing stream that glowed like copper, and they rode through the water a good half mile before climbing up the bank on the other side. Sliding back against him, she inhaled his scent and felt safe and protected. By the time they started the ascent to his cave, her hands were on his, and she was nestled so far back into his chest it felt like they were one person. The smell of his sweat was an aphrodisiac.

When, at last, he stopped Reba, it was in a small green hollow beside a sky-scraping waterfall that glittered in the sun. "Wow. Rivendell."

Laughing, he slid down off the horse then held up his hands to catch her. She swung her right leg over the horse's neck and leapt down into his arms.

"You're right. There are nature spirits here just like the elves of Middle Earth."

Planting her hands on his shoulders, she let her head fall back. Her lips reached out to his. *Kiss me. Kiss me now. This is the perfect moment.*

Instead, he laid his palm across her forehead and looked into her eyes. "No fever, even in this heat. That's good." Taking a step back, he broke the spell. Then he slipped the halter off the mare and gave her a gentle slap. "Be free, girl."

"So we're here?"

"My cave's up there." He gestured with his chin. "But this is our first stop. It's a good place to cool off." His wet skin shone in the sunlight, and sweat dripped from his temples. "It's so hot the blackflies are hovering in the shade."

The sun was directly overhead and the temperature scorching. "I just want to go stand under that waterfall."

"Let me have a look at your wound first."

She walked through the lush grass over to the rocky pool, then stood and stripped off her khakis—watching him watching her. "Well, come on. It's not getting any cooler."

Carefully, he pulled back the gauze and examined the wound. "Looks good. You're cleared to swim, but after you'll have to dry it thoroughly in the sun and then—"

"Shush," she breathed, touching her finger to his lips. "Let's just enjoy the moment."

Grasping the bottom of her navy tank, she pulled it up over her head. Then it was panties off, and she was wading in gingerly and screaming, "Oh my God! It's freezing!"

Laughing, he tore off his buckskin pants and jumped in. When he smiled like that, innocent and real, her heart bounced. They splashed and played like kids as they moved toward the waterfall. The closer they came, the louder the roar, until all Jesse could hear was the thunder of water on rock.

"I've never been this close to a waterfall," she shouted. "This place is magical."

Jed caught her in his arms and bent her back, gently gazing into her eyes. Her hands caught his jaw and brought his lips to hers. Closing her eyes to his kiss, she opened to him. Nothing else mattered. She wanted to burrow inside of him. Wanted him inside of her. Pressing her pelvis against his cool wet body, she felt how much he wanted her. Yesterday's shame and apprehension vanished in this magical place.

When at last they broke away, he held her face between his warm palms. "You are a gift, Jesse Jardine."

She didn't know how to respond to that. She just stared into his eyes. *If I'm a gift, open me. Here. Now. I'm yours.*

For a moment, he pressed his forehead to hers, and then he grabbed her hand. "Come on. There's something I want to show you."

ONE-EYED JACK

Ira glanced up and down the road to see if anyone was watching, then stared up at the sign above the blood-red door: Hank's Roadkill Café—*Food so fresh you can hear its heart beat.* Hank was as much of a ham as the meat hanging from hooks behind the counter. A butcher by trade, he didn't shrink away from displaying animal parts. The windows of his coolers were polished and neatly stacked with every kind of meat in every possible cut. His twelve blends of German sausage were legendary. And it was rumored the president had once stopped by for the Elmer Fudd: a rabbit stew so thick Hank served it with two homemade biscuits sticking up from the gravy in the shape of ears. Ira swayed toward the simpler fare—hash browns, double cheeseburgers, and anything with bacon.

He peered through the glass window to see who was in there noshing and shoved open the wooden door with his shoulder. The bell jingled to signal his entry, and Hank looked up from the roast beef he was carving to give Ira the nod. Ira was a good customer, and Hank showed his appreciation by giving him the occasional piece of pie on the house. There was a fresh lemon meringue, as dazzling as the sun, sitting on the counter.

Ira nodded and looked for a place to park himself. The few tables and chairs around the wall were full, but he made a beeline for a single empty seat in the far back corner near the man-can. His ma had packed him full of oatmeal and fruit, but his mouth was watering for something more substantial.

Hank brought him his regular order in record speed. He'd just picked up his fork and started digging into the bright-yellow egg yolk with the thick crusty toast when the door to the man-can opened and a stink worse than the back alley wafted out with the offender. *Sheriff Flanagan.*

Ira glanced down. Not a portion of his plate was visible beneath the extra hash browns and three-inch piles of bratwurst and bacon.

"Christ, Ira. Does your mama know you're in here shoveling in that one-eyed jack like it's your last meal on death row?"

If his mama found out, it very well could be. At least he'd lose his desserts for a month and his mama would give him that disappointed look. Nervously, Ira glanced up at the smug face of the sheriff. He swallowed and wiped the sticky yolk from his lips with the back of his fist. "Hey, sir."

He'd never got around to calling Sammy's dad Sheriff Flanagan, or anything else but sir, which is what Sammy'd always called him to avoid a backhand.

The sheriff stood in the cramped aisle, stinking of Winstons and man-can deodorizer that didn't do much but emphasize the problem, and stared down at Ira. It made further eating impossible.

The sheriff took off his gray Stetson and raked his fingers through his thinning brown hair. "You seen Sam? He ain't answering his phone, and he ain't at the office. What's he up to?"

Ira set down his fork, rubbed his chin, and shrugged. "I don't know."

That was an odd piece of news. Sam rarely missed a day of work. He always said the F in Samuel F. Flanagan stood for *fastidious.* Insurance was the backbone of the community, and you never knew when someone would need to upgrade their policy. His old man knew as much.

"Well, when did you last speak?"

"Last night." Since his jail stint, anyone remotely connected with the law made Ira sweat, even when he'd done nothing wrong.

"Did he say anything about today?"

Ira sniffed and pulled his lips sideways. "We're meeting for a bite later."

"Well, when you see him, you tell him I'm looking for him."

"Yes, sir. I will."

"Oh, and one more thing."

Ira glanced up and sniffed again. The stench of the cigarettes irritated his allergies.

"You ever get rid of any of those wrecks you got out there in your dad's lot?"

"Sometimes people buy 'em. Why?"

"Is my wife's old Chevy still there, or did you send it out for scrap?"

Jenny Flanagan had driven that old rust heap until she died a few years ago, and Ira knew exactly where it was. He'd had his first kiss in the back seat of that '85 Celebrity, and it wasn't on the lips either. Margie MacDougall. Her pale hair had slipped like corn silk through his fingers. He drifted for a moment in the memory.

"Ira?"

"Yeah, it's still there. Why?"

"Just curious. I'll be out to have a look at it later. You know where it's sitting?"

Ira shrugged. "I could find it."

He didn't particularly want to find it; in fact, it was running through his head to hightail it back to the farm and get rid of that Chevy. There was no good reason for the sheriff to want to see it after all these years. Especially coming on the heels of that news about Ruby Little Bear. He thought about her holding that wee skeleton. He'd been thinking about that a lot and was wondering if the sheriff's need to see Mrs. Flanagan's Chevy had something to do with the discovery of Ruby's body. He was about to ask when the sheriff turned and walked away. Shaking off the thought, Ira picked up his fork and dove back into his one-eyed jack.

Then the sheriff stopped and turned with a smirk on his face. Pulling out his cell phone, he snapped a photo of Ira and his plate of contraband, then made a chucking noise. "Just in case."

"Goddamn it," Ira cussed. Then he felt bad for blaspheming on top of breaking his no-macaroni diet and lying to his ma—cause that's what he'd do when she asked him where he'd been today. Flanagan knew he was more afraid of her than anything else. Ira speared a round of bratwurst and shoved it into his mouth. The salty, spicy pork did wonders for his mood.

The bell jangled as the sheriff sauntered out the door. Ira watched him through the glass pane as he stood and cupped his hands around a Winston. Ira hated cigarettes and was glad Hank's had become a smoke-free establishment. Obviously Flanagan didn't think that included the man-can.

Sammy smoked almost as much as his old man. Acted like him too, even though he was always cussing him out. Sammy had even talked about running for sheriff once; then his old man found out and put an end to that. He wouldn't have won the election anyway. Sheriff Flanagan had enough dirt on the citizens of Lure River to stay in office until he decided to retire.

But where the hell *was* Sammy? When he'd taken care of the Chevy, he'd drive out to the cave. *He better not be trying to cheat me out of my share.* The thought sent a burst of acid through Ira's gut, and he belched. He nodded his apology to the ancient Miss Lily Spring, who'd taught him in grade two, and her younger sister, Miss Viola, whom he'd narrowly avoided as his English teacher in high school.

But the thought stayed stuck. It would take a few more rounds of bratwurst and a vat of coffee to wash it down.

RIVER WALK

Sam awoke curled up on the bench seat of his pickup. It was hot as hell, his head was pounding, and his tongue felt like burnt toast. Tasted like it too. It might have been the rye. He closed his mouth when he noticed the damp spot on the wine velour where he'd drooled. *Jesus Christ. Didn't even make it home last night. Haven't done that in years. Passed out thinking about that girl.*

Sitting up, he rubbed his face with sweaty palms. Then he cranked open the door, bent over casually, and threw up. *Christ, it burns.* After wiping his mouth, he lit up a Winston and took a quick look at his cell phone. 6:30 a.m. *Black coffee. Damn. Still too early for Hank's.*

VanHouten and the girl were likely still asleep, but he might as well take a look since he was here anyway. He came around the corner of the house but stopped short and ducked behind a rose bush. They were both out in the backyard, standing near the horse—the girl wearing a black-and-green ball cap with her blonde hair caught up sporty-like in a ponytail, and VanHouten, scrubbed clean with his hair slicked up like one of those goddamn celebrities. The girl's feet were bare, and she was favoring her left leg. Maybe he'd hurt her already, and that was why they'd come to the doc's office. He heard the odd words . . . "Seattle" and "rainy." She limped out of sight then reappeared, and VanHouten boosted her up on the horse. Leaping up behind her like a rodeo star, he threaded his arms through hers possessively and rested his hands on her hips.

Sam scowled. How was he going to warn her about VanHouten when they were cuddled up like that? She was the spitting image of Sam's mother, and every time he looked at her, all he could think about was how the old man used to come up close behind her and she'd get that look of fear on her face. He was too young to save her from the bastard then. Oh, he'd tried, and got many a beating for his efforts, but he'd never quite saved her. Men who hurt women needed to be locked up for good.

He waited until they left—the old Appaloosa clomping down the gravel—then got back in his truck and glanced at his watch. He really needed that coffee, but Hank held firm to his hours and wouldn't open for another twenty minutes. Maybe he'd just follow them for a while at a distance and see what VanHouten was up to. He was likely taking her back to the reservation. Did the girl know the cops were out by her cabin digging up a body? Goosebumps riveted up his arm, and he shivered and spit.

He watched them till they were nearly out of sight, then followed along discreetly in Pearl, his mouth dust dry and tasting like an old turd. He lit up a Winston and then had to pull over for his morning cough. Once he spit up, he was all right. But to ease things a hair, he twisted the cap off his flask and took a couple of gulps. That, at least, changed the taste in his mouth and gave him enough of a buzz to soothe his headache.

He watched them cross the bridge and head toward the reservation trail. Then VanHouten came to a cut in the trees and urged the horse through. It was obviously some kind of unmarked path, perhaps one he used for forays into town.

Sam parked the pickup on the gravel shoulder and climbed out. He walked off, then hurried back to get his cell phone and make sure the truck was locked. It was early for thieves, but you never knew who was still hopped up from the night before. Plus, the moon had been full last night, and crime always increased on a full moon. He ought to know. He did the payouts. A carload of wasted teens could wreak havoc on an abandoned vehicle, and Pearl was as old a friend as Ira.

But the girl drew him like a bee to pollen, and he just couldn't let her out of his sight. He followed on foot as they wound through the woods. It was hot, pushing ninety, and the mosquitoes were thick and biting where he roused them from the long grass.

When they came to the river, VanHouten urged the horse in and kept going straight upstream. It was wide and shallow at this point, the bottom a mass of round flat stones. It hadn't rained for the last two months, so the current was slow moving. Still, there were spots where it surged between the rocks.

Sam followed along the bank, dodging the dense scrub, swatting bugs. Stopping, he bent down in the shallows at a sandy shoal, splashed cool water on his face, and took a long drink. When he looked up again, they'd crossed through the rougher water and over to the other side. *Damn.* It was wider here, and, with the rushing current, there was no way he should try crossing the river on foot. Still. He watched them continue on up another five hundred yards or so. When they were nearly out of sight, VanHouten urged the horse into another cut in the trees. Sam marked it as best he could, gauging it by a couple of closely stacked boulders that towered over the rest.

Just turn around and go home. Forget the girl. She chose VanHouten, and if he hurts her like he hurt the other one, well, that's just natural goddamn consequences. But Sam's mother hadn't deserved what she got for marrying a man who turned out to be a monster. Sam couldn't save his mother, but he was a man now, and he could at least try and save this girl. Plus, if he did, she might be grateful enough to want to get to know him better. And he'd like that. Yes, he would.

Sweat dripped in his eyes and stung. Sitting on the riverbank, he took off his cowboy boots and socks and put his feet in the water. It felt so good he stood on the bank and stripped off his jeans and boxers. He took off his button-down shirt and packed his clothes and cell phone inside it. He rolled everything up and stuffed it inside his boots. Then, hoisting them high in one hand, he stepped off the bank into the sandy shallows.

Keeping his eyes on the far side of the river, he stumbled along, feeling the bite of the stones on his bare feet, scrunching up his face, and letting the odd curse slip out to lessen the pain. Halfway across, he was up to his waist, and the river tugged at his loose parts. The sensation was half-good and half-terrifying, like the river was a woman with her mind set on him—like his was set on the girl. She was such a pretty thing, and she looked so innocent in that pink T-shirt. VanHouten had somehow charmed her with his wild-man routine. But he'd only end up hurting her. *Christ, he didn't even fight to keep his kid.*

Sam crossed without a slip and climbed out the other side near the cut where he'd seen the horse enter. He walked a while naked, in the more open patches where the bugs weren't as bad, and let the sun dry his skin. Then he stopped to put his clothes back on and headed into the bush. It was easy enough to follow the trail left by the horse. VanHouten was heading on a diagonal route up a low hill.

Sam followed, thinking about his mother and how the two of them used to go hiking in the hills when he was young. She could have been an actress. People said she was a dead ringer for Kate Winslet in *Titanic*. She loved the sun and being out in the bush. For a while, he'd forgotten that, but now it came back, and *she* came back as clear as when she was alive. *"You're a good boy, and you were meant to help people,"* she'd say. That's why he took up his granddaddy's insurance business. Helping people who'd lost something precious—whether it was a vehicle or their home or some heirloom stolen by thieves—always made him feel good. If he couldn't return it to them, he could at least offer compensation and a kind ear.

When his stomach growled, Sam realized he was starving. He pulled his phone from his jean's pocket and gasped. *Ten thirty! Christ!* VanHouten and the girl were clear out of sight. He tried to mark the place, thinking he might come back this way and take up the trail again later, when he'd eaten and had proper clothing, maybe a pack and water.

But when he turned around, the river was miles and miles away. He thought he could see a place closer to the water if he cut through a rock-strewn field, but halfway through he realized it was impossible to traverse. He headed back toward the trail but couldn't find it. *Damn!* He wandered, picking his way through the scrub and rocks for what seemed hours. When at last he spied the river, a silver glint in the sun, he was elated, but also near delirious for want of food and water. His head was hollering again, and images of coffeepots kept drifting through his mind.

Then he tripped on a rock and landed on his hands and knees. Standing up, he brushed off his palms. His jeans were ripped, and blood drizzled out where he'd hit the sharp edge of a rock. He finally slid down the hill to the river, half on his feet and half on his ass, and glanced up and down. He was nowhere near where he'd crossed before, but he could see the church steeples from Lure poking up through the trees in the distance. If he could make it across, he'd be able to follow River Road back to his truck. If he hurried, he could make it into work this afternoon.

Stripping off again, he repacked his jeans, boxers, socks, and cell phone in his shirt. He tied the shirt sleeves around his neck like a pack and was half-proud of himself for thinking of that. Now he at least had his arms for balance as the boots were much lighter and he could hold them in one hand. Halfway across, he was doing all right.

But when he slipped into the dip, he went under before he'd even had a chance to close his mouth. He took in a hefty breath of river water and bobbed up, coughing and sputtering. Then, just like that, he was caught in the current and swept downriver. His boots got wrenched from his hand and careened off in the froth. Reaching out, he grasped a rock and hung on until the panic subsided and he could breathe again. *Goddamn VanHouten! The man is a curse!*

At last, he found his footing and ambled back across to the Lure side, clinging to rocks one after the other. He came up under the bridge and had to pick his way back up the side of the river naked, his wet clothes knotted around his neck like a noose. Leaning back, he wound up and chucked his ruined cell phone into the river, where it might catch up to his best pair of boots.

When he got back to his truck, there was something stuck against the windshield under the wiper like a parking ticket. Picking it up, he squinted to read the words.

I KNOW WHAT YOU DID.

A rush of adrenaline sent his body tingling, and he crouched down by the rearview to catch his breath. There was only one man who had access to blank parking tickets and printed in big boxy capital letters like that. His old man. Sheriff Flint Flanagan. But what exactly did the old man think he had on him? *I KNOW WHAT YOU DID.* Sam hadn't done anything recently that would warrant a threat like that, and that's exactly what it was. The old man had either followed him here or run across his truck while driving his rounds. Either way, his father knew Sam wouldn't be able to shake it off. It just wasn't in Sam's nature.

His naked body betrayed him by breaking out in a sweat. He looked around to see if the old man was hiding in the bushes, watching and laughing. He might just be messing with him. He did that sometimes. But this felt more serious than the usual kibitzing, like maybe he knew about the mine and the fact that Sam had forged ownership papers for it. No one had ever checked them, and no one had ever noticed him and Ira in that cave on the reservation.

But even if the old man knew, Sam couldn't let anyone stop him now. He was too damn close.

He climbed into his wet jeans and tossed the dirty underwear in the back. He'd pretty much had his morning shower in the river anyhow. His socks were soaked, but he had a worn pair of sneakers in the cab. Sitting on a rock on the side of the road, he wiped his feet and pulled them on, his mind buzzing.

The office would have to wait. If the old man was on to him, he'd have to pick up the pace before things went awry. A couple of full days with the pick and shovel and he could bag all he needed. The mine was high up on the reservation, northwest of the girl's cabin. If the old man came out there, well, he'd just have to deal with him. After all the beatings he and his mother had endured, he often fantasized about putting a pick through the old man's head.

Feeling a little calmer now he had a plan, Sam hopped up into the cab, shoved his key in the starter, and kicked her up. Once he had the rest of the gold bagged, he'd disappear from this town and go someplace where the old man could never find him or hurt him again.

If only his mom had stayed alive long enough to see this day.

Never mind. He'd take the girl in the pink shirt. Rescue her from VanHouten and this godforsaken town. She might not come willingly, but, in the end, she'd thank him.

CAVE CROCUS

Hawk wasn't sure why he wanted to show Jesse the sacred plant so badly, apart from the fact that he was going to use it to heal her wound. But as he took her hand and pulled her out of the pool, he trembled with apprehension. The jagged rocks that led behind the waterfall were slippery with algae, and he couldn't risk her falling again. She might survive it, but his heart wouldn't. He had to keep her safe. Protect her. Share this miracle with her.

He hoped she'd feel the same sense of awe he'd felt when Joe brought him to this place for the first time twenty years ago. "You must never tell anyone about this plant, Little Hawk. It's a sacred gift from the Creator. If people knew about it, they'd exploit it like they do everything else, and its secret would be gone forever."

Hawk knew Joe was right. The pharmaceutical companies would steal it and clone it. Look what they'd done to the rainforests. So he never told a soul. Not even Shen. By the time they came back, she was pregnant, and he couldn't risk bringing her up here. And though he loved her, he wasn't sure she'd appreciate it like he did. Shen was devoted to Western medicine. She loved the doctor in him but didn't know the real man inside. They'd met at college where it was all work, and there'd been no time for anything else. He hadn't told her about his time with Joe and Effie in the bush, or about how Joe had trained him to be a healer and not just a doctor.

But Jesse got it. She got *him*. There was something about her that he trusted, and he knew intrinsically that Joe would be all right with it . . . with her. Maybe it was her love of nature. Her compulsion to save the deer and otter impressed him, though at first he'd laughed at her. Even the way she worked with the horse told him she'd never put any sentient being at risk, be it plant or animal.

"Are you ready?" he asked, and she nodded eagerly.

He squeezed her hand tightly as they walked through the waterfall. Jesse screamed as the cold water crashed down on her head. He held her tightly, and she clutched his arms to steady herself on the other side.

"Oh my God!" Her hair was plastered down around her face, water dripping from the end of her nose. Her lashes were stuck together below her bangs, but her eyes were wide and dancing with a thrill he understood.

She turned and stared out through the coursing veil of water. Then she reached back through it and watched the shimmering water make trails in the wavering sunlight. He stood behind her with his hands on her shoulders, afraid she'd fall and break a bone. He couldn't handle it if she got hurt again, but he didn't want to stop her either. She was feeling like a kid, and he felt like a kid watching her.

But when she bobbed her head under and screamed, he yanked her back. "Jesse!"

"Man! What a rush! Do it. Do it with me."

His heart beat like a powwow drum. "Okay. Okay." Grasping her outstretched hand, he held his breath and stepped under the falls with her. Her scream cut through the veil of water. Then they both stepped back, and she collapsed into his chest, laughing. Wrapping his arms around her, he held her close. He could feel her trembling. "Are you cold?"

"Kiss me again and warm me up." Leaning down, he brought his mouth to hers and caught her cool lips with his. Then, scooping her up in his arms, he stepped deeper inside the cave behind the falls. He was aware of their naked bodies, the curve of her breast against his chest, the desire he felt for her. If her hand strayed . . . if she touched him, he knew he'd never be able to control himself. His body was ready, but his mind was not.

If they had sex now, it would change everything. Things he didn't want to change. Like his loyalty to Shen. His reclusive life. And he wanted more than sex with Jesse. He wanted the friendship he'd never had with Shen. With Shen, it had all been fast and frantic. The first night they met they had sex, and every night after. And then she was gone. He couldn't go through that again.

"I want to show you something," he said, putting Jesse down.

"What?" Fragments of sunlight danced on the dark cave wall.

"Do you see this plant?"

She ran her fingers over the twisted, gnarly vine that grew up the crack in the rock. "Weird. Is it alive? It looks ancient, like some fossilized remnant of Precambrian times."

Hawk smiled. That's exactly the response he'd hoped for. "Joe showed it to me when he first brought me to this place twenty years ago. It grows nowhere else, and it's like no plant I've ever seen."

Jesse bit her lip as she examined it. "You mean it's some rare vine?"

"More than that. It's a sacred gift from the Creator. A contrary plant."

She glanced up, her eyes narrowing curiously as she searched his face. "Contrary?"

"It grows in the dark from a cleft in the rock, and it spreads down rather than up. It's the earliest plant to bloom in spring. Over one week, its scarlet petals open to bright-orange stamens, and in the last three days, long white glittering stigmas shoot out. It attracts bees for miles. They're drawn to it even though it's here in the dark behind the waterfall. Bees fly through the veil of water, intoxicated by its scent, and dance in its essence. They're willing to risk death for it."

She cocked her head. "You're messing with me, right?"

He shook his head.

"The bloom sounds like a saffron crocus. Have you asked a horticulturist about it?"

"No, and I never will. Joe made me promise never to show it to anyone."

She looked at him strangely. "Are you planning to kill me now that I've seen it? Or don't I count?"

"You count. I wanted you to see it because I'm going to use it to heal your wound."

"How?"

"The dried, ground stigmas will heal a wound almost instantly. And you're right. The flowers look similar to crocuses, but they grow on this twisted vine. And the bulbs and leaves are nothing like a crocus. Plus, saffron spice is a rare delicacy, but this plant is poisonous. Joe warned me never to eat it."

Jesse glanced down at the wound on her thigh. "But you'd put it in an open wound?"

He nodded. "If I'd had some with me two days ago, you'd be totally healed by now. Organically. No need for all the pain you suffered the last couple of days. No scar."

Her eyes sparkled. "So it's a miracle drug."

"Yes. Which is why you can never tell anyone about it. This is the only plant I've ever seen, and if the pharmaceutical companies find it, they'll steal it to clone. Swear to me that you'll never tell anyone."

She looked at him oddly. "Is it so bad to clone it? Think how many people it could help."

"No. This has to remain our secret. This is Anishinaabe land. The Creator gave it to them to use. Sometimes, people come here and take a pinch when they need healing. And I only take a pinch when I need it too. Swear to me you'll never tell anyone."

"God, you're intense." She flashed her green eyes. "Okay. I swear."

"It not only heals wounds. It can shrink a tumor. When Effie had skin cancer, Joe used it to heal her. It's a topical remedy and only works on the surface of the skin. Effie's lesions disappeared within days."

"And you have some?"

"Yes. That's why I wanted to bring you here. Will you let me heal you?"

"How can I say no to a handsome doctor with a miracle drug?" A corner of her lip turned up in a grin. Reaching up, she touched his shoulder, and then she turned back to the waterfall. "But you'll have to catch me first."

A surge of panic hit his gut as he watched her turn and bolt straight for the waterfall. She ran beneath the veil, screaming, then leapt off the cliff into the rock pool below. He stood staring, momentarily stunned. There were sharp upturned rocks in the bottom of the pool—rocks that could cut her or break her bones or give her a concussion, or worse.

"Stop!" he yelled, but his voice was lost in the rush of the falls. How could he keep her safe when she kept running headlong into danger? He'd never met a woman so reckless and impulsive.

Taking a deep breath, Hawk shook his head. And then he jumped.

MRS. FLANAGAN'S CHEVY

Sweat poured down Ira's forehead, drizzled into his eyes, and made them sting. He swiped at it with the back of his hand. It had to be a hundred degrees and still only mid-morning. With a quavering belly stuffed with one-eyed jack, hash browns, and fried pork, he pushed his way past Hank's counter. He'd left the cash on the table as usual.

"Ira."

He glanced across the counter at Hank, who was holding out a Styrofoam container.

"Take this, and screw Flanagan."

Ira took it, noticing a fat slice was missing from the lemon meringue. The saliva gathered in his mouth, and he licked his lips. "Thank you."

The butcher shrugged. "Sometimes your mama asks if you've been in, but I can never remember."

When Ira grinned, his lip trembled. "God bless you, Hank."

The butcher nodded and went back to frying his bacon.

Ira climbed into the cab of his truck and started her up. The pickup was a hodgepodge of vehicle parts stripped from various wrecks and soldered together onto a 1960 Chevy three-quarter-ton frame. Sammy called it Frankenstein, and Ira figured he was right—it was something of a monster. But it hadn't cost him a buck to build, and the cab was grand enough to allow him room to move—not like some of the newer trucks with their bucket seats and four on the floor. He slipped it into gear and eased out onto the road.

Sammy was on his mind, as was Sammy's mother's car. He scratched his bearded chin with his knuckles. If the sheriff was looking for Sammy and that old Chevy, he must have a reason. It was Monday morning, and Ira's mother was out cleaning the church for the priest. She did it every Monday and every Friday and sometimes in between if there was some extra function like a supper or a christening. She wouldn't be home for hours. He wanted to spend some time with Mrs. Flanagan's Chevy before the sheriff arrived to do whatever it was he was bent on doing. That car had been good to him.

The Griswold's old farmhouse sat well back from the side road. His great-grandpa Lynch had bought the farmland and built the house after he emigrated from Belfast in the 1840s. Lynch was a Protestant, but if it hadn't been for him and his dream, they wouldn't have this land, the house, the barn, and the fields of wrecks that sprawled like rusting coffins all the way to the river.

That's where Mrs. Flanagan's Chevy sat. Hidden under a tarp, the '85 Silverado had a good view of the river but was protected by willow scrub. Sam's mother had always been good to Ira, and he liked to think of her sitting at the wheel, calm and happy and gazing out at the rippling water. The sheriff used to beat her and Sam. Everyone knew it, and no one did anything about it. Ira's ma said that even the priest feared Sheriff Flanagan. Now Mrs. Flanagan was free of him, at least, and her car was too.

Ira turned up the driveway, caught the two-wheel track in the field, and drove all the way down to Mrs. Flanagan's Chevy. Sometimes, if he was very still and prayed, God spoke to him. God told him that Sammy would betray him if he got the chance. That's why he was wondering about the gold and where Sammy was right now. He could have gone out to the mine to check, but God told him to come here first.

After pulling the tarp off the Chevy, he opened the back door. Ira always sat in the back because Sammy always sat in the front, just like Sammy always got the prettiest girl. Usually the blonde. Ira couldn't argue, though, because it was Sammy who did all the talking to get them girls at all. If it were up to him, he'd never have been kissed in his life, let alone down there. He glanced down at the bulge in his crotch. When he was known as the Griz and winning all his boxing titles, the girls in Lure River seemed to like kissing him down there. When he came home after doing ten years in prison for manslaughter, a few came by to see if he'd changed, and they always ended up right here in Mrs. Flanagan's Chevy.

Grabbing the Styrofoam square from the bench seat, he clambered into the back of the Chevy and shut the door. Leaning back, he popped open the container. Good old Hank. Scooping the pie up gently with one hand, he took a bite, making sure to get some of the pastry and the tart lemon filling and the meringue, which was as light as heaven. *Goddamn, that's good. Sweet and sour. Smooth and flaky. The meringue like sugar mountains.* Closing his eyes, he ate the rest of it blind, relishing the delicious decadence of it. Knowing he wasn't allowed to eat it made it all the better.

Licking the meringue from his lips, he remembered a big strong girl named Sue who'd said she'd never been able to find a boy who was man enough for her. She'd pushed him down on the back seat that night and climbed right on top of him. He almost suffocated, kissing her giant breasts, and then suddenly he was inside her and she was bouncing and laughing and Faith Hill was singing "This Kiss" on the radio, and she let him finish like nobody else ever did, groaning and howling and—

Goddamn it! His pants were gooey. He hadn't thought of that time with Sue for years. If Flanagan took away this car, what would happen to his memories?

When the car door opened, Ira jumped and covered the stain with the pie container.

Sheriff Flanagan leaned in and smirked. "Found you, Ira . . . and the car."

"What do you want?" His stomach churned, and he swallowed hard to push back the burning acid.

"Just to talk, boy, that's all."

The sheriff slid into the back seat beside him, which jacked up Ira's discomfort level about two hundred percent. That one-eyed jack was looking for any means to escape and was planning to take the pie with it.

"Ruby Little Bear," the sheriff said, and sniffed. "Tell me about her."

"Tell you what?"

"I know you boys used to borrow Jenny's car . . . *this* car . . . when you went out cruising for girls."

Ira bit his lip. "I don't know anything about that."

The sheriff cleared his throat, pulled his gun out of his holster, and stroked it with his thumb.

"I saw this car drive off the reservation that night."

Ira squirmed in his seat. "What night?"

"Prom night, 2000. The night Ruby Little Bear was murdered. I thought it was Sam, so I kept that information to myself. A scandal like that would have ruined my chances of re-election." He ran his finger up the cold metal of the gun. "But now I'm thinking maybe it was you."

Ira's mouth flew open. If Sheriff Flanagan decided to pin Ruby's murder on him, he'd land back in prison for good. "It wasn't me!" he said.

He imagined the girl's dirt-flecked skeleton and the pale bones of a tiny animal where her heart would have been. Then another image appeared in his mind: a cardboard box full of mewling kittens in Sammy's attic. Ira's mother had said he could have one, and then they were gone. He belched a big one, and the car filled with the stink of undigested pork.

Sheriff Flanagan coughed and rolled down the car window.

"So, which one of you was driving? Was it you or Sam, or were you both there?"

Ira felt cold and couldn't get a breath, just like when his asthma attacked.

The sheriff pulled out one of his Winstons and lit up.

Ira's hand flew over his mouth and nose, where a trickle of air was still getting through.

"I just want to know the truth about what happened that night."

Reaching over, Ira squeezed the handle of the back door and shoved it open. He scooted across the seat and climbed out into the fresh air.

The sheriff did likewise and stood on the other side staring across the dusty roof. "The thing is, Ira, if Ruby Little Bear was in this car, even for a few minutes, it's likely she left an imprint—a hair or a few skin cells. You can bet her DNA will be here somewhere. That's what we call evidence. And that, coupled with my witness statement, will be enough to put whoever was with her that night in prison."

"It wasn't me. You got it wrong."

"Maybe. But maybe not." The sheriff threw down his cigarette and made a production out of grinding the butt into the ground. "If it was an *accident*—if she said no when you were bent on yes— that might change things. Especially if you told the truth now." He paused, waiting to see if Ira would suddenly blurt out a confession. Then he shrugged. "I think maybe the two of you were there that night and Ruby Little Bear got scared. Maybe she thought you were going to gang up on her. And maybe you were."

"No. That's not . . . I-I wasn't there."

"Even second-degree murder could get you up to forty years, and with your manslaughter record, you know the judge will give you the max. You wanna go back to prison?"

Ira's hand flew to his heart. It was thumping right out of his chest.

The sheriff walked around the back of the Chevy and stopped within an arm's length. "Look, I know what girls are like. They all want it. And a big strapping boy like you was back then, with all them boxing titles, they was all over you. I remember. There's probably little Griswolds all over town."

Ira scratched his chin and glanced down at the wet spot on his canvas pants. It was starting to itch.

"I wouldn't blame you for getting mad if the girl teased you and then changed her tune."

"It wasn't me. Please, just stop talking." His head was starting to pound. The sheriff would never give up. He needed someone to blame so he could look good, like he solved a twenty-year-old murder.

"Killing a young girl is a whole lot worse than killing a drunk at Billy's Bar. What will your mama think? She'll likely have to give up her job at the church, and then what'll she do for money? Your mama will be shamed, branded the mother of a murderer. Once people find out—"

Ira's fists came up with surprising ferocity and caught the sheriff, one, two, right square in the mouth. The hand that was holding the gun started to rise, but the next punch sent it sideways. Then Ira was on him and pounding and pounding, his knuckles slipping in the blood. But still he kept on pummeling the sheriff's face. "Don't talk about my ma. Just stop talking!"

And then he did.

Ira fell back on his butt beside the sheriff's body and stared down at the bloody mess that was his face. He'd seen Sammy's face look like that plenty of times after the sheriff had put the fists to him, but still he knew it wasn't right.

He touched his palms together at his mouth and whispered,

"Dear God, what do I do now? I didn't mean to hurt him, and I didn't hurt that girl. Help me. Please."

The answering voice swept through his head like the announcer at a hockey game underscored by organ chords. *The car. The DNA. The sheriff. They all have to go.*

Now that they'd found Ruby Little Bear's body, everyone would start asking questions. The sheriff was a horrible man, but he wasn't wrong. Had he told his deputy he was coming here? Likely not. This was personal.

In the quiet that enveloped Ira, he suddenly heard the river rippling over the rocks below. Just beside the willow scrub was a pathway that led to a swimming hole. He and Sammy had tied a rope and hung a tire from a huge elm tree there so they could swing out over the river and cannonball into the deep water.

Standing up, Ira took a breath and wiped his bloody knuckles on his pants. He was breathing easier than he had in a long while. Picking up the sheriff's body, he shoved it into the back seat and closed the door. Then he put the Chevy in neutral and started pushing.

STRAWBERRY MOON

Perhaps it was the shock of the cold water or the rushing hormones of newfound love or the realization that Jed had just shared a precious secret with her, but as Jesse jumped from the rock ledge, she forgot entirely about her wounded thigh. In midair, she pulled her knees tightly into her chest and then cracked the water like it was plate glass. Her feet plunged until their soles hit rock, and the force propelled her upward. Bursting through, she expelled a rush of elated laughter.

A second later, Jed popped up beside her with wide frightened eyes and a gaping mouth. It was only through his terror that she remembered her injured thigh. Without a word, he hustled her to the side of the cold pool, hoisted himself up, and pulled her up beside him.

When she glanced at the blood streaming down her leg, the pain hit with its initial force, and she fought the dizziness that threatened to take her out.

"I'm sorry," she said, bursting into tears.

He tied the gauze tightly around the gaping wound, then caught her head in the crook of his arm and pulled her against his chest. He held her as she cried, tears falling like the waterfall that echoed in her brain.

"It's all right. We have the plant."

Scooping her up in his arms, he carried her uphill in the blazing sun, past scrub and rock. Her lips were buried in his neck. Her eyes watched the world over his shoulder. At the dark mouth of the cave he paused, and she turned her head. Then he carried her over the threshold.

He laid her down on a bed of buttery doeskin and covered her. Even in the late afternoon heat and humidity, she shivered.

"How bad?" She was afraid to look.

"The sutures are frayed and the wound gaping. But it will heal and give you a chance to see how miraculous this plant really is." Taking another piece of doeskin, he pushed against the wound. "Hold this firm."

"I'm sorry. I . . . That pool . . . You . . ."

Leaning over, he kissed her gently on the forehead. "I'm going to get the medicine. Remember, firm pressure to stop the bleeding."

She lay there, holding the bloody doeskin and thinking how reckless she'd been. He hadn't chastised her, but after everything he went through to save her life, she'd all but destroyed it in one impulsive moment. How could he be so patient and understanding?

When Jed returned, he'd tied a skin around his waist and looked as primal as he had that first day in the woods when he killed the deer. Despite the pain of her wound, her body responded, and she ached for him. He carried a red clay dish, and, when he took the cover off, she saw that it contained a thin layer of dust, like a scattering of poppy seeds.

"That's it? Is that all you have?"

"It's all I need. Once I put the seeds in the wound, I'll pull it tight and bind it so it seals. You won't need stitches this time, and the skin will heal completely without even leaving a scar. I promise. You won't believe it."

Part of her didn't believe it, though she wanted to. "You shouldn't have to use it on me. A plant like this should go to someone who didn't foolishly injure herself."

"Rest," he said, in his authoritative doctor tone.

Lying back, Jesse closed her eyes and felt the comforting heat of his hands as he worked over her wound. Then she felt him rise and step away, and a cool vapor rushed between them.

"Where are you going?" She didn't want to be away from him, not even for a moment.

"Just rest. You're my guest. I'm going to cook for you."

"But—"

"You may not *feel* tired, but trust me, you're in shock. Sleep and let your body heal."

He didn't say *again*, but she heard it.

The afternoon sun streamed through the cave mouth, but everywhere else, edges fell to shadow. Behind her, in the blackest corner, she heard water trickling. Was that the water feature he'd joked about? She wanted to explore but dared not move. After a while, her eyes grew heavy and she slept.

Awaking abruptly from a fragmented dream, she saw a flash of white pass through the maw of the cave. A wave of adrenaline slammed up her legs to her groin, and her damp skin burst out in goosebumps. "Wolf!" she whispered. "Jed!"

The white timber wolf sauntered through the sunbeams, staring with deep turquoise eyes. This was *his* wolf, and Jesse was a usurper in its cave. Wolves were territorial, lived in familial packs, and respected a hierarchy. Jesse did not belong.

But the wolf didn't attack. It simply lay down about six feet from her, nose to paws, and watched—an act far more intimidating.

"Jed!" she said again, in a deep, throaty, whisper.

He walked in with her backpack slung over his shoulder. In his hands, he carried a basket full of plants.

"Wolf." She gestured with her head.

He turned to the wolf. "So, you finally decided to come home."

"Will she hurt me?"

"If she wanted to hurt you, you'd already be shredded. I've seen her hunt. Just be gentle and honest with her."

"Honest?"

"Sister's more intelligent than either of us, and her instinct is much keener. She can read your thoughts and energy as well as your body language, so be careful what you think." He pulled his lips into a grin and busied himself with the food in his basket. "She already knows you're a vegetarian and not much of a threat to her food supply."

Jesse wanted him to stop working, to come and sit beside her and talk. She wanted to touch him, to know everything about him.

She said his name aloud. "Jedediah VanHouten."

He glanced over. "Joe called me Little Hawk. You can call me Hawk or whatever you like. Anything but Jed."

That seemed overly dramatic, and she couldn't think of a response. He obviously still carried enough baggage for a world cruise.

He brought her a tin cup full of water and two pieces of jerky. Perhaps *he* was a mind-reader too. "You must be hungry. I'll get a fire going and make a stew."

"More bunny broth?"

"Venison with wild onions, lamb's quarters, and mushrooms. I eat from the land."

"Hunter-gatherer," she said.

He scoffed.

Jesse bit into the jerky. It wasn't sweet and salty like some she'd tried as a kid. She wondered what it would be like to never eat salt or sugar again. Never go out to a restaurant. She decided to change the subject. "Tell me about your wolf."

"For starters, she's not *my* wolf. I call her Sister because we've lived together in this cave for three years. I found her abandoned the first winter. She was just a runt, cowering and whimpering in the corner."

"She's beautiful."

"Yes, and ready to join her own pack. She won't be here much longer."

172

"Won't you be lonely without her?" The unanswered question billowed in the room. Reaching over, she took his hand. "I don't mean to pry. I just want to understand."

"Why I live alone in a cave in the middle of the wilderness? It's simple. I love it here. Joe and I came here every summer for years when I was a kid. It's full of good memories. And I have everything I could possibly need."

Jesse wanted to be one of his good memories. Something he needed. She wanted his plant to work its magic. She wanted him to be happy and love her.

"I brought your backpack. You still have clothes in there. Do you want to get dressed?"

"No, I want you to kiss me again."

His blue eyes flashed as a corner of his lip curled. Lying down on his side, he caught her chin and cheek in his palm. "You're bold, woman. I like that *most* of the time." When his mouth found hers, she shared his breath and opened to him.

His lips were soft and warm, then hard and demanding, then hot and pliant and speaking the sultry language of love. Closing her eyes, Jesse sank into the rhythm of his soul, arcing up to touch him when he towered over her then turning to slide over him, squeezing his hard muscles in her hands and kissing every bit of bare skin she could find.

They kissed on and off for hours in the silence of the darkened cave, yet every time her hand strayed to the strained deerskin around his hips, he gently pushed it away. She'd never wanted a man so much, but something held him back, and she didn't have the nerve to ask what it was. She feared the answer.

He caught her hair in his hand, smelled it, and sighed. "So why is a beautiful woman like you out here alone in the woods?" It was the first time he'd asked anything about her past, and he did it so casually she didn't see it coming.

"Oh, my fiancé. Alec. He died." She chewed her lip.

"Ah, Alec." His brow furled. "I'm sorry. I didn't mean to—"

"It's all right. I want to tell you about him."

"Was he sick?"

"No, just audacious." She didn't realize until that moment that the same could be said of her. She wasn't as wild as Alec, but she took risks too. Look what she'd just done, jumping off the edge of the waterfall. "Alec was a stuntman, and he wanted a job in a new movie about Everest. He went to Nepal to get some firsthand experience and pad his résumé."

"He climbed Mount Everest?"

"He tried. There was an avalanche. Someone in the party sent a photograph."

"You couldn't say goodbye." His silvery eyes flared, and the wave of understanding that passed through his face softened every pore. "That's why you came to tell me about Joe."

She squeezed her eyes tight to dispatch the snowy image. "They never recovered his body."

That confession ended in a flurry of kisses that continued until it was time to either slow down or race for home. She hoped for the latter, but Jed pulled away. "Time to make that venison stew."

She laid there and watched him work like a chef in his cave kitchen. He built a fire in a hollow near the mouth and hung a cast-iron pot over the flame. Her mouth watered when the breeze carried the scent her way.

"It smells delicious."

"I'm glad you're not a vegetarian anymore. I don't think I could keep you alive on last year's hazelnuts, wild rice, summer weeds, and mushrooms."

"That sounds wonderful."

By the time they finished eating, night was falling. He presented her with a bark bowl full of wild strawberries. Two chocolate digestive cookies stood by the side of the bowl.

"They're my mother's favorites," he explained.

She thought of the strawberries each having a spirit as strong as the deer, as they ate the juicy fruit together with their fingers. The strawberries were sweeter and sharper than any she'd ever eaten, and the chocolate cookies simply decadent.

"Are you close to your mother?" He didn't seem close to his father. She could feel an invisible wall between them.

He nodded slowly. "I'm searching for a way to heal her with the plant. She's in horrible pain. Rheumatoid arthritis."

"Have you tried a tincture? Maybe a salve or a balm?"

"The tincture evaporated too quickly. I'm going to try making an infused oil. Next time I see her, I'd like to have some for her to try."

Is that why he didn't want to see his mother last night? Could he not stand to see her in pain?

"You could mix the infused oil in beeswax and add essential oils to make it smell lovely," she said, remembering a salve she'd made once for Alec's bruises.

Their minds drifted for a few moments in silence.

"Do you think I can walk now? I need to use the bushes."

He laughed. "Let's have a look." Pulling back the doeskin, he nodded his head. "Beautiful."

"Let me see." The edges of the wound had sealed with a pink line, but the skin looked neither infected nor raw. "Wow." She felt a little in awe of him, though she knew he hadn't invented it. Still. The healing was incredibly fast. She started to get up. "I'm a little desperate."

He laughed again. "Of course. You've been stuck here for hours." He stood, then bent down and helped her to her feet. Leaning into him, her lips grazed his bare chest, and he kissed the top of her head. "You're fortunate there's a full moon tonight."

"Come with me?"

"Put this on." He helped her into a loose deerskin shirt that fell to her knees. "If you go out there naked, the bugs will eat you alive."

After, they lay outside, bundled together beneath a blanket of skins, and stared at the silver-shadowed moon that hung in a sky surrounded by stars. A great gray owl swooped overhead from the silhouette of a tall fir tree. It was the most beautiful moment she'd ever experienced.

Turning to him, she touched his lips with her finger and then kissed him. Deep. Long. Lush. "I want you . . . Hawk. I want to make love to you. Here. Now. I ache for you."

"I feel it too."

He returned her kisses with equal intensity, his hands and mouth exploring as he allowed hers the same freedom. As their breath quickened and fell into sync, she felt his fears diminish. He was opening to her and she to him. Before the night was over, they'd be joined. She could feel it.

Suddenly, he paused and pointed to the sky. "Look, a meteor!"

"This *is* an auspicious night. Our own meteor, and there to the northwest, you can see Mercury and Mars."

"Our own planets." He laughed.

"Yes, and just to the right are Pollux and Castor, the Gemini twins. Can you see them?"

He kissed her again. "What else do you see, Jesse Jardine?"

"Way over there, in the southeast, is Jupiter. It's the brightest star in the sky."

"It's bright, but not nearly as bright as this moon."

"That's because it's the strawberry moon . . . June 17."

"What?" Pulling back, he narrowed his eyes.

"Of course. You don't keep a calendar, do you? I read the almanac as light reading." She laughed. "This year, June 17 is the strawberry moon. That's today."

Sitting up, he moved away from her, lowered his gaze, and raked both hands through his hair.

"We should go."

"What? Why?" What had she done wrong? Everything seemed good. Had she pushed him too far too fast? A tingling sensation passed up the back of her neck and scalp, and then her gut flipped.

"We should go in now," he repeated. He stood, reached down, and pulled her to her feet, but he refused to look her in the eye.

They ate in silence. The rest of that long night, he lay on his side, facing away from her, hiding his face, caved in on himself. She lay awake for hours, stiff and embarrassed. She'd thrown herself at him and been rejected. He didn't want her. How could she ever face him again?

Lying there, she felt like a thin sheet of ice, frozen and brittle. If she moved, she'd shatter into a million tiny shards and melt into the earth.

He was awake too. She could hear his short breaths. After several intolerable hours, his breathing lengthened into soft snores, and she realized he'd finally fallen asleep.

Creeping from the skins, she took off his deerskin shirt and grabbed her backpack as she slipped outside, naked, into the night. By the light of the strawberry moon, she pulled on her turquoise sweater, panties, and khaki pants. The wound was almost healed. If she was careful, she'd be all right. Sitting on a rock, she pulled on a pair of wool socks and her moccasins.

She was going home. She'd rather take her chances in the wilderness than stay with a man who didn't want her. Her broken heart eclipsed her fear as she headed down the path, one foot following the other.

PROM NIGHT 4

June 2000

By the time he found the girl, she was standing in her bra and panties on a huge flat rock beside the lake.

"*Damn.* This is beautiful." He wanted to say *you're beautiful*, but he didn't want to spook her.

Spreading her arms, she leapt off the rock. The splash soaked his clothes. Peeling them off, he jumped in behind her. They played around, splashing each other, laughing and yelling.

Then she hoisted herself up on the rock, gathered her long hair to one side, and squeezed out the water. The side closest to him was pure neck, and that vibrant medicine-wheel earring swaying hypnotically. He sprang up beside her and then realized his wet boxers weren't doing much to hide the fact that he liked her. Nervously, he ran his hands through his short hair to spike it up.

She flashed her dark eyes. "Wanna kiss me?"

"Hell, yeah." He caught the back of her head in his hand and pulled her face to his. She smelled as fresh and clean as the lake. But her lips and tongue were hungry. He'd had enough experience with girls to know when they were ready to take it further. The kitten girl definitely was.

Moving his other hand behind her back, he popped open her bra. She wriggled out of it without taking her lips off his. The wriggle made him pant inside. He wouldn't last if he touched her. Maybe even if he looked. *Shit.* He needed to get her into position. Couldn't lay her down on the rock. Couldn't take her back to his mother's car. Couldn't stop either.

Releasing his grip on the back of her head, he pulled his lips free to gulp in a couple of deep breaths and slow himself down.

Not understanding, she picked up her bra and slung the straps back over her shoulders.

"What are you doing?" His boxers were strained. His voice husky.

"Come on. Let's swim some more."

"But—"

She pushed herself off the rock and landed back in the lake. The water came up to her waist. The bra was back on tight.

"Eagle Rock's about fifty yards out. I'll race you."

Then she turned and dove into the water and was gone.

"Hey!" He strained his eyes. He could see nothing that resembled a rock, or the kitten girl. He held his breath and felt like he was swimming underwater beside her, waiting for her to surface so he could breathe again. He pushed himself up to his knees and then stood. "Hey, where are you?"

HAUNTED

The pan Sam was using to separate the precious gold bits from the silt, sand, and gravel in the underground stream was another one of his great-granddaddy's tools. He'd found it, along with a scrawled note and a faded, illegible map, in a burlap sack buried in a pile of well-used implements in the attic. That was four years ago—the day after his mother died just one month before her fiftieth birthday. Jenny Flanagan had died of heart disease, but Sam knew that was just doctor-talk for a broken heart.

The note in the sack simply said, "I ran out of time. Don't you."

Aw, hell. Sam had sat on the dusty attic floor and cried into that note for over an hour. He'd give anything to bring his mother back for even one more day. Jenny Crisp had been pretty and smart and talented, but she didn't stand a chance after she started dating Flint Flanagan in high school. Sam had seen the prom photo. Flint was the football captain, mostly because he was violent and intimidating. His team won games, or he made them pay. He was feared but not liked, except by Jenny, who was drawn to him by some inexplicable force Sam refused to call love. He figured that a woman went for a forceful man because biology told her he could protect her and their family. Sam spit. *Bullshit.* Jenny never finished school because she got pregnant when she was just sixteen. Then she ended up needing Sam to protect her from Flint.

Millie, who owned the beauty salon, was Jenny's best friend growing up. Millie used to do his mother's hair for free and give her sample colognes and shampoos because she knew Flint wouldn't let her spend money on herself. Jenny loved this one cologne called Vanilla Dreams. It was exotic, she said—vanilla, musk, amber, and just a breath of jasmine. It was Sam's favorite. When she died, Sam went to the drug store and bought two bottles—one that he hid in her coffin and another that was still in his socks-and-boxers drawer. When he was really missing her, he'd take it out and smell it.

He could imagine the girl in the pink T-shirt wearing Vanilla Dreams. She looked an awful lot like his mom did when she used to take him to ball games and movies whenever the old man was working late.

Sam was built small like his mother—only five foot six when he stretched—but as far back as he could remember, he'd been trying to rescue his mother from his father and get them both out of Lure. That he hadn't succeeded was his one big regret. Now that she was gone, there was no reason for him to stay.

Before she was even in the ground, the old man had tasked him with clearing out the attic. He wanted to sell the house—which had been in her family for generations—and move into his cabin out at the lake. He spent most of his time there anyway. All that "junk" her dead family left behind had to go to the dump.

That's when Sam found the traps and started setting them out in the bush, wishing it was the old man with his neck broken instead of some rodent. Trapping otter, beaver, and muskrat in the ponds had become an inexplicable compulsion. He felt bad about it but couldn't seem to give it up.

Sam's great-granddaddy had run out of time. And his mother had run out of time. But Sam sure as hell wouldn't. He was still young—only in his mid-thirties. He was fit and smart and determined to get out of Lure. With the cash from this gold mine, he could do it in style. Though how he'd ever found the mine from the scrawls on that map was still a mystery. If Sam believed in such things, he'd say he was being guided by his great-granddaddy's ghost.

In the beginning, he'd suffered with backaches and exhaustion due to the hard physical work. He was, after all, a fine-fingered businessman more accustomed to detecting insurance fraud than working a fraudulent gold mine. But, after a while, he got the hang of it. He also began to collect a fair number of the bright-yellow nuggets. They were small but mighty, like Sam.

When he realized how much gold might be lurking in this hidden hill stream, he decided to share his secret with Ira. It was no fun digging alone or having a secret you couldn't share, and how rich did a man need to be, anyway? It wasn't the Black Hills, but Sam figured they'd get enough eventually to leave Lure and go somewhere warm. Maybe find those "California Girls" the Beach Boys used to sing about.

The mine was hidden up in the northwest sector of the reservation. Sam liked to think that his great-granddaddy had found the cave before the reservation came into being in the 1850s, but he didn't really know. All he knew was that he'd inherited a gift that day, and he intended to use it to make his escape. The Chippewa didn't seem to know or care about it, so he figured he might as well help himself. There was plenty left if they ever did discover it.

Now that his father was threatening him with exposure, he needed to speed things up. The old man would never actually have him arrested. That would reflect poorly on him, and he cared more about his reputation than he did about his son. But the old man was not averse to harassment, intimidation, and blackmail. The threat on his windshield was how he operated. Threats and fists. That's all he knew.

Sam's stomach was rumbling, and he was feeling light-headed when he finally decided to take a break.

He'd told Ira to meet him at Hank's for a bite around five. When Sam didn't show up, it was hard to say what Ira would do.

Likely fill up on ham and then go home to sleep it off. Without a cell phone, Sam didn't have much choice. He'd have to hunt down some food, maybe find a pay phone and try calling Ira. He didn't fancy driving all the way into town. He couldn't take the chance of running into the old man or being spotted by one of his goons. His father had the goods on pretty much everyone in town, and he used it at his discretion, which wasn't all that discreet. Sam would have to settle for the convenience store on the reservation. Cold meat, string cheese, and chips. At least that's what he was craving. Maybe a can of beans or ravioli, if he could find one with a pop top, and a vat of coffee to get him through the night.

Sam revved up Pearl and headed down the side road with the country station blaring and his tires kicking up dust. At dusk, shadows blurred the edges of the road. He got so far into singing along with the country oldies his mother loved that he didn't realize where he was until he saw a floodlight through the trees. This was the cabin where the girl in the pink T-shirt was staying. Slowing Pearl, he peered down the driveway. Beneath the floodlight, they were taking down the tarps that had been set up around the shed and folding them up.

Sam wondered if they had a positive identification on Ruby Little Bear yet. She'd gone to his high school but was a couple of years younger, so he'd never really noticed her. He sat for a moment with the engine idling, wondering what she'd felt in that moment when she died, and if her spirit still haunted this part of the reservation.

Since people started speculating that it was Ruby in that shallow grave, they'd been telling stories. About seeing her ghost hovering over the lake like a massive misty shadow. About hearing screams like the cry of a young cougar coming from the woods. About near drownings, where the victim had felt something pulling at their legs underwater—fingers squeezing and then, at the last second, letting go. The folks on the reservation used to swim and picnic at this lake, but no more. They were calling it Ruby's Lake now, and were doing smoke ceremonies to pacify her spirit.

When Kenny Rogers suddenly came on the radio singing "Ruby, Don't Take Your Love to Town," Sam damn near pissed himself.

He sat stiff to the end of the first chorus then pushed the button to turn off the radio and jammed his foot down hard on the gas. The tires thrashed the gravel and spun. Then, as the truck lurched forward, his headlights caught a white-and-black shape skittering across the road right in front of him.

Skunk? No. Cat!

Instinctively, he slammed his foot down hard on the brake. One word sprang from his trembling lips as the tires spun and squealed.

"Tippy!"

The left front tire caught the soft shoulder, and the ditch sucked his pickup in and over, all in a flash. He couldn't even catch a breath. The rolling truck slammed him against the door, and then his lights went out.

LOST

By late morning, the heat and humidity were so intense Jesse was forced to take shelter in a wooded valley. Her mouth was dry, her chest tight, her thoughts racing. Spying a small creek almost hidden by dogwood and willow, she squatted and cupped her hands to sip the pure, clear water. The bottom was sandy and pocked with rocks that caused the rushing stream to burble and sing. Her gaze darted to the chickadees that flitted and buzzed through the scrub. In any other circumstance, she'd have found it romantic. But not today. Jesse was lost—so lost she might never get out of here alive.

In another impulsive moment, she'd run from Jed and the safety of the cave. She didn't know what she'd said or done to trigger the change in him. One moment they were kissing under the stars, and the next he'd shut down completely. From hot to cold. He wouldn't talk to her. Wouldn't even look at her. How could she stay there after she'd thrown herself at him and been rejected like that? Embarrassed and humiliated, all she wanted to do was run home and hide. And run she did.

She should have thought to find Reba and ride out rather than try to walk. The problem was, she hadn't been thinking, just running. And *should*s were no good now.

The wound on her thigh was nearly healed, just as Jed had promised. A faint pink line was all that remained of the gaping wound. His sacred plant was indeed a miracle cure. She understood his fears of exploitation, but if he could get it to the *right* people, it could help millions. Ah, but it was not her secret to tell. He'd trusted her with it, and she'd made a promise. Even if she never saw him again, she couldn't break that trust.

Her stomach growled. She was starving but hadn't brought food, not even a few pieces of his venison jerky. Searching through her pack, she discovered two small cans of baked beans that had fallen to the bottom beneath the clothes. She ripped the top off one tin right away and ate the lukewarm beans with her fingers.

After rinsing the tin in the stream, she packed it away in her bag. "Leave no trace." That was one of the seven principles both Alec and Jesse had followed in all their backcountry adventures. *Alec. Oh, God.* She'd always teased him about being a risk-taker, but she was just as impulsive as he was. And look what had happened to him. Jesse shivered. Her mind was racing, the sweat dripping in her eyes.

After scanning the surrounding area again and seeing no one, she stripped off her clothes and stepped into the creek. Ironically, it was the first time in days she'd felt almost *normal*—uninjured at least. She waded in up to her waist, then bent her knees and sank below the surface. The cold water eased some of the frantic mania she felt. She couldn't be that far from Lure River. If she didn't find someone, someone would find her.

After drying herself in the sunlight, she dressed in a clean tank top, panties, and khaki shorts, then put on socks and her moccasins. Seized by a newfound determination, she tried to make a plan. She wanted to go back to her cabin, but that might mean going into town first. In town, she could phone Rainy.

An image of the skeletal hand rose in her mind, and she thought suddenly of the body buried in the shed.

Was it really Ruby Little Bear? Perhaps by now they'd identified her and contacted the family. Then she had another thought. If it *was* Ruby, there was a murderer on the reservation, or at least there had been twenty years ago. Was the killer still around, living among them, no one the wiser? An image of the two creepy men back in

186

Lure River flashed through her mind.

Get a grip, Jesse. You'll never find your way if you don't focus.

She glanced up at the sun. It was directly overhead and didn't give her any sense of direction. Perhaps, if she followed the stream, it would eventually lead to the river they'd traversed on their way in. Before she left, she took a dirty sock from her backpack and tied it securely to a tree branch near the stream. If Jed was tracking her, she wanted him to find her.

The man had been living like a hermit in a cave for almost four years. How could she expect him to suddenly act like a normal guy out on a date? He had stuff, baggage, just like she did. If anything was ever going to happen between them, they'd have to talk it through—once he was ready to talk. In the light of day, taking off seemed childish.

"I'm sorry," she called out. "Jed, help me, please."

There was no way she could find her way back to him, but with his bush skills, he might find his way to her. And she wanted to see him—not just because she was lost, but because she missed him. They'd spent every minute together the last few days, and she felt like a part of her was missing. Running had been a stupid mistake.

By mid-afternoon, she realized she was traveling southeast, away from the sun. The stream had forked and changed direction. Her scalp quivered as the hair lifted on the back of her neck. She was definitely lost. Couldn't find her way into town. Couldn't find her way back to Jed.

A childhood story came to her, and she remembered all the images from a long-ago picture book. When Hansel and Gretel's stepmother tried to lose them in the woods, Hansel left a trail of white stones that they were able to follow home. Jesse smiled. She needed to leave a trail of white stones for Jed to follow.

Should I keep going or stay here and wait? But what if he isn't following me? If I keep going, surely, I'll find a cabin or a trapline or something. It's the reservation. People live here. Rainy lives here. A sense of calm washed over her at that moment, and she could think again.

She kept a pen and notebook in her pack. After searching around, she found the gel pen, though the notebook was gone. She scooped a smooth flat gray rock from the stream and, after it dried in the sun, she wrote on it in capital letters.

LOST. FOLLOW TRAIL ALONG STREAM. JESSE

She propped up the rock so the words were visible, then took handfuls of pebbles from the stream and dropped them in a circle around the rock. If Jed came this way, he couldn't miss it. Then she gathered as many round pebbles as she could and drew an arrow on each one. Taking the empty bean can from her bag, she filled it with the rocks. Who said fairy tales taught you nothing?

She was almost sure they'd ridden northwest the day they left town. If she kept going southeast, she should eventually hit the river that separated the reservation from the town of Lure River. It wouldn't get her back to the cabin, but it would lead to people.

Keeping the creek on her right, she tramped through the bush, crushing down the grasses and leaving the marked pebbles visible every twenty paces or so. But after a couple of hours, her feet were swollen and her back was aching. She was used to hiking, but not all day. She needed a place to rest and camp for the night. Maybe a sheltered space near the creek with enough dry wood to keep a fire going.

For a moment, she panicked and squeezed the front pocket in her pack feeling for her lighter. *Yes! I still have it.* She'd packed it days ago and forgotten about it. When Jed was around, she didn't have to think. He was one of those men who took care of everything. If only he were here to take care of her now. As much as she prided herself on her independence, she was lost, exhausted, and a heartbeat away from desperation.

Another mile or so downstream, she found a flat, sandy bank—

a perfect place to launch a canoe if only she had one. The sun was sinking over the hills before she had collected enough wood to build a small fire encircled by rocks. She used the bushes and then washed as best she could before sitting cross-legged in front of the campfire.

She was just about to eat her second can of beans when a great gray owl glided in, its immense wings two dark shadows against the dusky sky. With a whoosh it settled on a blue spruce branch. Its face resembled a huge black heart etched on a moon-round head. Two luminous golden eyes stared from the center of two black discs. Jesse took a slow breath and stared back. A silky white scarf and black mark on its chin further embellished the enchanted face. Time stopped as she stared into the oracular gaze of the owl. Then, in a rush of wind, it flew skyward, and she was left alone.

What did owls symbolize in stories? Owls were solitary, never seen in pairs. Was she destined to live alone? Shivering, she rubbed her arms and stared at the fire. In some Indigenous cultures, the owl was the messenger of death. Her gaze followed the smoke as it streamed straight up in a plume then seemed to split in two. Closing her eyes, she prayed that Jed would see the smoke.

ANGEL GIRL

Ira trudged back to the farmhouse bathroom and turned on the shower. His hands were stiff, his knuckles cut and bruised. He glanced in the steamy mirror. He was soaking wet with river water, but his clothes and skin were still stained with the sheriff's blood. He'd left his old truck down by the river, so as not to infect her with any of that evidence the sheriff talked about.

You did the right thing, Ira. Sheriff Flanagan liked to hurt people, and you stopped him. Sammy will appreciate what you did. Now, go clean yourself up.

Ira nodded. He could feel the warm breath of the angels around him. God had sent them to help him. He stripped off his bloody clothes, rolled them up, and shoved them into a black plastic garbage bag along with his work boots. Then he stepped into the shower and used plenty of the green-striped soap. The strong scent cut through the wafts of steam as he scrubbed himself clean, opening his eyes to watch the blood circle down the drain.

He didn't regret what happened. The sheriff had laughed at him and said mean things about his ma. The only thing he regretted was having to push Mrs. Flanagan's Chevy into the river. His good memories had vanished in that whirl of river water, and he might never get them back.

When he got out of the shower and brushed back his red hair, he noticed a few thick white hairs. They'd been pushing out of his eyebrows and beard at wild angles the past while, but this was the first time he'd seen them in his hair. He used deodorant and put on his long-sleeved button-down shirt—the white one with the flowers curling down the shoulders and chest that his ma liked—clean blue jeans creased down the middle, and his best leather belt with the silver bull-head buckle. He pulled out his steel hunting knife and checked the sharpness of the blade against his thumb, then slipped it into the leather sheath and attached it to his belt. He wanted the angel girl to feel safe.

The moment he'd seen her in Lure, he knew she was special. Sammy thought she was just a pretty girl who looked like his ma, but Ira knew better. God had sent her for him because he was doing God's work. This time, Sammy wouldn't get to choose the girl. This time God had chosen for Ira.

For the first time in a long time, his breathing was easy, so he didn't take his asthma medicine. He didn't need it. He'd surrendered to God, and God would see him through this with the help of the angel girl.

You're going to leave your ma for a while, but she'll be fine. The angels will watch over her too. Go gather up your stuff. Pack your canvas satchel with everything you need for a bush walk. Then get the garbage bag, go outside, and take care of the Sheriff's truck. All of that needs to disappear.

Sheriff Flanagan's black Ford F-150 was parked right in front of the farmhouse in plain view of the road. That's how he'd snuck up on Ira down by the river. Anyone driving by the last hour or so could have seen it, and everyone knew his truck. With *SHERIFF* and a big gold star emblazoned on the side, it was hard to miss. Well, there was nothing he could do about that now but move it as fast as he could.

Luckily, the sheriff had left his key in the ignition. And the idea slipped into Ira's brain like one of Hank's over-easy eggs. In the far back corner were several wrecked transports that had jackknifed on the highway and been written off. All he had to do was open up the back of one of them, let down the ramp, and drive the truck up inside. No one would think of looking there. If anyone mentioned seeing the pickup out front, he'd just say the sheriff had come by looking for Sammy. Hank could back him up by saying the sheriff had come into the café earlier asking about Sammy.

By the time Ira finished, it was nearly suppertime, and he started to worry that his ma might be home any minute.

God told him to leave his truck there at the farm. It was best if he just walked into the bush. Before he left, he dusted off his square-toed cowboy boots and put them on.

Just put one boot in front of the other, Ira. Keep walking and have faith.

He backtracked down to the river to make sure Mrs. Flanagan's Chevy was still submerged. The surface of the water was as calm as any other summer day. The river rippled as it flowed down from the hills, birds sang in the trees, and a slight breeze cooled the world after the intense heat of the afternoon. He took a few deep breaths and headed upriver.

It was a relief not to have to think for himself. Thinking made him tired. All he had to do was put one boot in front of the other. He glanced down as he walked and listened to the sound of the river. A butterfly flitted across his path, and he stopped short and glanced up. *Tiger swallowtail.* He remembered that from Miss Spring's class. He'd caught one in his cheesecloth net, put it in a jar of mothballs, and then pinned it to a Styrofoam tray. She smiled when she saw it. This one fluttered off into the paper birch trees.

Farther away, he saw the massive oak and elm trees he loved to climb as a kid. This was where he came when his father was angry. He'd built a treehouse and hid here for hours until it was safe to go home again. As he walked by, he saw the broken boards had fallen in a heap on the ground. When he was locked away in that cement prison, he used to dream of these trees.

Prison had been that sheriff's fault too. All Ira had done was hit a drunk who was bothering one of the waitresses, and the next thing he knew, Flanagan had him in cuffs. The waitress had been Sue. Yeah, he hadn't thought about that in years. The guy kept touching Sue, and she kept pushing him away. Finally, Ira just let him have it. Sue thanked him later. She even came to the prison a few times and sat with him. The last time, she told him she was going to college in Minneapolis to become a social worker. She said she'd write. But she never did.

By the time Ira came to the narrow, flat-rock crossing in the river, dusk was settling. The moon was full and the sky filled with stars. He crossed gingerly and walked up the embankment onto the reservation, one boot after the other. The moon cresting the hill called to him, and he followed. At the top, all he could see were tree-covered hills. Paradise.

He walked and walked, and then he smelled the smoke. In the calm distance it rose straight up into the dusky sky and then split into two plumes that looked like the wings of an angel.

His heart pounded as he thundered down the side of the hill.

He was panting by the time he reached the birch copse and saw her sitting beside the fire at the edge of the river.

"Thank you," he said aloud, looking up at the stars.

She'd been staring at the fire but looked up when she heard his voice. Her eyes and mouth both widened, and she scooted backwards, then jumped up.

"Don't be afraid. It's me . . . Ira."

"Ira?" Her eyes narrowed.

"I saw you in Lure. God sent me."

In the distance, the sound of sirens startled them both.

"Look, I appreciate your offer, but I'm fine. I don't need help. My friend will be here any minute. I think that's him now." She pointed up into the pine trees on the hill above the river.

Ira pulled his hunting knife out of the leather sheath. He wasn't prepared to share the angel girl with anyone else. "Sit down."

She bolted then, and he sprang.

Clearing the fire, he caught her in six strides and wrapped his arm around her neck. Her breath came in quick gasps, like his did when the asthma was attacking. She shook and struggled, trying to get away. He squeezed harder, and the knife quivered in his fist. "It's all right. God sent you for me, angel girl."

She made funny sounds and thrashed about, so he squeezed harder. "Stop moving."

When she finally did stop, her body sank against him, and he panicked and dropped the knife. Then he eased her down to the ground and stared at her. Her face glowed beside the flames of the fire. She was, without a doubt, an angel. But she didn't seem to know it.

Kneeling, he leaned over and put his ear to her mouth. Her breath came in quiet little soughs. He opened his backpack and took out the rope God told him to bring. After tying her wrists and ankles, he tethered her to a tree and sat down beside her. He was tired and hungry.

"What should I do now?"

But God had stopped talking.

TRACKER

Hawk awoke at dawn, sensing that something was wrong. Turning, he reached out to touch Jesse. But the space was empty. He took in a quick breath as his chest tightened. Where was she? Gone to the bushes? Perhaps the plant had worked, and she was feeling well enough to wander outside on her own. He walked to the mouth of the cave and looked outside, but she was nowhere in sight. Then he glanced down to the space where he'd set her backpack. It was gone. Jesse was gone.

His gut ached like he'd been punched. *Damn her. Why? Why would she leave?*

He knew she wanted to make love. He did too. But after she told him what day it was, how could he? June 17 was Shen's birthday. Once he knew that, he couldn't even look at Jesse, let alone touch her. It wasn't fair, but it was the truth.

It's my fault. I should have talked to her. I should have explained.

But all he could think about was Shen and the night she died. All through her pregnancy, Shen had been having regular checks. She was healthy and strong, and the baby was healthy too. The delivery would be a natural childbirth. For two almost-doctors it would be simple.

But the one thing they'd neglected to do was check the family history because Shen still refused to speak to her parents. She hadn't told them about him or the baby. So neither he nor Shen knew that heart disease ran in Shen's maternal line. Her grandmother had nearly died in childbirth, which was why Shen's mother was an only child. She'd survived only because she'd given birth in one of the biggest hospitals in Houston. He found that out later. If he'd known, even suspected, that a heart attack was possible, he would never have agreed to deliver the baby himself in Joe's cabin in the woods.

Shen was a seemingly healthy woman, but during that final push, she suffered a heart attack so severe he couldn't revive her, let alone get her to the hospital in time to save her life. She'd felt pressure and discomfort in her chest and stomach near the end, but he'd attributed it to the transition phase. And he'd never forgive himself for that fatal error. Not even a doctor, yet he thought he knew everything. He was so confident in their limited experience and knowledge that he'd set her up to die. He'd messed up and run off, and now he had to atone.

In three months, on the seventeenth of September, it would be four years since her death and his son's birth. Four years of guilt and shame. Four years of knowing he should have fought harder to keep his boy. At the time he'd had no strength to fight, but now the regret tied a knot in his belly and squeezed. It hadn't been his idea to tell the parents she hated about what had happened, but Sheriff Flanagan took it upon himself to notify her next of kin. Then they'd swooped in with their money and lawyers and threats, and left with everything.

If Shen knew he'd left their son to grow up in her childhood home with the parents she'd detested, she'd be livid. She wouldn't be out in the bush, kissing a stranger; she'd be in court, railing against them and finding a way to get their son back.

Maybe it was time.

Time to fight. Time to stop feeling sorry for himself. Time to ask his family for help.

But first he had to find Jesse. He'd brought her here, and he couldn't just leave her alone in the bush. She'd never find her way back to town. The cave was well hidden, which is why no one, save him and Joe, had ever been here.

When he found the Appaloosa mare grazing down in the valley by the creek, he exhaled loudly. Maybe Jesse hadn't left at all. Maybe she was just sitting somewhere in the sun or had gone for a walk. But why take her backpack? He sauntered back to the cave, searching for signs. A few feet down the path, he found a partial imprint in some soft ground. She was clearly walking away from the cave. He followed down the trail to the pool. Perhaps she'd gone back to the waterfall.

Yesterday, for a moment behind that streaming veil, he'd felt a love for her as strong as the water that rushed from the rocks. Jesse was impulsive—an adventurer like the man she'd loved and lost—but she was also strong and resilient, intelligent and brave. That love had grown as he watched her throughout the day.

By nightfall, he wanted to make love to her so badly his teeth ached, but something held him back. And when he realized the date, he was glad he'd waited. How could he make love to another woman on Shen's birthday? He'd only spent two birthdays with Shen, but he couldn't tarnish those memories. If he could have found the words to explain, surely Jesse would have understood. Instead, he'd gone silent and abandoned her to draw her own conclusions.

As he wandered through the rocks, watching for signs of Jesse's trail, he struggled to remember those memories of Shen. They'd been studying for their summer term exams both years. Had they done anything special? Yes, candles stuck in the pizza and sex in the park. Which year was that? He couldn't remember. All he really remembered was needing to pass those exams. He did pass. They both did. And now neither of them were doctors.

And Jesse was gone.

He found the mare's halter and led her down the trail. Jesse mentioned wanting to go home. Would she try and find her way back to the cabin? Yes, she would. She'd come looking for him with no plan and no clue as to where he was. It was a gnarly and dangerous journey he knew only because he'd spent years traversing this landscape. He could run from the cave to the cabin in two hours, but he knew the land and the myriad pitfalls in between.

Turning the Appaloosa, he stared out into the wooded hills and valleys to the northwest that stood between him and Jesse's cabin.

Two hours later, he'd traversed half the distance and seen no sign of her. Another thought tugged at his consciousness. Maybe she'd try to find her way back to Lure because that's where they'd come from. In this heat wave, she wouldn't be able to walk far. She'd need to take shelter before noon.

"Can you find her, Reba? You found me once when Jesse needed me. Now we must find her. I need her." The words surprised him. "Come on, Reba. I need her," he repeated. The thought buoyed his spirits, and the mare perked up her ears.

Turning again, he urged the horse into a slow trot and backtracked.

The Appaloosa walked on another two hours southeast before she veered off the trail and began to bounce in small steps down a steep grassy hill. Hawk leaned back and let her have her head while he watched for signs: a turned rock, a print in the dirt, crushed grasses, a broken plant. He tied his hair up and felt the sun on his neck and back as the temperature soared.

He heard the laughing creek before he saw it. Hidden behind a dense screen of willows and dogwoods, the narrow coppery creek flowed southeast from the high hills. He followed along, grateful to the horse, who pushed her way through the ferns and tall grasses until the rocks became denser and an opening appeared. It led down to the stream.

Dropping the reins, he slid off the horse and let her wander. Both parched from the heat, they found their way to water. Hawk knelt in the mud and slick rocks along the bank, cupped his hands, and drank deep. He washed the sweat from his face and shoulders with sweeping strokes. Reba had drunk and stood calmly staring into the water, no doubt glad for the break and the shade of the tall leafy trees that edged the stream.

He stood and went to the mare. "You think she came this way?" He stroked her nose, and she returned his gesture with a snort.

Picking up the reins, Hawk mounted, and they walked together along the edge of the stream for another mile before he saw it. His heartbeat drummed loudly in his chest. With a whoop and a slap to the horse's neck as he leapt off, he grabbed Jesse's sock from the branch. Scanning the bank, he discovered her prints in the wet earth. He could imagine her stopping here, squatting by the stream, and drinking.

"Thank you," he said, squeezing the sock in his fists and turning his face to the heavens. "She left this for me. We're going to find her soon, Reba. I can feel it."

As he followed the trail, he began to see signs of Jesse: crushed grasses, the odd scuff in the rocks, the shallow indent of a moccasin print. And then, just when he was thinking they should stop and rest for the night, he came across the flat gray rock.

LOST. FOLLOW TRAIL ALONG STREAM. JESSE.

Yes, I'm following you. I'm coming.

"We can't stop yet, old girl. She can't be that far ahead. We need to find her before dark."

Not long after, he found the first stone. She'd drawn an arrow on it.

It was almost dark when he saw the pale plume of smoke rising up into the clear moonlit sky. As if calling him, it seemed to split into a pair of hawk's wings.

Squeezing the mare with his thighs, he urged her on. "I'm coming, Jesse. I'm coming."

He was riding at the top of the rise, maybe fifty yards from the fire, when he heard voices.

Slipping off the mare, he tethered her to a tree branch and made his way through the bush on foot.

His heart drummed when he saw Jesse's ashen face shining in the light of the fire. She was leaning back stiffly against a tree, her wrists and ankles bound with ropes. In front of her stood a huge man. Hawk saw the look of terror in her bulging eyes.

Pursing his lips, Hawk moved closer.

The man turned suddenly and pointed up at the sky. "The smoke. It was a sign. I saw your angel wings in the sky."

Ira Griswold. Holy shit.

Hawk clenched his fists. *Boxing Champion. Violent temper. Killer.*

Ira Griswold was at least a decade older than Hawk but his story, like Hawk's, had become part of the small-town folklore of Lure River. Hawk had just graduated from high school when Ira was released from prison. Some drunken hunter manhandled a waitress in the parking lot at Billy's Bar. When no one intervened, Ira stepped in and beat the man into the ground in full view of the patrons, who were all heading home. The Griz was said to have iron fists.

A verdict of first-degree manslaughter got Griswold fifteen years and a fifteen-thousand-dollar fine that cost his parents their life savings. His father died shortly after from a stroke, and his mother took refuge in the Catholic church. When Ira was released ten years later, he too had found God.

As far as Hawk knew, he hadn't hurt anyone since then, but then again, he hadn't had a reason. This was a man capable of deadly violence who suffered with head injuries. And he had Jesse.

Awakening

The grating squeal of metal on metal brought Sam back to a cloudy sort of consciousness. The noise was deafening and the truck vibrating, and then mercifully, it stopped. Sam's ears rang. Opening his eyes, he stared through a web-cracked windshield into a topsy-turvy world.

What the hell happened? I was driving and then that . . . that thing . . . that ghost cat ran in front of my high beams. Tippy. It had to be Tippy!

He hadn't thought of Tippy in years, not since . . . *Oh, God. Not since that day when—*

"Hey, Sam. Do you know who I am?"

Sam's eyelids fluttered and he focused left, just enough to recognize Gus VanSickler peering sideways through the window. He'd known Gus for years, but not like this. Gus owned the gas station and was the local mechanic. He was a good one too. But today he was wearing a strapped-up helmet and dressed in his firefighting gear.

"It's Gus VanSickler with the Lure River Volunteer Fire Department."

Why's Gus upside down? No, wait. He isn't upside down. I am. Christ! I'm hanging from the goddamn belt! Did I roll the truck?

Sam trembled with the realization. He tried to speak, but his mouth wouldn't work. He blinked several times to hold back the tears.

"Good. That's good. We've worked together on this pickup of yours plenty of times over the years. Now, tell me. Who are you? What's your name?"

Sam blinked again. *Sam. Sam F. Flanagan. F for fucked.* He thought it and then instantly regretted it. His mother hated that word.

"Sore mouth, I know. You hit the steering wheel. You're breathing fine, though. Clear airways, and that's good. Do you remember what happened?"

A mad dash of black and white flashed through Sam's mind, and his eyes widened.

"I'll tell you what, Sam. We're gonna examine you and then get you out of Pearl and off to the hospital in St. Paul. The helicopter is on its way."

Gus's face disappeared, and all Sam could see was the bottom of his brown canvas pants taped with fluorescent green.

He kept his eyes on that neon green until he felt something on his right side. His eyes shifted to take in another fireman, who'd climbed into the cab through the open door and was squirming toward him.

"Hey, Sam. It's Jake. I'm gonna check you for injuries. I'd say hang tight, but I can see you're already there." Grinning, he touched Sam lightly on the shoulder, and Sam wanted to punch him.

Jake Hendricks. Jackass Jake. He hasn't changed since high school.

Sam tried to yell as Jake patted him down, squeezing and checking for injuries in a way that made Sam think he was enjoying himself far too much. When he got to his left leg, Sam howled pitifully, and the sound caught in his throat. *Get me out of here now!* But his mouth wouldn't work. There was pain and bitterness as something metallic drizzled down his throat. *Blood.* With the realization, he choked and coughed. His eyes bulged. He shuddered. He thought he was going to puke but couldn't operate his mouth, and that led to another spasm. He was going to choke on his own blood and vomit and die.

To slow the panic, he focused on the lime-green tape at the

bottom of Gus's pants. He could hear the metal wrenching as Gus worked the spreader, then realized what he was doing. *Gus is prying open the hinges to take the door off. How can he do this to Pearl?*

Closing his eyes, Sam tried to make it all disappear. The pain in his leg, his busted mouth, the destruction of his precious truck. A surge of acid burst into his mouth and he belched it out his nose. *Damn, that burned.* Then his left arm suddenly fell free, and he realized the driver's door was gone. *God. That door was like a piece of me.* How many years had he driven around town with his elbow jutting out that window? Eyes stinging with tears, he reached up and tried to wipe them away with a shaky knuckle.

Gus appeared again, crouching down. "You with me, Sam?"

A few wet blinks.

"Jake's going to cut you out of that seatbelt, and we're gonna ease you down and lay you on the backboard. Just relax and let us do what we do."

Sam felt hands on him, supporting him, easing him down. Then more bodies crowded around, and several hands laid him on his back. When Gus put on the neck brace, he relaxed a tad with the sense of security it brought. And then they strapped him down and he felt a sudden surge of paranoia.

"Flanagan, is it? Sam Flanagan? My name's Chase. I'm the police chief here on the reservation. Do you remember what happened?"

Reservation. Yeah, I was driving. Getting food. Passed that cabin where the girl . . . And then Tippy . . .

Closing his eyes, Sam saw an image of them all as clear as day, sitting beside him in his mother's '85 Chevy Silverado—Tippy and Marmalade and the mama cat and the girl. Twenty years had passed. Twenty years, and he hadn't remembered a goddamn thing. And now? Why was he suddenly remembering now? *I have to tell Chase about that night . . . about the girl.*

Sam stared at the police chief and tried to form words. His

tongue rolled and pushed, but nothing happened. *Damn it! What's wrong with my mouth? Is my jaw busted?*

Images flashed through Sam's brain, and then his eyes stung again. He remembered the girl's beaded earring swinging as they drove, the bright red and yellow, the black and white. *It was a beaded medicine wheel. Yeah, that's what it was.* He liked the way she cradled Marmalade to her breast. And he liked the kiss she gave him just before she jumped in the . . .

"Wa-wa," he stuttered.

"You want water?" Chase shook his head. "I'm sorry, but we can't give you any water in case you need surgery. You understand?"

"L-l-l," Sam repeated, but it came out in small wet breaths. He tried to raise his hand and point to the lake. He could see the girl under the water, her eyes wide open. He was holding his breath, trying to untangle the rope, trying to save her life.

The fingers on Sam's right hand moved as he worked to untangle that old wet rope. He closed his eyes as the tears ran down his cheeks. When he opened them again, Chase had disappeared, and Gus was squatting beside him, dabbing his face with a piece of gauze.

"You're lucky to be alive, Sammy. Old truck like this? No airbags?" Gus wrinkled his brow. "Someone's watching over you, boy."

Sam felt a shiver career up his legs and hit him in the groin. *Was it her? Was she still here, like Tippy, watching him?* He felt like he was an actor inside a movie he couldn't participate in. But he wanted to. He had to. His whole body shook to free itself. He opened his eyes again and searched for the police chief. Chase. Where was Chase?

When Chase appeared again, shoving his phone into his pocket, Sam exhaled. "Medevac in five. We just might beat the golden hour." He turned to Sam. "You're lucky the forensics team was still on site and heard the crash."

Sam's gaze shifted through the stubble of roadside trees, searching for the black-and-white cat. How could Tippy still be alive? That kitten would be twenty years old now. Or had he seen Tippy's ghost? It sure as hell seemed real. Then another thought. Maybe the kittens had survived, and he'd seen Tippy's great-grandson. That thought made his heart swell in a strange, eerie way.

He'd left them there that night, the mama cat and all the kittens, except for that one he . . . *Jesus*. His fingers tingled with the memory of what he'd done to that little warm orange body. But what choice did he have? He couldn't leave the girl all alone in the shed, and she'd liked that kitten so much. Marmalade, she'd called it.

The helicopter props whipped up gravel and dust as the pilot put down on the side road. For a moment, the noise was deafening, and then he heard shouting beside him.

"Your boy's gonna be all right, Sheriff."

Sheriff?

Gus nodded, and Sam's gaze shifted.

Shit! The old man's here. How the hell did he get here so fast? Of course, the old man never missed a call out, even when it was on the reservation where he had no jurisdiction and no business being. But he looked like he'd been in some kind of brawl. Like maybe he'd done three rounds with a UFC contender and lost. His eyes were red and bruised and nearly swollen shut. His lips were cut up and fatter than his head. Sam could see lines of stitches here and there on his tanned skin. He wanted to know who and how and why. He'd never seen his father take a beating before, and the thought sent a rush up his arms.

First the old man had left that cryptic note on his windshield, and then he'd been pummeled.

The sheriff went into his lawman stance, narrowed his eyes, and scowled. "Been lookin' for you, boy," he shouted over the roar of the helicopter propellers.

Sam closed his eyes and sniffed. How was he going to get close enough to talk to Chase with his father hanging around?

"Thanks for the ride, Depp. I'll go with him in the medevac."

Sam opened his eyes wide in protest, and he tried to block with his hands, but the paramedics had jumped out of the chopper.

Gus was talking. "Sam Flanagan. Airways clear. Breathing irregular. In and out of consciousness. Facial contusions. Possible break left leg, maybe rib cage. Possible internal injuries. Sheriff Flanagan here is Sam's father and has asked to ride with you."

"Appreciate the concern, Sheriff, but that's against regulations. I'm sure you know that."

The old man scowled, and Sam was suddenly in love with the paramedic.

She knelt down, and all he could see were her big blue eyes and pale hair. Leaning in, she spoke to him quietly, like it was just the two of them out there on the road. His eyes read her lips. "Hello, Sam. My name is Susan Halstead and I'm an EMT. We're going to do our best to get you safely into the chopper and off to hospital. Can I examine you?"

A whimpering sound came from Sam's throat as he blinked.

"Any place you feel pain?"

Another whimper. There was pain in his leg now that Gus had said it was injured, and his face was throbbing like maybe his nose was broken, or his jaw, or both.

He blinked slowly. *One for yes. Wasn't that the way it was done?*

"Looks like your nose and mouth took the brunt of the impact with the steering wheel. Can you wiggle your toes?"

Sam's toes wiggled at the mention, and he blinked his eyes again affirmatively. He was tired suddenly. Really tired.

"Good. That's good." Taking a pair of surgical scissors, she cut down the side seam of Sam's pants. She said something to the other paramedic then prodded Sam shoulders and chest. When her fingers hit his rib cage, he winced.

"I'm going to give you something for the pain, Sam. You're going to feel it pretty quick. Then we're going to lift you onto the stretcher. Just relax now."

Sam willed his muscles to wilt. His mouth still felt stuffed with wet copper, and each breath sent a sharp pain through his core. The needle was nothing going in, but on its way out, Sam drifted to a far better place than the one he'd started out in. A swirly, painless place. And then he was gone.

PROM NIGHT 5

June 2000

"Eagle Rock's about fifty yards out. I'll race you." The girl turned and dove into the water and was gone.

"Hey!" Sam strained his eyes. He could see nothing that resembled a rock, or the kitten girl. He held his breath and felt like he was swimming underwater beside her, waiting for her to surface so he could breathe again. He pushed himself up to his knees and then stood. "Hey, where are you?"

About twenty yards out in the lake, a burst of bubbles broke the surface. "What the hell?" Diving in, he felt the cold rush of water along the sandy bottom. He opened his eyes and swam as far as he could. There was a mess of debris in the lake. Rocks and branches, old fishing rods, even a couple of traps.

When Sam found her, she was entwined in several feet of rope and tethered to the bottom. Her mouth and eyes were open wide. The rope was attached to the bow of a sunken rowboat. Somehow she'd got the rope caught around her leg. It looked like she'd tried to untangle it but ended up making it worse.

He shot up to the surface and gulped air. Looked back to shore. Looked for Eagle's Rock. Saw something rising from the surface another thirty yards out.

Diving down several times, he went at the rope methodically, untwining what he could and finally finding where it had snagged and knotted and cinched tight just above her knee. With both hands, he pulled it down, and slid it off the end of her foot. She looked like a mermaid, suspended there in her bra and panties, her long hair and earrings swaying with the water. He caught her neck in the crook of his elbow, pulled her in tight, and swam one-armed to the surface. He popped her head up, hoping she'd open her mouth and gasp.

"Come on. Breathe."

He blew air into her mouth like you did for CPR, but still nothing happened. Hooking his arm around her head, he towed her back to the flat rocks. He picked her up in his arms and laid her out on the rock. Then, kneeling beside her, he tried pushing his palms against her chest and counting to thirty like he'd been taught in P. E. class. He did it till his arms ached. In the movies, the drowned person always coughed up water and lived.

But not the kitten girl. He felt the artery in her neck. Nothing. He leaned in, hoping to feel her breath against his ear. Nothing.

"Damn, girl." Sam crushed his face in his fists to stop the tears. "What the hell am I supposed to do now?"

REDEMPTION

Jesse awoke, her head aching. She couldn't think. Then she remembered the big red-haired man. He'd choked her out. She kept her eyes closed. If he was here, she didn't want him to know she was awake. She tried to move her body and realized her hands were bound together in her lap. Instinctively, she twisted her wrists to see how tightly they were tied. Opening her eyes just a flutter, she gazed down to discover that both her wrists and ankles were bound with some sort of scratchy jute rope. She was seated on the ground and tethered to a tree with more rope. He'd wound it around her waist several times.

The giant was sitting on the ground beside the fire, looking awkward and uncomfortable, like his knees couldn't bend properly in those tight jeans. His fancy white shirt and big silver cowboy buckle glowed luminescent in the moonlight. He hadn't noticed she was awake, and perhaps she could use this to her advantage—at least delay whatever was coming until she had a chance to think.

He'd said his name, Ira, and something about God and angels. Now he was shaking his head and babbling incoherently about the sheriff and Sammy and Mrs. Flanagan's Chevy and Ruby Little Bear and kittens. "It wasn't me. Sammy was driving. I didn't kill her. God knows." He kept repeating it like an incantation.

This was the red-haired man she'd seen in Lure River. Was Sammy the other man, the creepy one who'd talked to her? She still had his card in the pocket of her jeans, though she hadn't done more than glance at it. But she remembered the name Flanagan. The cowboy sheriff. His name was Flanagan too. An image of the skeletal hand in the shed flashed through her mind, and she suppressed a scream as shivers ran up her arms. These two. She knew there was something off about them. Had they killed the girl and buried her in the shed? And what did the sheriff have to do with it?

Ira was stuck in a loop now, repeating those last two words over and over: "God knows. God knows."

If he was a religious extremist, there was a chance she could talk him out of whatever he was planning. She'd gone to Sunday School when her mother was alive and could recall a few Bible verses, though none were coming to mind now.

Closing her eyes tightly, she silently called out to Jed.

Her stomach panged, and she curled her shoulders forward over her chest to help ease the acid churning in her gut.

When her captor threw another log on the fire, the clatter startled her, and she flinched and opened her eyes. He noticed, and she looked away, feeling the sweat break out on her face.

"Don't be afraid. God sent me." He pointed to the smoke with one of his huge hands. "I saw your angel wings in the sky."

Jesse's stomach rolled, and she swallowed back the sour taste in her mouth. When he stood and took a step forward, she shook her head wildly from side to side. "Love is patient. Love is kind." The long forgotten verse came out like a prayer, and she continued to repeat it.

* * *

Hawk had two things tonight that he didn't have the night he'd fought the bear: space, and the element of surprise. Every muscle in his body was fueled by fury. Poised at the top of the hill and hidden by trees, he stared down. Nothing stood between him and his target. He took a deep breath, and ran, leapt, and launched himself on Griswold.

The force of the attack unbalanced the red-haired giant, and he staggered sideways into the stream with Hawk on his back. Hawk squeezed and squeezed, trying to choke him out. He knew how to do it; he just couldn't get beyond that bull neck to the artery below. In the background, he could hear Jesse's voice, though he couldn't comprehend what she was saying.

Then Griswold's fist came up and caught Hawk's right temple. For a moment, the light flickered, and he thought he was going down. Mercifully, he recovered, but the fist came up again and again, hammering him hard. Hawk let go, landed on his feet, and wavered sideways several steps into the stream. Griswold splashed in after him and, swaying above Hawk, narrowed his eyes and shook that massive head.

Hawk took the moment to roll sideways, push out of the water, and check his balance. Pulling his knife from the sheath, he swirled it through the firelight to make sure the big man saw it. "I don't want to hurt you. Just let her go."

Griswold's rage eclipsed his confusion. Lips pulled back, he bared his teeth, then bellowed and charged. Lowering his head, he hammered it into Hawk's gut.

Hawk reeled backward. He tried to take a breath and couldn't. *Diaphragm spasm.* Backing up, he dropped the knife in Jesse's lap. He knew the spasm would subside, but if the madman took him down, she needed a fighting chance.

When Griswold came at him again, lowering his head and raising his fists to strike, Hawk deked into the stream and scooped up a rock in his fist. Griswold's right hook caught him in the jaw but, as the pain spiraled, he bashed the rock against the side of the big man's temple. The giant wobbled and shook his head.

At last, Hawk's diaphragm relaxed, and he sucked in a breath. "Christ, man! We don't have to do this. Just let her go!"

Griswold's eyes narrowed. "She's mine."

As the man lurched toward him, Hawk pulled one of the

flaming logs from the fire. With blistering fingers, he waved it in the air like he might to scare off an attacking animal. When that had no effect, Hawk knew there was only one thing left. He waited until those massive fists came up into boxer stance, then lunged sideways, turned, and cracked Griswold over the head with the flaming log.

The scent of burning hair was nauseating. The man's eyes rolled up in his head, and he wavered and fell into the fire. Grasping his arm, Hawk yanked him out. He'd seen too many burn victims to leave any man to suffer that fate. Then his knees gave way and he fell on his ass.

"Jed!"

Turning, he saw Jesse standing by the tree, clutching his knife in her fist.

"Look out!" she yelled and ran at them just as Griswold grabbed Hawk's calf and yanked hard.

Jesse rushed in and stabbed Griswold hard in the fleshy part of his gut.

Griswold bellowed, looked down at his bloody white shirt, and touched the blood.

"Didn't expect that from your angel, did you?" Jesse leapt back. Eyes wide. Delirious.

Both men were on the ground, and Hawk hoped that knife wound would be enough to end it. But Griswold's eyes bulged in rage, and he lunged for Jesse.

Reaching out, Hawk grasped the burning log and cracked the man over the head again, once, twice, three times. At last, the giant gave way and collapsed.

"Jesus Christ!" Hawk placed two fingers against Griswold's carotid artery and felt his pulse beat. "Stay down, man. Just stay down."

For a moment, Jesse and Hawk stood staring, just catching their breath. Then he gestured to the rope.

"Hand me that."

Jesse stood, paralyzed and pale-faced, still clutching the bloody knife she'd used to stab Griswold.

"Here, give me that," Hawk said. Taking the knife from her trembling hand, he wiped the blood off on his pants and shoved it back in the sheath. "You're all right now." Catching her in his arms, he held her tightly. "I've got you." He could hear her stifled sobs and feel hot tears against his shoulder.

"I stabbed him." Her voice wavered in disbelief.

"You sure did." He tasted the salt on her cheek. "Don't worry, he'll survive. But before he gains consciousness again, we better truss him up." Hawk uncoiled the rope from around the tree.

Jesse reached out. "Here. Let me."

Seeing the look of determination on her face, he handed her the rope. "Hands behind his back, good and tight."

"I think they killed that girl," Jesse said, as she tightened the knots that bound his wrists and ankles.

"What?"

"Ruby Little Bear. He was babbling about her. Said her name. Said it wasn't him. It was Sammy. He mentioned the sheriff too. We have to tell the police." She took another length of rope and hogtied his wrists and ankles behind him. When she finished, she stood up tall and hoofed Griswold in the hip. "I keep seeing her bones in the dirt."

Hawk breathed deep and exhaled a shaky breath as Joe's voice played in his mind: *"That girl, she never left."* He sighed. Too many women missing. Too many murdered. It wasn't right.

He coughed to clear the lump in his throat. "The main road is just a couple of miles downstream. From there, it's not far to the tribal police station."

Jesse was suddenly tight against him, kissing him, and he forgot everything but her until Griswold moaned.

"That man has an iron skull," she said.

"And a hole in his gut." Hawk got down on his knees and examined the wound. "I can't tell for sure, but I think you just missed his spleen. We need to stop the bleeding."

Jesse was rifling around in Griswold's canvas satchel. She pulled out a large steel hunting knife in a leather sheath. "Glad he packed this away."

Hawk's eyebrows rose.

"He's got enough gear in here to outfit a hiking party. I wonder where he was going."

"I'm glad you didn't get to find out."

"This looks like a first aid kit."

"Pass it here." Hawk put pressure on the wound, poured peroxide into it, and stood back when Griswold flinched. "I hope he stays unconscious. I don't want to have to hit him again." He found enough gauze and adhesive to cover the wound and tape it up. "That'll have to do until the police arrive."

Jesse pulled a Bible from Griswold's satchel and sat it beside him on the ground. "He's crazy, you know. He kept saying I was an angel."

"I can understand him thinking that." Hawk ran his fingers through her soft blonde hair. "I left Reba grazing up in the hills. Let's go get her and ride out." He nudged Griswold's cowboy boot with his moccasined toe. "He needs proper medical attention, and he's not going anywhere."

"What if a bear comes along, or a pack of wolves?"

Hawk touched his stinging temple. "I pity any animal that tries to take *him* on."

He clasped Jesse's hand as they walked up the hill together. Two owls were calling to each other in the woods. Then a helicopter flew low overhead, and they both stared up.

After it passed, she stopped and looked into his eyes. "Look, I'm sorry I took off and you had to go through all this."

"*You're* sorry? It was *my* fault. I'm the one who's sorry. I should have talked to you last night. It's just that . . . when I realized . . ." His voice faded as his thoughts drifted back to Shen and the boy.

"What did you realize?"

"Last night . . . it was Shen's birthday. I didn't know until you said the date, and then I just couldn't—"

She touched his mouth with her fingers. "Oh. Oh, wow. I understand."

"It's not that I don't want to be with you, Jesse. I do. I just couldn't—"

She stopped his mouth with a deep kiss that set his senses reeling. What he hadn't been able do last night he was certainly ready to do right now if Ira Griswold weren't lying on the ground, bleeding like a stuck pig.

TRUTH

The next time Sam awoke, he was in a hospital bed. An intravenous needle was stuck in the top of his hand and taped down with adhesive. They must have been pumping some heavy drugs into him because he didn't feel any pain. He lifted his hand slowly and touched his face. His broken nose had been set, splinted, and packed. He was breathing through his mouth. His lips were fat. His mouth tasted of burnt copper. His throat felt parched, and the inside of his lips was raw where his teeth had slammed against them and the steering wheel. He wanted to get up but was hooked to the IV, and, when he shifted, he felt a sharp pain in his rib cage. The impact had propelled his body forward into the driver's door. He took a shallow breath through his mouth and winced. Likely busted ribs. *Did I roll my goddamn truck?*

He remembered someone saying he was lucky. *Was it Chase? I have to talk to Chase.*

Sam could remember everything that happened that night with the kitten girl. He'd never asked her name. They'd just talked about the kittens. And when she said she knew him from school, he was too embarrassed to admit he didn't know who she was. Now he knew.

Ruby Little Bear.

He'd done everything he could to resuscitate her, but it was useless. The girl was gone. Then he got scared. If anyone found out that he'd been there with her that night, it would affect his father, who was in the middle of his campaign. *Sheriff's Son Found on Reservation With Dead Chippewa Girl* would not make a good re-election slogan. The old man would take out his anger on Sam and his mom, and Sam just couldn't stand to see his mother beaten one more time.

Sam had done what he thought was best for everyone. He found a shovel in the shed, dug a grave, and buried Ruby Little Bear. She'd told him she liked it there, so he figured she'd be happy enough. Then he took Marmalade and . . . He'd cried then, and he cried again now, thinking about it. But he wanted her to have that orange kitten forever. He couldn't leave her all alone in that grave. When he'd filled it in, he got the box with the mama cat and the kittens from his mother's Chevy and left them inside the shed too. Tippy was making little mewling sounds as he shut the door, and Sam fell to pieces.

That night he went out and got drunk—drunker than he'd ever been before in his whole life. And mercifully, when he woke up the next day, he didn't remember any of it. It was like the memory had been erased from his brain. That was the honest-to-God truth. But how was it even possible? And why had it suddenly come back now? Whatever happened, he was ready to tell the truth and face the consequences.

"You finally woke up." The old man sauntered in, carrying a coffee.

Sam could smell the Winstons on him and, for the first time in his life, they made him want to puke.

"Were you DUI tonight, boy?"

"Nah." They'd likely tested him for alcohol, maybe even drugs. The old man would have known that, unless he hadn't bothered to ask. He was fishing.

"Why'd you leave that note on my truck?" Sam asked, casting a line himself. His voice sounded strange: low, raspy, garbled, like someone else was talking.

"I saw your mother's car drive off the reservation that night. I thought it was her, so I followed to see what she was up to. Then I realized it must have been you boys—you and Ira."

A light went off in Sam's brain. "Did Ira do that to your face?"

The old man smirked. "What I want to know is, which one of you killed that girl?"

Sam narrowed his eyes. "What?"

"Were you there together? Did she get scared and try to fight you off? Start screaming?"

"No." Sam was repulsed by his father's implication, but even more by the glint in his eye—like somehow the idea excited him.

"Well, I'll tell you what, boy. Here's how we're gonna play this. Ira Griswold borrowed my wife's car that night. He drove out to the reservation and hooked up with Ruby Little Bear. Then things got rough, and that temper of his took over. He killed her, and—"

"No, that's not—"

"You listen to me, boy. Ira Griswold's going back to prison for the rest of his life. That bastard tried to kill me today."

"What? Why did he—?" Sam's hand flew to his chest as he tried to catch his breath.

"Couldn't handle the heat."

"But Ira didn't hurt Ruby. He wasn't even there."

"Yeah, he was. And if you tell anyone any different, you won't be getting out of the next wreck alive. You hear me, boy? Griswold's going to prison anyway. Another killing won't make any difference. The Little Bears will get their justice, and you and I can go back to business as usual."

"No." Sam shook his head. That was no way to honor Ruby Little Bear. He had to tell the truth. She hadn't fought off a rapist and been murdered. She got caught up in the trash at the bottom of the lake and drowned. She'd been happy when she jumped in that lake. He didn't want her memory tarnished by his father's lies. "No. Ira had nothing to do with it. And what about his mother? It'll kill her if he goes back to prison, especially for something like that."

"Son, it's about time you learned that the only difference between a liar and an honest man is one of perception. People see what they want to see. And a smart man tells them where to look."

"But it's not right."

"Your buddy used his fists on me, knocked me out cold, then pushed the Chevy into the river with me in it. Your *friend* tried to drown me. That's attempted murder of a police officer, and that's God's honest truth. If the cold water hadn't revived me . . ."

Sam's eyes widened, and he almost laughed right out loud. *Good old Ira. What the hell?*

"Gus is winching the Chevy out of the river right now and taking it to the impound. Once forensics get a hold of it, they're sure to find something. DNA stays around. Just finding *one* of Ruby Little Bear's hairs in that car will put that madman away for good."

Sam took a quick intake of breath through his mouth and stared at the old man. This was an argument he couldn't win. Not now. Not like this. He had to get to Chase and explain. He had to tell the truth.

Once he did that, he'd beg Ruby Little Bear's family for forgiveness. He really had suppressed the memory of that night until he saw Tippy and it all came flying back.

But how the hell was he going to get to Chase with the old man hanging around?

It must have been the drugs. All night, as Sam lay in the hospital bed with his leg suspended in a cast, his face swelled like a mad baboon, and a mysterious liquid pumping through his veins, his mind spun visions of Ruby Little Bear.

She came to him as she had that afternoon so long ago, her long brown hair spun gold in the sunshine and her big brown eyes sparkling like smoky quartz.

"You sound like you're writing a romance novel," she said, and pulled the right side of her lip up into a grin. She was pure sugar.

"Maybe I am."

In the dream, Sam was tall and buff and young—the first two of which he'd never been. It was definitely a romance novel.

She pulled one of her beaded earrings out of her pierced ears and swung it in front of his eyes. The bright red reminded him of Pearl, but it was that mustard yellow that gave him shivers.

"You liked these. I think you should have them."

Sam scoffed. "I do like them, but I can't wear girl's earrings. Besides, I haven't got pierced ears."

"Yeah, you do," she said, and when he swung his head from side to side the earrings swayed. "See. They suit you."

He sighed. His big heart was crammed with so much sadness he thought it might explode. "Ruby, I'm so sorry. If I'd gone swimming with you that day, maybe—"

"It wasn't your fault, Sam. It was never your fault."

"I tried to bring you back." An image of her pale watery face took his breath away.

"Don't," she said, and, leaning forward, she took both his cheeks in her hands and kissed him on the mouth.

He closed his eyes and felt their tongues swirl. "Jeez, Ruby."

"You did your very best by me, Sam. I couldn't have asked for anything more."

"I should have taken you home. I was just . . . I was scared of what he'd do."

"It's all right. I'm grateful for what you did. That's why I've been looking out for you."

"You've what?" He was suddenly embarrassed. What had she seen?

She giggled, and his heart sang. "Don't worry, Sam. I haven't watched you do *that*. I just made sure you were all right. Sometimes, I whispered in your ear and came to you in your dreams like I'm doing now."

"I wish I could remember." If things had turned out differently, he'd like to have got to know Ruby Little Bear. She was a girl he could love . . . Maybe he even did love her a little bit.

She leaned in close and kissed him again, and they fell over on their sides in a grassy field and kept on kissing. After a while, she leaned back and flicked him on the nose with her finger.

"Who do you think told you about the gold mine, Sam Flanagan?"

"No one told me. I followed my great-granddaddy's map, and there it was."

Ruby shook her head. "That map was nothin'. Just some old man's dream."

Sam considered this. It seemed real enough. "I probably shouldn't have taken that gold. It's on Chippewa land." He was feeling a little guilty, her being Chippewa and all.

"You're smart. You'll figure out what to do with it."

"Hey, Ruby, that night when I rolled my truck, were you there?"

When she winked, she looked as cute as a girl could look.

"And was Tippy there too, or was that his ghost?"

"That place is swarming with cats. You wanted to find them a home, and you did." Ruby kissed him again. "You're a good man, Sam. You always have been, even though you never believed it."

"Well, you're right about that. I've left junk in the rivers and ponds for years—junk like the stuff that killed you."

"That's cause you've been trying to get caught for years. Part of you was scared, but the other part wanted everyone to know what really happened. You wanted people to clean up all that junk. It's not just here. There's junk across this whole country."

"Yeah. Yeah, there is."

"So what are you gonna do about it?"

Sam narrowed his eyes and cocked his head. "Clean it up?"

Ruby flicked his nose again.

"Ow. Stop doing that. My nose is broken."

"Just tell them the truth about me, silly. That's all you need to do."

RESURRECTION

Chief Chase was pulling into the tribal police station just as Jesse and Jed rode up on Reba. They both slid off, and as they walked toward him, leading the tired mare, Jesse grasped Jed's hand. She'd held him tightly as they rode those last few miles and didn't intend to let go now.

Chase nodded to Jesse. "I just came from your place. Bad accident out there tonight. We had to call for a medevac."

"We heard the helicopter. I hope the patient's doing all right."

Chase shrugged, then stared at Jed, who stood stiffly in his blood-stained clothes. "You're Joe's boy. Your dad's the doctor in Lure River, isn't he?"

Jed nodded and stretched out his hand. "That's right. I'm Ha— Jed. Jedediah VanHouten."

Chase shook his hand. "You're a doctor too, aren't you?"

It was Jed's turn to shrug.

"Fortunately, yes." Jesse moved closer to Jed. "We were attacked in the woods. We got away, but our attacker is still out there."

"Where's that, exactly?" Chase pulled out his cell phone.

"Beside the stream about two miles north of the bridge. Big man. We had to restrain him. Head injuries. Knife wound to the abdomen. I did the best I could to staunch the bleeding, but he needs medical assistance."

Chase made a call, and a minute later a female officer came out of the station and joined them. "Ambulance is on its way with Search and Rescue."

"That your blood or his?" Chase said, glancing at Jed's ruined shirt.

"Both." Jed stared down and then touched his head wound.

"I'll need to take your clothing into evidence."

Jesse glanced nervously at Jed. They were the victims. She hadn't considered they might be charged if Griswold didn't survive. "The man tried to abduct me."

Chase cleared his throat. "You knew your attacker?"

"Not really. I've seen him a couple of times in town."

"His name's Ira Griswold. He's violent and volatile. Delusional," Jed said. "He told Jesse she was an angel sent to him by God."

Chase cocked his head. The officer spoke up then. "Sir, we received an APB about an hour ago for a suspect named Ira Griswold. Sheriff Flanagan's looking for him in connection with two felony charges. You must have missed it when you were out at the cabin."

Chase's lips flattened. "This incident happened on the reservation. Griswold will stay in our custody. Flanagan won't like it, but he's got his hands full anyway. I just saw him. It was his son who rolled his truck tonight."

So far, Jesse had never seen the police chief riled. She wondered what it would take to ruffle him.

"Griswold also talked about Ruby Little Bear," she said. "He kept saying 'it wasn't me.' And he mentioned the sheriff and his son Sam. I think they were involved in whatever happened to her out there. Something about kittens and Mrs. Flanagan's Chevy." She rubbed both her arms and crossed them over her chest. "Is it really her?"

Chase's eyes widened, and he nodded several times. "We haven't made it public, but we've informed the family. It's definitely Ruby Little Bear."

Jed took a deep breath and exhaled.

"Thanks for this information. We're going to need a statement from each of you."

"Could it wait until morning?" Jesse asked. "I'd really like to get back to my cabin." She couldn't wait to get alone with Jed somewhere they could clean up and finally relax.

"Fortunately, we were just finishing up out there when the accident happened." He turned to the officer. "Marie, could you run these two out to the cabin after we get those clothes?"

"Thanks, but we've got Reba," Jesse said, turning back and stroking the mare's nose.

"My horse trailer's still hooked up to my truck." Chase gestured across the lot to the white pickup parked under the light. "And this poor old mare looks worn out."

Jesse was feeling worn out herself. She was beginning to really like Chief Chase. He was all business but in a pleasant, thoughtful kind of way.

"I'll come by around noon tomorrow and get a statement from each of you." He looked at Jed, who was looking sheepish, his deerskin clothing soaking wet and covered in blood. "But I will need—"

"I don't have any other clothes," Jed said.

Jesse opened her backpack and pulled out a hot pink T-shirt and a pair of loose khakis.

"You're kidding me, right?"

"I think they'll fit . . . just till we get home," she said, flashing him a grin.

* * *

"I've only got a single bed," Jesse said, as she opened the door to the cabin.

"Well, we'll just have to squeeze in nice and tight." When Jed glanced up at the wall above the door, Jesse's gaze followed.

"What's that?" She squinted at the white shape stuck between the chinks in the logs. "I never noticed it before."

"Makwa's tooth." Jed bit his lip. "Please don't get mad at me. I had a dream about you and a bear I fought once." He threw up his hands. "I thought you needed protection."

"When did you do that?" She didn't like that he'd come into her cabin and hidden the tooth, but there was something so gallant in the action that she couldn't be mad at him.

"Sometime in between kissing you on the porch and finding you injured in the bush."

"Which time?" She grinned. "So much has happened since then."

"I know. I feel like a different person."

Jesse touched his chest. "You *look* like a different person. You're pretty in pink, but I'll need my shirt back sometime."

He grasped the bottom of the T-shirt, pulled it off over his head, and tossed it.

She stared at his tanned pecs and ran her hands over his shoulders and down his arms. "Did the bear do this?" With a finger, she traced one of the long scars down his bicep.

"Makwa. He wanted to sleep in my cave and wouldn't take no for an answer."

Leaning in, Jesse kissed the pale scar and wavered with the musky scent of him.

"Your turn," Jed said. He grasped the bottom of her tank top and pulled it off in one fluid motion. "God, you're beautiful. I've been wanting you since the moment I saw you in the woods that day."

"That day you shot my deer," she teased. Her lips whispered along his neck, and then she lifted her face to catch his lips with hers.

His hands slid down her back to her glutes, and he pulled her in so tight she could feel every inch of him through the thin khakis.

"Technically, it was *my* deer."

"Shut up," she said, and then she shut him up with a kiss that sent them reeling back against the log table. The khakis didn't last. They landed in a pile on the floor, and when he lifted her onto the edge of the table, all she could feel was Jed. She clung to his strong arms and opened her body and soul to him. Jed. He was everywhere. Everything. When he picked her up off the hard wood table, she clung to him, burying her face in the hollow of his collarbone, gasping with the sheer joy of feeling him inside her. They crashed onto the soft wool of the cot, rhythm racing until there was nothing but skin on skin and breath on breath.

Do you have any clothes that aren't made of deerskin?" Jesse ran her fingers through Jed's hair, combing out the knots with her nails. It was thick and wavy and beautiful.

"At my parents' place. I was thinking about going to see them tomorrow afternoon."

"Yeah?" Jed certainly was changing. That night in his dad's office he hadn't been ready, but now . . .

"Tea?" Jesse was curious about his change of heart but didn't want to pry. A cup of tea always seemed a good way into a tough talk.

"Yes, please. Do you have black tea? I've been craving it since that night at my dad's office."

"But of course. Orange pekoe."

Jesse wriggled out of his arms reluctantly and slipped on a long loose T-shirt. After lighting the propane stove, she put the iron kettle on to boil. She was suddenly starving. She found some crackers that weren't too stale and a jar of peanut butter and put them on a tray with the mugs. "Could you light us a fire?"

"A metaphorical fire or . . . ?" He winked.

"A real fire to go with the metaphorical fire."

As she put down the tray, Jed crouched, lit a match, and held it to the dry wood already stacked in the fireplace. She loved watching him walk around her cabin naked. His body was as chiseled as a Greek statue. She remembered watching him hoist that buck over his shoulders. "Mountain man," she whispered.

Swinging around, he caught her in his arms. "This mountain man is yours as long as you want him." He touched her hair, then pulled several strands to his face and inhaled. "Ah, forest and woodsmoke. Two of my favorite scents." His gray eyes flickered.

She touched the swelling along his temple. "How's your head?" The wound was red and swollen, and his eye was partially closed. "Would your miracle plant heal this wound?"

"It would, but I left so quickly I didn't bring it. I need to keep some in my pouch so I'm never without it," he said, clutching his totem bag.

"Sit," she directed, and kissed the bump lightly. "What's the pain level on a scale of one to ten?"

"Zero when you look at me like that."

"I never want to stop looking at you." Straddling his lap, she wrapped her arms around his neck and kissed him.

The whistling kettle interrupted their kiss, but neither of them tasted the orange pekoe tea that night.

In the morning, Jesse awoke with her cheek warm against Jed's bare chest. Sliding in against him, she woke him with a kiss. Their bodies fit together in perfect symmetry, and she couldn't get enough of him.

"Tea?" she asked.

"Not just yet." He breathed across her skin, awakening every nerve. "Maybe never if it means either of us ever leaving this bed." His eyes were lazy and full of mischief, his blond hair mussed from her fingers.

But the sound of a vehicle outside sent a surge of adrenaline sweeping up her legs. "Get dressed. That's Rainy's Jeep. She might have your brother with her."

Jed stood up and climbed into her khaki pants, as she did likewise.

There was a scratching on the cabin door just as Jesse lit the propane stove and set the kettle on to boil.

Jed, who was closer to the door, opened it.

Rainy's eyes bugged when she saw him standing there, shirtless and wearing Jesse's pants. "Oh my God! Jed!" She sprang to hug him, then caught herself and backed up awkwardly.

"What's happening, friend?" Jesse asked. Rainy was clearly in distress.

"I, uh—"

Alec bounced through the door.

Gasping, Jesse dropped the tin cup she was holding in her hand and grasped the back of the chair. "Alec?" Jesse's breath caught. She glanced from Rainy to Jed and back to Alec and finally exhaled.

Alec's brown hair was buzzed military short at the sides and spiked on top. His skin glowed, and he'd got new ink—a full sleeve from shoulder to wrist in what was undoubtedly a Nepalese design. The tattoo was fully visible, as were his muscles. The monstrous dragon face had a sharp, geometric pattern. It was tribal and suited him, but made Jesse's stomach flip.

Rainy found her voice and started babbling. "Alec arrived yesterday, and I didn't know if you were back yet, but he wanted to see where you were staying, and here you are."

"You-you were—"

"Dead. I know. But as you can see, that rumor isn't true." Stepping up, he grasped Jesse and pulled her to his chest in a hug.

She stood stiffly, caught between duty, relief, rage, and repulsion, but she couldn't let go for fear of falling.

Glancing over Alec's shoulder, she saw Jed's naked back as he walked out the door.

"Jed! Wait!" she called, but he didn't turn or even pause.

Rainy looked from Jesse to Jed and back again. "I'll go." She raced after Jed, leaving the door open behind her.

Alec held Jesse at arm's length. "You look different. Healthier and, dare I say, happier? Is it because of him?"

Jesse glanced over his shoulder. Jed was walking, and Rainy was running along beside him. Finally, he stopped. Jesse couldn't hear the conversation, but hands were waving emphatically.

"So it *is* about him." Alec picked up her left hand, the one with the obviously missing engagement ring, and glanced out the door. "I get it. You thought I was dead, and I've been gone a long time."

"Where have you been? The last I heard, you were buried under an avalanche in the Himalayas."

"That I was."

When he hugged her again, his scent kindled a kind of familiarity, but Jesse's skin tightened as a wave of goosebumps careened down her arms. *This can't be happening.*

"Can we sit and drink coffee like we used to? There's so much I want to tell you."

Jesse stared out the open door. When she saw Jed climb into the passenger seat of Rainy's Jeep, she exhaled deeply. *If he walks into the bush now, I may never see him again. I'll never find my way back to that cave . . . that beautiful waterfall. I have to trust that Rainy can keep him in town. He mentioned going to see his parents. Please let her take him to Matt.*

"Jesse?"

She flinched when the Jeep started up and pulled away. Then she glanced at Alec and slowly closed the door. "What?"

"Do you have coffee? When we left, the café wasn't open yet. Hank's Roadkill Café?" He snickered. "God, this town is so hick."

No, it's not, she thought. *I like Lure River and its characters. Well, most of them.* She shoved the cans around in her larder. She hated coffee. All she wanted was a steaming cup of orange pekoe. And Jed.

When Alec edged up behind her again and touched her shoulder, she stepped back, repulsed. "Where have you been all this time, Alec? It's been months. Why didn't you call? Or write? You couldn't find some way to get a message to me? Some way to tell me you weren't dead? Do you know how many nightmares I had, where you were buried under a mountain of snow and I couldn't find you?" Her hand swept through the air, but inside she was trembling with rage. Slamming the coffee tin down on the sideboard, she stared into his incredulous eyes. "You don't get to look at me like that! I thought you were dead for the past year and a half. And now you saunter in here like you went on a casual weekend ski trip?"

"I'm sorry," he said, rubbing her shoulder.

She pulled away. "Don't. Don't touch me. Unless you were in a hospital somewhere in a remote mountain village with amnesia and too many broken bones to move for the last year and a half, I don't want to hear it."

"We've been friends forever, Jesse. Won't you at least hear me out?"

Jesse sighed. "Give me the brief version—and make it real." Alec's stories were legendary, but most of them he'd spun with gold.

"I did fall in the avalanche. I was badly injured and taken in by a Nepalese family who looked after me for several months."

"Is that where you got this?" She pointed at the hideous dragon.

He nodded. His eyes clouded for the first time since he'd walked in the door. "Jesse, I know you've met someone. Well, the truth is, I met someone too. She saved my life, brought me back from death, and nursed me back to health."

"Where is she now?" Jesse growled through gritted teeth.

"Still there, in Nepal. She's waiting—"

"Jesus, Alec!"

He hung his head sheepishly. "Jesse, we've been best friends forever. I couldn't just phone or email or text something like that. I wanted to tell you in person."

Best friends forever. That much was true. Their relationship had never been a heart-pounding, lustful romance. It just happened because they'd been together so long.

"I don't care if you want to break up over some woman in Nepal, but how could you let me think you were dead for over a year? Friends don't do that!" She picked up her quill box from the dresser, opened it, and plucked out the diamond engagement ring he'd given her the Christmas before he left. Shaking her head, she threw it at him. "Leave now and take this with you."

He scooped up the ring and held it out to her. "Jesse. Please."

"Oh, don't beg, Alec Treacher. You're the most narcissistic man I've ever met. I can't believe I never saw it before." Turning her back on him, she said it at last. "Goodbye, Alec."

Quiet settled over the room like a thick dark cloud. Jesse heard the door open and then close, and with it came a sense of relief. It was finally over. The waiting. The worrying. The wondering. And then she heard a sigh.

When she turned, her eyes blazed fire. "You're *still* here?"

"Rainy left. How do I—?"

An incredulous choke. "Start walking. I hope you have to walk all the way back to Nepal." Grabbing a thick chunk of wood from the pile, she hurled it at him to satisfy her itching palm.

Alec dodged, and it hit the log wall with a force that shook Makwa's tooth right out of the chink above the door. The tooth hit the floor and bounced.

Jesse scooped it up and held it between her palms.

"I'm sorry," Alec said, as he opened the door.

"Go, Alec. Go and live your dreams." Jesse squeezed the bear's tooth tightly. "I don't need you or your dreams anymore. I've got dreams of my own."

CEREMONY

Several days later, the usually calm and quiet woods surrounding Jesse's cabin bustled with people of all ages. The community was holding a special ceremony to honor Ruby Little Bear. The sun shone bright and warmed their skin. The lake rippled harmoniously. Children ran barefoot, laughed, and splashed in the water. Sage burned and drums beat. People sang and hugged and cried and laughed. And Jesse watched it all while seated on the porch step. She was feeling lost and very out of place. If it weren't for Rainy, who huddled beside her, she'd have hidden inside.

Special equipment had been brought in to clear the garbage from the lake a few days after Sam Flanagan confessed that he was with Ruby Little Bear when she drowned while swimming here at the cabin.

"That's him there." Rainy gestured to a small man who looked even smaller hunched over on crutches. His leg was in a cast, his face a mass of bruises. Jesse's suspicions were confirmed. Sam Flanagan was the man she'd seen in town with Ira Griswold.

"So he's the one who buried Ruby Little Bear in the shed with the kitten." Jesse sucked her bottom lip. She wasn't quite sure how she felt about that. She'd certainly seen the feral progeny of the kittens he claimed to have left in the shed that day. And the notion that he'd left the poor girl with one of them curled up close to her heart was tragically romantic.

Rainy nodded. "Apparently, Ruby got tangled up in a rope attached to a sunken rowboat. He was able to tell them exactly where it was."

Jesse had watched the battered boat disappear, with the rest of the junk, in the back of a trailer. She wondered if they'd do anything with the object that was somehow responsible for Ruby's death.

"The poor man has been holding onto that story for twenty years. Can you imagine? He was even able to tell Chief Chase about the beaded earrings she was wearing that day. Medicine wheels. Ruby taught beading at the Friendship Center. Everyone loved her." Rainy sighed. "I heard they found the earrings in the grave and they're giving them back to the Little Bears."

Jesse shivered as Rainy talked on.

"I suppose it was a blessing that he suffered with dissociative amnesia all this time."

"*If* he really did." Jesse wasn't sure such a thing was possible. Besides, Sam Flanagan had given her the creeps in Lure River, and she couldn't quite forget that. Or that his best friend had tried to abduct her. "Why's everyone being so nice to him?"

"Because they believe he did what he thought was right at the time. The accident jogged his memory, and, once he remembered, he told Chief Chase the truth. He could have kept quiet, but the man took a big risk, and that kind of honesty goes a long way around here. Then he went to the Little Bears and begged them to forgive him. He's paying for all of this—the equipment to clean up the lake and several other ponds and streams where he's seen garbage."

Seen it, or put it there? Jesse thought.

"And he's created a special annual scholarship for Indigenous youth to go to college in Ruby's name. A full free ride."

A model citizen, Jesse thought, and her hand strayed to her hip. She wasn't ready to let Sam Flanagan off quite that easily. The garbage in one stream had nearly killed her. If Reba hadn't found Jed, she could have disappeared in the woods just like Ruby and never been seen again. Did Sam know about those traps like he knew about the others? Tears clouded Jesse's eyes, and she sniffed.

The Little Bears had obviously forgiven Sam. He sat beside them in a huge circle of lawn chairs. "It must have been so hard for her family." Jesse wiped the tears from her cheeks.

"For Sam too. He's the sheriff's son."

"Yeah." Jesse remembered how the cowboy sheriff had harassed her and Jed that night at the doctor's office. And her heart softened a little for the small man whose father was a big jerk.

"Sam told Chief Chase that the sheriff wanted to lie about it. He was going to blame everything on Ira Griswold. Say he murdered Ruby. Sam refused. He wanted to honor Ruby by telling the truth."

Ira Griswold. Jesse shivered at the memory of the big man choking her out and tying her to a tree. She didn't want to imagine what might have happened if Jed hadn't come along when he did. She'd decided not to press charges after Chief Chase told her that Griswold was locked up in prison, awaiting trial for attempting to kill Sheriff Flanagan. She just wanted to forget.

As the afternoon wore on, Jesse felt more and more like a squatter on someone else's land, which in her heart she knew she was. This was Anishinaabe territory and always had been. If it hadn't been for Rainy, who seldom left her side, she would have run away. She didn't know how much longer she could stay here, alone in the cabin, knowing that Jed was in town at his parents' house. Seeing all the families together made her feel even more desolate. She touched the tooth in the pocket of her skirt and wished that Jed would magically appear.

When it was time for the feast, the Elders were served first, and then the men served the women and children. Jesse politely accepted the plate of salads, fry bread, and grilled fish from Chief Chase, but inside she was dying.

She turned to Rainy. "I have to go to him."

"As your best friend in the whole world, I'm telling you, Jesse, just wait. Matt says that Jed has been in intense discussions with his parents and their lawyer for days. He's going after custody of his son. They're preparing a case, and it's a really big deal."

It *was* a big deal. Jed had changed so much from the hermit who lived alone in the woods, she could hardly believe it. Maybe Rainy was right. It wasn't just about her. Jed had a three-year-old son in Texas, plus a lot of catching up to do with his family.

"And he knows that Alec's gone for good, right?"

"I told you, girlfriend, he knows and he's thrilled." Rainy put her arm around Jesse and hugged her. "Aw, come on. He's just giving you both some time to process what happened. I saw the look on his face when Alec walked through the door. It was like his world fell apart. Again."

"Oh, don't say that."

"Look. Jed loves you. But, when fiancés rise from the dead, it turns everyone's world upside down."

Jesse sighed. "I'm going to check on Reba. After all the pony rides she gave today, she deserves a pail of oats." She set her half-cleaned plate on the porch step, stood up, and smoothed out the rose floral dress Rainy had loaned her for the day. It buttoned down the front and was cinched at the waist with an embroidered leather belt that matched her beige cowboy boots.

Reba was grazing in the thick grass by the edge of the lake, but as Jesse walked toward her, the mare raised her head and stared down the driveway. A chill ran up Jesse's arms, and she looked to see what had caught the horse's attention.

Jed! Jesse's heart thrummed in her chest. The bottom half of his handsome face was pale where he'd shaved his beard off, but laughter brought a flush to his cheeks. Reaching out, he slapped his brother on the back, and they laughed as they walked up the driveway together.

When he saw her, Jed stopped laughing, stood very still, and seemed to peer inside her soul. Then the corner of his lip pulled up in a naked grin.

Jesse bolted, leapt on him, and wrapped her legs around his waist. Burying her face in his shoulder, she inhaled that scent she'd missed so much—that scent that was pure Jed.

"On a scale of one to ten, how do you feel?" he whispered.

"Off the charts, and I don't ever want to be away from you again."

He lowered her to the ground and held her hands as she took in the whole picture. He was packed into denim jeans and a pale-blue T-shirt that turned his eyes a silvery blue. His long blond hair caught the lake breeze and shone in the sun. The tan cowboy boots and turquoise-studded belt buckle were a surprise.

"I didn't know you were a cowboy."

"I didn't know *you* were a cowgirl." Standing back, he admired her in the fancy pink dress, then whistled. "Mercy, woman."

She felt her face flush, but, standing there in Jed's arms, her feet itched to dance.

"I'm sorry I've been gone so long. I went back to the cave to get medicine for my mother. And my father and I talked to our lawyer. I'm going after my son."

"That's fantastic." Throwing her arms around his neck, she leaned up and kissed him long and hard.

When she finally let him go, he broke out in that lopsided grin. "I brought you something," he said, as he pulled a tiny blue box from the pocket of his jeans. "And seeing you like this, I think I got it right."

Jesse's heart caught in her chest and for a moment she couldn't breathe. Then she opened the box and gasped. A pink stone heart, set on a silver chain, glittered up at her.

"Oh my God. It's perfect."

"It's a sapphire that belonged to my mother. When I told her about you, she insisted I give it to you. Once I get working, I'll buy you something of your own. I'll buy you the moon."

"This is all I need," she said. "And you." Taking it from the box, she passed him the chain and turned so he could clasp it around her neck. When he kissed the back of her neck, the warm brush of his lips sent her reeling. Turning her face, he caught her mouth with his.

"If you don't mind, I'd like to stay here at the cabin with you for a while. So much has happened, I just need . . ." His voice faded as he looked into her eyes. "I need *you*, Jesse Jardine."

"I don't know what to call you."

He held out his hands and caught hers between them. "You can call me anything you want." Bringing her hands to his lips, he kissed them as he stared into her eyes. "My parents named me Jedediah, after one of my ancestors. I'm a local boy, born and raised right here in Lure River. And I'm yours as long as you want me."

Jesse's heart swelled and she laughed to cover the tears that stung her eyes. "I'm pleased to meet you, Jed. Won't you come in and stay awhile?"

ACKNOWLEDGEMENTS

I wrote the first draft of Jesse and Hawk's story thirty years ago when I lived in rural Ontario.

I was something of a wild child and quit high school with only grade ten. In my mid-thirties, when my kids were young, I felt the need to graduate. So, I returned to high school by registering in one correspondence course at a time. Along the way, I enrolled in a course called Native Ancestry 11 that changed my world.

One night, I was sitting at my kitchen table reading the chapter on Animism—the belief that all beings, be they rocks, trees, deserts, fish, or winds are alive with spiritual force. *I know this*, I thought. *This is who I am.* That epiphany rocked me to the core and set me on a new path.

I'd just started my BA in Indigenous Studies at Trent University when I wrote the story of Jesse and Hawk. I was reading books by Basil Johnston and Eddie Benton-Banai, both who were Anishinaabe (Ojibwa) leaders and storytellers; learning with traditional teachers and Elders; going to powwows and feasts; attending ceremonies; and soaking up a culture I loved and felt at home with. I want to acknowledge this time because I'm grateful to everyone who touched my life in those days. You helped me change. You helped me heal.

It took me several years to complete my degree, as a single mother, and part-way through, my seventy-five-year-old mother said casually, "I'm not surprised you're into this. My great-grandfather married an Indian. She was Tuscarora and he was Dutch." That great-grandfather's last name was VanSickler, so I named Gus, the mechanic, after him because my great-grandparents and their children ended up running one of the first garages in Toronto. I was shocked by my mother's remark and wondered why I'd never heard this story before. I don't know if there's such a thing as ancestral memory, but perhaps my mother was right. While researching my ancestry, I connected with a previously unknown line of the family who confirmed my mother's story and sent me a tin-type photograph of my Indigenous great-great-grandmother.

While I was studying at Trent, I was invited to a Three Fires Lodge ceremony in Wisconsin on the shore of Lake Superior. Later, I drove through the American Midwest on my way to British Columbia. And that's where I set the fictional town of Lure River.

I asked subscribers to my seasonal newsletter for help creating names and businesses for the town and got wonderful replies. I want to thank Tara, Heike, Jackie, and Marci for your responses. You'll see some of your suggestions in this book.

Lure is a town I'd love to call home and the main characters are closer to me than any I've written yet. I've always wanted to live in the cabin Jesse rents for the summer on the reservation. And I've always felt like I was born in the wrong time and place, just like Hawk.

I found the manuscript of the thirty-year-old draft, wrapped in brown paper, a couple of years ago while packing to move. When I read it, I was surprised and intrigued. I started to rewrite it, then Jesse found the bones of a missing Indigenous girl in her shed. Ruby Little Bear started to speak, and the story took off in another direction. Still, the essence of the major characters remained, even Sam and Ira, and for that, I'm grateful.

Much has been written about Missing and Murdered Indigenous Women. In Canada, many of these homicides occur in urban areas and most remain unsolved, especially when the offender is a stranger. In British Columbia, where I live now, this came to light in the Robert Pickton serial murder case, and, also through the inquiry surrounding the Highway of Tears. Indigenous women are vulnerable, but strong. Much more work needs to be done to find those who are missing and stop victim-blaming, so Indigenous women and girls no longer must live in fear.

Though this is a suspenseful light-hearted romantic adventure, and not a non-fiction book on this topic, Ruby Little Bear shared her story with me, as some characters do, and I thank her for that. Ruby shines a light, not just on Missing and Murdered Indigenous Women, but on Respect for the Land.

A special thank you to Indigenous mentor, activist, and motivational speaker, Alexa Blyan. Alexa took time out from her work to read and respond to *Lure*. Alexa is working on a new video project, *Digital Voices*, that encourages people who've experienced trauma to reclaim their stories by speaking out. She often speaks to the issue of Missing and Murdered Indigenous Women. Find her at alexablyan.com.

I want to acknowledge Eileen Cook, who helped me craft this book with her developmental edit, and Amanda Bidnall, who did an amazing final copy edit. I met both these talented women through a supportive group of authors called The Creative Academy. Also from TCA, are romance writers, CJ Hunt and Danika Bloom, and supernatural thriller writer, JP McLean. Though they are extremely busy women, they all took the time to read my book and write something wonderful for me.

Finally, I want to acknowledge my publicist, Mickey Mikkelson from Creative Edge Publicity, who amazes me with the promotional opportunities he sends my way.

ABOUT THE AUTHOR

W. L. Hawkin writes romantic adventures, often charged with "myth, magic, and mayhem" from her home near Vancouver, Canada.

Her Hollystone Mysteries series features a coven of West Coast witches who solve murders using ritual magic and a little help from the gods. The books—*To Charm a Killer, To Sleep with Stones, To Render a Raven,* and *To Kill a King*—follow Estrada, a flawed magician and coven high priest as he endeavors to save his family and friends while sorting through his own personal issues.

Her latest, the Lure River Romances, is a small-town romantic suspense series set in the American Midwest, in the fictional town of Lure River. The first, *Lure,* tells the story of Jesse & Hawk.

Hawkin graduated from Trent University with a BA in Indigenous Studies. It was then she discovered her great-great grandmother was an Indigenous woman. Wendy went on to study English literature at Simon Fraser University in British Columbia, and then teach high school. She found her voice publishing poetry and Native Rights articles in Canadian news magazines and is now an Indie author/publisher at Blue Haven Press.

For the past few years, Wendy has been a book reviewer for the Ottawa Review of Books. A member of the Federation of BC Writers and the Writers Union of Canada, she actively engages with readers and writers at conferences, and is represented by Creative Edge Publicity.

As an intuitive writer, Wendy captures on the page what she sees (visual scenes) and hears (conversations) and allows her muses to guide her through the creative process. She needs to feel the energy of the land, so although she's an introvert, in each book her characters go on a journey where she's traveled herself. If you don't find her at Blue Haven Press, she's likely wandering the woods with her beautiful yellow dog.

Did you enjoy this book? Reviews keep books and authors alive. Please take a moment to leave a few words with your favorite retailer and/or at Goodreads or Bookbub. Thank you.

Are you curious to know more?

Check out the Hollystone Mysteries:
To Charm a Killer
To Sleep with Stones
To Render a Raven
To Kill a King

Come by www.bluehavenpress.com and subscribe to my seasonal newsletter for more "myth, magic, and mayhem."

Find and follow me on:
Instagram @wlhawkin
Twitter @ladyhawke1003
Facebook @wlhawkin
Pinterest @W.L. Hawkin
Bookbub @w.l.hawkin

blessings and all good wishes.
Wendy

Made in the USA
Monee, IL
23 January 2022

88949270R00148